PENGUIN BOOKS

# THE SMALL BACHELOR

P. G. Wodehouse was born in Guildford in 1881 and educated at Dulwich College. After working for the Hong Kong and Shanghai Bank for two years, he left to earn his living as a journalist and storywriter, writing the 'By the Way' column in the old *Globe*. He also contributed a series of school stories to a magazine for boys, the *Captain*, in one of which Psmith made his first appearance. Going to America before the First World War, he sold a serial to the *Saturday Evening Post* and for the next twenty-five years almost all his books appeared first in this magazine. He was either part author or sole writer of the lyrics of eighteen musical comedies including *Kissing Time*; he married in 1914 and in 1955 took American citizenship. He wrote over ninety books and his work has won world-wide acclaim, being translated into many languages. *The Times* hailed him as 'a comic genius recognized in his lifetime as a classic and an old master of farce'.

P. G. Wodehouse said, 'I believe there are two ways of writing novels. One is mine, making a sort of musical comedy without music and ignoring real life altogether; the other is going right deep down into life and not caring a damn . . .' He was created a Knight of the British Empire in the New Year's Honours List in 1975. In a BBC interview he said that he had no ambitions left, now that he had been knighted and there was a waxwork of him in Madame Tussaud's. He died on St Valentine's Day in 1975 at the age of ninety-three.

P. G. WODEHOUSE

# THE
# SMALL
# BACHELOR

PENGUIN BOOKS

## PENGUIN BOOKS

Published by the Penguin Group
Penguin Books Ltd, 27 Wrights Lane, London W8 5TZ, England
Viking Penguin, a division of Penguin Books USA Inc.
375 Hudson Street, New York, New York 10014, USA
Penguin Books Australia Ltd, Ringwood, Victoria, Australia
Penguin Books Canada Ltd, 2801 John Street, Markham, Ontario, Canada L3R 1B4
Penguin Books (NZ) Ltd, 182–190 Wairau Road, Auckland 10, New Zealand

Penguin Books Ltd, Registered Offices: Harmondsworth, Middlesex, England

First published by Methuen & Co. 1927
Published in Penguin Books 1987
5 7 9 10 8 6 4

Printed in England by Clays Ltd, St Ives plc
Typeset in Plantin

# PREFACE

I have three reasons for being particularly fond of *The Small Bachelor*.

I suppose authors generally have a special affection for those of their books which come out easily. It is not that we mind work —we are always ready to give our all for our Art—but it is nice when we are occasionally spared the blood sweat and tears, and there are few things more agonizing than the realization, after one has written 50,000 words of a novel, that as a theatrical manager I knew used to say of a play which seemed to him to fall short of perfection 'it don't add up right'.

Few people, for instance, liked *Thank You, Jeeves*, as much as I do, but I love it because it came out as smooth as treacle gurgling out of a jug and never gave me a moment's anguish from the opening paragraph of Chapter One. I actually wrote the last twenty-six pages—about 5,500 words—in a single day between breakfast and dinner, and felt fine when I had done it.

*The Small Bachelor* was one of the easy ones. I wrote most of it in a punt on a lake at a country house in Norfolk with gentle breezes blowing and ducks quacking and all Nature, as you might say, pitching in to make my task more pleasant.

My second reason for being fond of the book is nostalgic. So much of the action takes place in the Greenwich Village sector of New York, where I lived between 1909 and 1914. I have not visited it for fifty years and everybody tells me it has been ruined by hippies and drug addicts, but when I was there it was a charming spot entirely different from anywhere else in New York. I was very hard up in my Greenwich Village days, but I was always very happy. There were trees and grass and, if you wanted to celebrate the sale of a story, two wonderful old restaurants, the Brevoort and the Lafayette, which might have been invented by O. Henry. Prohibition, which killed them both, was unheard of then, though it enters largely into *The Small Bachelor*: everything such as food and hotel bills was inexpensive: one could live on practically nothing, which was fortunate for me because I had to.

The third reason for my affection for this book is that it is based on a musical comedy I have always had a weakness for, a thing called *Oh, Lady*, the second of the shows which Guy Bolton, Jerome Kern and I did for the Princess Theatre on 39th Street.

Making a novel out of a play is not the simple job it might seem to be. You can't just take the dialogue and put in an occasional 'he said' and 'she said'. *Oh, Lady* for instance, ran—exclusive of musical numbers—to about 15,000 words. A novel has to be between seventy and eighty thousand. I wrote 50,000 words of *The Small Bachelor* before I came to the start of *Oh, Lady*. When I did, I admit that things eased up a lot, though even then the fact that I had added so many threads to the plot made it impossible to use the dialogue as it stood. Sigsbee Waddington, the false necklace, Officer Garroway and the oil shares were not in the play, and Mrs. Sigsbee Waddington was an entirely different character.

For the record, *Oh, Lady* was produced during a printers' strike, so we got no newspaper notices, but in spite of that it was such a success that while it was running at the Princess Theatre another company was formed to play it at another New York theatre simultaneously, with four companies out on the road. And when it was done at Sing-Sing with a cast of convicts, it was, so I am told, a riot.

The only thing missing from it was a real song hit. Jerry's music, as always, was enchanting, but what we felt we needed was an outstanding song hit. There was a number for the heroine in the second act called 'Bill', but we all thought it was too slow, so it was cut out. It was not till it was done in *Show Boat* six years later that we realized that, like Othello's base Indian, we had thrown away a pearl richer than all our tribe.

As the fellow said, that's show biz.

P. G. WODEHOUSE

# CHAPTER ONE

## I

THE roof of the Sheridan Apartment House, near Washington Square, New York. Let us examine it. There will be stirring happenings on this roof in due season, and it is as well to know the ground.

The Sheridan stands in the heart of New York's Bohemian and artistic quarter. If you threw a brick from any of its windows, you would be certain to brain some rising young interior decorator, some Vorticist sculptor or a writer of revolutionary *vers libre*. And a very good thing, too. Its roof, cosy, compact and ten stories above the street, is flat, paved with tiles and surrounded by a low wall, jutting up at one end of which is an iron structure—the fire-escape. Climbing down this, should the emergency occur, you would find yourself in the open-air premises of the Purple Chicken restaurant—one of those numerous oases in this great city where, in spite of the law of Prohibition, you can still, so the *cognoscenti* whisper, 'always get it if they know you.' A useful thing to remember.

On the other side of the roof, opposite the fire-escape, stands what is technically known as a 'small bachelor apartment, pent-house style.' It is a white-walled, red-tiled bungalow, and the small bachelor who owns it is a very estimable young man named George Finch, originally from East Gilead, Idaho, but now, owing to a substantial legacy from an uncle, a unit of New York's Latin Quarter. For George, no longer being obliged to earn a living, has given his suppressed desires play by coming to the metropolis and trying his hand at painting. From boyhood up he had always wanted to be an artist: and now he is an artist: and what is more, probably the worst artist who ever put brush to canvas.

For the rest, that large round thing that looks like a captive balloon is the water-tank. That small oblong thing that looks like a summer-house is George Finch's outdoor sleeping-porch. Those things that look like potted shrubs are potted shrubs. That stoutish man sweeping with a broom is George's valet, cook, and man-of-all-work, Mullett.

And this imposing figure with the square chin and the horn-rimmed spectacles which, as he comes out from the door leading to the stairs, flash like jewels in the sun, is no less a person than J. Hamilton Beamish, author of the famous Beamish Booklets ('Read Them And Make The World Your Oyster') which have done so much to teach the populace of the United States observation, perception, judgment, initiative, will-power, decision, business acumen, resourcefulness, organization, directive ability, self-confidence, driving-power, originality—and, in fact, practically everything else from Poultry-Farming to Poetry.

The first emotion which any student of the Booklets would have felt on seeing his mentor in the flesh—apart from that natural awe which falls upon us when we behold the great—would probably have been surprise at finding him so young. Hamilton Beamish was still in the early thirties. But the brain of Genius ripens quickly: and those who had the privilege of acquaintance with Mr. Beamish at the beginning of his career say that he knew everything there was to be known—or behaved as if he did—at the age of ten.

Hamilton Beamish's first act on reaching the roof of the Sheridan was to draw several deep breaths—through the nose, of course. Then, adjusting his glasses, he cast a flashing glance at Mullett: and, having inspected him for a moment, pursed his lips and shook his head.

"All wrong!" he said.

The words, delivered at a distance of two feet in the man's immediate rear, were spoken in the sharp, resonant voice of one who Gets Things Done—which, in its essentials, is rather like the note of a seal barking for fish. The result was that Mullett, who was highly strung, sprang some eighteen inches into the air and swallowed his chewing-gum. Owing to that great thinker's practice of wearing No-Jar Rubber Soles ('They Save The Spine'), he had had no warning of Mr. Beamish's approach.

"All wrong!" repeated Mr. Beamish.

And when Hamilton Beamish said 'All wrong!' it meant 'All wrong!' He was a man who thought clearly and judged boldly, without hedging or vacillation. He called a Ford a Ford.

"Wrong, sir?" faltered Mullett, when, realizing that there had been no bomb-outrage after all, he was able to speak.

"Wrong. Inefficient. Too much waste motion. From the muscular exertion which you are using on that broom you are obtaining a bare sixty-three or sixty-four per cent. of result-value. Correct this. Adjust your methods. Have you seen a policeman about here?"

"A policeman, sir?"

Hamilton Beamish clicked his tongue in annoyance, It was waste motion, but even efficiency experts have their feelings.

"A policeman. I said a policeman and I meant a policeman."

"Were you expecting one, sir?"

"I was and am."

Mullett cleared his throat.

"Would he be wanting anything, sir?" he asked a little nervously.

"He wants to become a poet. And I am going to make him one."

"A poet, sir?"

"Why not? I could make a poet out of far less promising material. I could make a poet out of two sticks and a piece of orange-peel, if they studied my booklet carefully. This fellow wrote to me, explaining his circumstances and expressing a wish to develop his higher self, and I became interested in his case and am giving him special tuition. He is coming up here to-day to look at the view and write a description of it in his own words. This I shall correct and criticize. A simple exercise in elementary composition."

"I see, sir."

"He is ten minutes late. I trust he has some satisfactory explanation. Meanwhile, where is Mr. Finch? I would like to speak to him."

"Mr. Finch is out, sir."

"He always seems to be out nowadays. When do you expect him back?"

"I don't know, sir. It all depends on the young lady."

"Mr. Finch has gone out with a young lady?"

"No, sir. Just gone to look at one."

"To look at one?" The author of the Booklets clicked his tongue once more. "You are drivelling, Mullett, Never drivel— it is dissipation of energy."

"It's quite true, Mr. Beamish. He has never spoken to this young lady—only looked at her."

"Explain yourself."

"Well sir, it's like this. I'd noticed for some time past that Mr. Finch had been getting what you might call choosey about his clothes. . . ."

"What do you mean, choosey?"

"Particular, sir."

"Then say particular, Mullett. Avoid jargon. Strive for the Word Beautiful. Read my booklet on 'Pure English.' Well?"

"Particular about his clothes, sir, I noticed Mr. Finch had been getting. Twice he had started out in the blue with the invisible pink twill and then suddenly stopped at the door of the elevator and gone back and changed into the dove-grey. And his ties, Mr. Beamish. There was no satisfying him. So I said to myself 'Hot dog!' "

"You said what?"

"Hot dog, Mr. Beamish."

"And why did you use this revolting expression?"

"What I meant was, sir, that I reckoned I knew what was at the bottom of all this."

"And were you right in this reckoning?"

A coy look came into Mullett's face.

"Yes, sir. You see, Mr. Finch's behaviour having aroused my curiosity, I took the liberty of following him one afternoon. I followed him all the way to Seventy-Ninth Street, East, Mr. Beamish."

"And then?"

"He walked up and down outside one of those big houses there, and presently a young lady came out. Mr. Finch looked at her, and she passed by. Then Mr. Finch looked after her and sighed and came away. The next afternoon I again took the liberty of following him, and the same thing happened. Only this time the young lady was coming in from a ride in the Park. Mr. Finch looked at her, and she passed into the house. Mr. Finch then remained staring at the house for so long that I was obliged to go and leave him at it, having the dinner to prepare. And what I meant, sir, when I said that the duration of Mr. Finch's absence depended on the young lady was that he stops longer when she comes in than when she goes out. He might be back at any minute, or he might not be back till dinner-time."

Hamilton Beamish frowned thoughtfully.

"I don't like this, Mullett."

"No, sir?"

"It sounds like love at first sight."

"Yes, sir."

"Have you read my booklet on 'The Marriage Sane'?"

"Well, sir, what with one thing and another and being very busy about the house . . ."

"In that booklet I argue very strongly against love at first sight."

"Do you indeed, sir?"

"I expose it for the mere delirious folly it is. The mating of the sexes should be a reasoned process, ruled by the intellect. What sort of young lady is this young lady?"

"Very attractive, sir."

"Tall? Short? Large? Small?"

"Small, sir. Small and roly-poly."

Hamilton Beamish shuddered violently.

"Don't use that nauseating adjective! Are you trying to convey the idea that she is short and stout?"

"Oh, no, sir, not stout. Just nice and plump. What I should describe as cuddly."

"Mullett," said Hamilton Beamish, "you will not, in my presence and while I have my strength, describe any of God's creatures as cuddly. Where you picked it up I cannot say, but you have the most abhorrent vocabulary I have ever encountered. . . . What's the matter?"

The valet was looking past him with an expression of deep concern.

"Why are you making faces, Mullett?" Hamilton Beamish turned. "Ah, Garroway," he said, "there you are at last. You should have been here ten minutes ago."

A policeman had come out on to the roof.

II

The policeman touched his cap. He was a long, stringy policeman, who flowed out of his uniform at odd spots, as if Nature, setting out to make a constable, had had a good deal of material left over which she had not liked to throw away but hardly seemed able to fit neatly into the general scheme. He had large, knobby wrists of a geranium hue and just that extra four or five inches of neck which disqualify a man for high honours in a beauty competition. His eyes were mild and blue and from certain angles he seemed all Adam's apple.

"I must apologize for being late, Mr. Beamish," he said. "I was detained at the station-house." He looked at Mullett uncertainly. "I think I have met this gentleman before?"

"No, you haven't," said Mullett quickly.

"Your face seems very familiar."

"Never seen me in your life."

"Come this way, Garroway," said Hamilton Beamish, interrupting curtly. "We cannot waste time in idle chatter." He led the officer to the edge of the roof and swept his hand round in a broad gesture. "Now, tell me. What do you see?"

The policeman's eyes sought the depths.

"That's the Purple Chicken down there." he said. "One of these days that joint will get pinched."

"Garroway!"

"Sir?"

"For some little time I have been endeavouring to instruct you in the principles of pure English. My efforts seem to have been wasted."

The policeman blushed.

"I beg your pardon, Mr. Beamish. One keeps slipping into it. It's the effect of mixing with the boys—with my colleagues—at the station-house. They are very lax in their speech. What I meant was that in the near future there was likely to be a raid conducted on the premises of the Purple Chicken, sir. It has been drawn to our attention that the Purple Chicken, defying the Eighteenth Amendment, still purveys alcoholic liquors."

"Never mind the Purple Chicken. I brought you up here to see what you could do in the way of a word-picture of the view. The first thing a poet needs is to develop his powers of observation. How does it strike you?"

The policeman gazed mildly at the horizon. His eyes flitted from the roof-tops of the city, spreading away in the distance, to the waters of the Hudson, glittering in the sun. He shifted his Adam's apple up and down two or three times, as one in deep thought.

"It looks very pretty, sir," he said at length.

"Pretty?" Hamilton Beamish's eyes flashed. You would never have thought, to look at him, that the J. in his name stood for James and that there had once been people who had called him Jimmy. "It isn't pretty at all."

"No, sir?"

"It's stark."

"Stark, sir?"

"Stark and grim. It makes your heart ache. You think of all the sorrow and sordid gloom which those roofs conceal and your heart bleeds. I may as well tell you, here and now, that if you are going about the place thinking things pretty, you will never make a modern poet. Be poignant, man, be poignant!"

"Yes, sir. I will, indeed, sir."

"Well, take your note-book and jot down a description of what you see. I must go down to my apartment and attend to one or two things. Look me up to-morrow."

"Yes, sir. Excuse me, sir, but who is that gentleman over there, sweeping with the broom? His face seemed so very familiar."

"His name is Mullett. He works for my friend, George Finch. But never mind about Mullett. Stick to your work. Concentrate! Concentrate!"

"Yes, sir. Most certainly, Mr. Beamish."

He looked with dog-like devotion at the thinker: then, licking the point of his pencil, bent himself to his task.

Hamilton Beamish turned on his No-Jar rubber heel and passed through the door to the stairs.

### III

Following his departure, silence reigned for some minutes on the roof of the Sheridan. Mullett resumed his sweeping, and Officer Garroway scribbled industriously in his note-book. But after about a quarter of an hour, feeling apparently that he had observed all there was to observe, he put book and pencil away in the recesses of his uniform and, approaching Mullett, subjected him to a mild but penetrating scrutiny.

"I feel convinced, Mr. Mullett," he said, "that I have seen your face before."

"And I say you haven't," said the valet testily.

"Perhaps you have a brother, Mr. Mullett, who resembles you?"

"Dozens. And even mother couldn't tell us apart."

The policeman sighed.

"I am an orphan," he said, "without brothers or sisters."

"Too bad."

"Stark," agreed the policeman. "Very stark and poignant. You don't think I could have seen a photograph of you anywhere, Mr. Mullett?"

"Haven't been taken for years."

"Strange!" said Officer Garroway meditatively. "Somehow—I cannot tell why—I seem to associate your face with a photograph."

"Not your busy day, this, is it?" said Mullett.

"I am off duty at the moment. I seem to see a photograph—several photographs—in some sort of collection . . ."

There could be no doubt by now that Mullett had begun to

find the conversation difficult. He looked like a man who had a favourite aunt in Poughkeepsie, and is worried about her asthma. He was turning to go, when there came out on to the roof from the door leading to the stairs a young man in a suit of dove-grey.

"Mullett!" he called.

The other hurried gratefully towards him, leaving the officer staring pensively at his spacious feet.

"Yes, Mr. Finch?"

It is impossible for an historian with a nice sense of values not to recognize the entry of George Finch, following immediately after that of J. Hamilton Beamish, as an anti-climax. Mr. Beamish filled the eye. An aura of authority went before him as the pillar of fire went before the Israelites in the desert. When you met J. Hamilton Beamish, something like a steam-hammer seemed to hit your consciousness and stun it long before he came within speaking-distance. In the case of George Finch nothing of this kind happened.

George looked what he was, a nice young small bachelor, of the type you see bobbing about the place on every side. One glance at him was enough to tell you that he had never written a Booklet and never would write a Booklet. In figure he was slim and slight: as to the face, pleasant and undistinguished. He had brown eyes which in certain circumstances could look like those of a stricken sheep: and his hair was of a light chestnut colour. It was possible to see his hair clearly, for he was not wearing his hat but carrying it in his hand.

He was carrying it reverently, as if he attached a high value to it. And this was strange, for it was not much of a hat. Once it may have been, but now it looked as if it had been both trodden on and kicked about.

"Mullett," he said, regarding this relic with a dreamy eye, "take this hat and put it away."

"Throw it away, sir?"

"Good heavens, no! Put it away—very carefully. Have you any tissue paper?"

"Yes, sir."

"Then wrap it up very carefully in tissue-paper and leave it on the table in my sitting-room."

"Very good, sir."

"Pardon me for interrupting," said a deprecating voice behind him, "but might I request a moment of your valuable time, Mr. Finch?"

Officer Garroway had left his fixed point, and was standing

in an attitude that seemed to suggest embarrassment. His mild eyes wore a somewhat timid expression.

"Forgive me if I intrude," said Officer Garroway.

"Not at all," said George.

"I am a policeman, sir."

"So I see."

"And," said Officer Garroway sadly, "I have a rather disagreeable duty to perform, I fear. I would avoid it, if I could reconcile the act with my conscience, but duty is duty. One of the drawbacks to the policeman's life, Mr. Finch, is that it is not easy for him always to do the gentlemanly thing."

"No doubt," said George.

Mullett swallowed apprehensively. The hunted look had come back to his face. Officer Garroway eyed him with a gentle solicitude.

"I would like to preface my remarks," he proceeded. "by saying that I have no personal animus against Mr. Mullett. I have seen nothing in my brief acquaintance with Mr. Mullett that leads me to suppose that he is not a pleasant companion and zealous in the performance of his work. Nevertheless, I think it right that you should know that he is an ex-convict."

"An ex-convict!"

"Reformed," said Mullett hastily.

"As to that, I cannot say," said Officer Garroway. "I can but speak of what I know. Very possibly, as he asserts, Mr. Mullett is a reformed character. But this does not alter the fact that he has done his bit of time: and in pursuance of my duty I can scarcely refrain from mentioning this to the gentleman who is his present employer. The moment I was introduced to him, I detected something oddly familiar about Mr. Mullett's face, and I have just recollected that I recently saw a photograph of him in the Rogues' Gallery at Headquarters. You are possibly aware, sir, that convicted criminals are 'mugged'—that is to say, photographed in various positions—at the commencement of their term of incarceration. This was done to Mr. Mullett some eighteen months ago when he was sentenced to a year's imprisonment for an inside burglary job. May I ask how Mr. Mullett came to be in your employment ?"

"He was sent to me by Mr. Beamish. Mr. Hamilton Beamish."

"In that case, sir, I have nothing further to say," said the policeman, bowing at the honoured name. "No doubt Mr. Beamish had excellent reasons for recommending Mr. Mullett. And, of course, as Mr. Mullett has long since expiated his offence,

I need scarcely say that we of the Force have nothing against him. I merely considered it my duty to inform you of his previous activities in case you should have any prejudice against employing a man of his antecedents. I must now leave you, as my duties compel me to return to the station-house. Good afternoon, Mr. Finch."

"Good afternoon."

"Good day, Mr. Mullett. Pleased to have met you. You did not by any chance run into a young fellow named Joe the Gorilla while you were in residence at Sing-Sing? No? I'm sorry. He came from my home town. I should have liked news of Joe."

Officer Garroway's departure was followed by a lengthy silence. George Finch shuffled his feet awkwardly. He was an amiable young man, and disliked unpleasant scenes. He looked at Mullett. Mullett looked at the sky.

"Er—Mullett," said George.

"Sir?"

"This is rather unfortunate."

"Most unpleasant for all concerned, sir."

"I think Mr. Beamish might have told me."

"No doubt he considered it unnecessary, sir. Being aware that I had reformed."

"Yes, but even so. . . . Er—Mullett."

"Sir?"

"The officer spoke of an inside burglary job. What was your exact—er—line?"

"I used to get a place as a valet, sir, and wait till I saw my chance, and then skin out with everything I could lay my hands on."

"You did, did you?"

"Yes, sir."

"Well, I do think Mr. Beamish might have dropped me a quiet hint. Good heavens! I may have been putting temptation in your way for weeks."

"You have, sir,—very serious temptation. But I welcome temptation, Mr. Finch. Every time I'm left alone with your pearl studs, I have a bout with the Tempter. 'Why don't you take them, Mullett?' he says to me. 'Why don't you take them?' It's splendid moral exercise, sir."

"I suppose so."

"Yes, sir, it's awful what that Tempter will suggest to me. Sometimes, when you're lying asleep, he says 'Slip a sponge of chloroform under his nose, Mullett, and clear out with the swag!' Just imagine it, sir."

"I am imagining it."

"But I win every time, sir. I've not lost one fight with that old Tempter since I've been in your employment, Mr. Finch."

"All the same, I don't believe you're going to remain in my employment, Mullett."

Mullett inclined his head resignedly.

"I was afraid of this, sir. The moment that flat-footed cop came on to this roof, I had a presentiment that there was going to be trouble. But I should appreciate it very much if you could see your way to reconsider, sir. I can assure you that I have completely reformed."

"Religion?"

"No, sir. Love."

The word seemed to touch some hidden chord in George Finch. The stern, set look vanished from his face. He gazed at his companion almost meltingly.

"Mullett! Do you love?"

"I do, indeed, sir. Fanny's her name, sir. Fanny Welch. She's a pickpocket."

"A pickpocket!"

"Yes, sir. And one of the smartest girls in the business. She could take your watch out of your waistcoat, and you'd be prepared to swear she hadn't been within a yard of you. It's almost an art, sir. But she's promised to go straight, if I will, and now I'm saving up to buy the furniture. So I do hope, sir. that you will reconsider. It would set me back if I fell out of a place just now."

George wrinkled his forehead.

"I oughtn't to."

"But you will, sir?"

"It's weak of me."

"Not it, sir. Christian, I call it."

George pondered.

"How long have you been with me, Mullett?"

"Just on a month, sir."

"And my pearl studs are still there?"

"Still in the drawer, sir."

"All right, Mullett. You can stay."

"Thank you very much indeed, sir."

There was a silence. The setting sun flung a carpet of gold across the roof. It was the hour at which men become confidential.

"Love is very wonderful, Mullett!" said George Finch.

"Makes the world go round, I often say, sir."

"Mullett."

"Sir?"

"Shall I tell you something?"

"If you please, sir."

"Mullett," said George Finch, "I, too, love."

"You surprise me, sir."

"You may have noticed that I have been fussy about my clothing of late, Mullett?"

"Oh, no, sir."

"Well, I have been, and that was the reason. She lives on East Seventy-Ninth Street, Mullett. I saw her first lunching at the Plaza with a woman who looked like Catherine of Russia. Her mother, no doubt."

"Very possibly, sir."

"I followed her home. I don't know why I am telling you this, Mullett."

"No, sir."

"Since then I have haunted the sidewalk outside her house. Do you know East Seventy-Ninth Street?"

"Never been there, sir."

"Well, fortunately it is not a very frequented thoroughfare, or I should have been arrested for loitering. Until to-day I have never spoken to her, Mullett."

"But you did to-day, sir?"

"Yes. Or, rather, she spoke to me. She has a voice like the fluting of young birds in the Springtime, Mullett."

"Very agreeable, no doubt, sir."

"Heavenly would express it better. It happened like this, Mullett. I was outside the house, when she came along leading a Scotch terrier on a leash. At that moment a gust of wind blew my hat off and it was bowling past her, when she stopped it. Sne trod on it, Mullett."

"Indeed, sir?"

"Yes, this hat which you see in my hand, has been trodden on by Her. This very hat."

"And then, sir?"

"In the excitement of the moment she dropped the leash, and the Scotch terrier ran off round the corner in the direction of Brooklyn. I went in pursuit, and succeeded in capturing it in Lexington Avenue. My hat dropped off again and was run over by a taxi-cab. But I retained my hold of the leash, and eventually restored the dog to its mistress. She said—and I want you to notice this very carefully, Mullett,—she said 'Oh, thank you so much!' "

"Did she, indeed, sir?"

"She did. Not merely 'Thank you!' or 'Oh, thank you!' but 'Oh, thank you so much!' " George Finch fixed a penetrating stare on his employee. "I think that is significant, Mullett."

"Extremely, sir."

"If she had wished to end the acquaintance then and there, would she have spoken so warmly?"

"Impossible, sir."

"And I've not told you all. Having said 'Oh, thank you so much!' she added: 'He *is* a naughty dog, isn't he?' You get the extraordinary subtlety of that, Mullett? The words 'He is a naughty dog' would have been a mere statement. By adding 'Isn't he?' she invited my opinion. She gave me to understand that she would welcome discussion on the subject. Do you know what I am going to do, directly I have dressed, Mullett?"

"Dine, sir?"

"Dine!" George shuddered. "No! There are moments when the thought of food is an outrage to everything that raises Man above the level of the beasts. As soon as I have dressed—and I shall dress very carefully—I am going to return to East Seventy-Ninth Street and I am going to ring the door-bell and I am going to go straight in and inquire after the dog. Hope it is none the worse for its adventure and so on. After all, it is only the civil thing. I mean these Scotch terriers . . . delicate, highly-strung animals. . . . Never can tell what effect unusual excitement may have on them. Yes, Mullett, that is what I propose to do. Brush my dress-clothes as you have never brushed them before."

"Very good, sir."

"Put me out a selection of ties. Say, a dozen."

"Yes, sir."

"And—did the boot-legger call this morning?"

"Yes, sir."

"Then mix me a very strong whisky-and-soda, Mullett," said George Finch. "Whatever happens, I must be at my best to-night."

## IV

To George, sunk in a golden reverie, there entered some few minutes later, jarring him back to life, a pair of three-pound dumb-bells, which shot abruptly out of the unknown and came trundling across the roof at him with a repulsive, clumping sound that would have disconcerted Romeo. They were followed by J. Hamilton Beamish on all fours. Hamilton Beamish, who believed in the healthy body as well as the sound mind, always did half an hour's open-air work with the bells of an evening: and, not for the first time, he had tripped over the top stair.

He recovered his balance, his dumb-bells and his spectacles in three labour-saving movements: and with the aid of the last-named was enabled to perceive George.

"Oh, there you are!" said Hamilton Beamish.

"Yes," said George, "and . . ."

"What's all this I hear from Mullett?" asked Hamilton Beamish.

"What," inquired George simultaneously, "is all this I hear from Mullett?"

"Mullett says you're now fooling about after some girl up-town."

"Mullett says you knew he was an ex-convict when you recommended him to me."

Hamilton Beamish decided to dispose of this triviality before going on to more serious business.

"Certainly," he said. "Didn't you read my series in the *Yale Review* on the 'Problem of the Reformed Criminal'? I point out very clearly that there is nobody with such a strong bias towards honesty as the man who has just come out of prison. It stands to reason. If you had been laid up for a year in hospital as the result of jumping off this roof, what would be the one outdoor sport in which, on emerging, you would be most reluctant to indulge? Jumping off roofs, undoubtedly."

George continued to frown in a dissatisfied way.

"That's all very well, but a fellow doesn't want ex-convicts hanging about the home."

"Nonsense! You must rid yourself of this old-fashioned prejudice against men who have been in Sing-Sing. Try to look on the place as a sort of University which fits its graduates for the problems of the world without. Morally speaking, such men are the student body. You have no fault to find with Mullett, have you?"

"No, I can't say I have."

"Does his work well?"

"Yes."

"Not stolen anything from you?"

"No."

"Then why worry? Dismiss the man from your mind. And now let me hear all about this girl of yours"

"How do you know anything about it?"

"Mullett told me."

"How did he know?"

"He followed you a couple of afternoons and saw all."

George turned pink.

"I'll go straight in and fire that man. The snake!"

"You will do nothing of the kind. He acted as he did from pure zeal and faithfulness. He saw you go out, muttering to yourself . . ."

"Did I mutter?" said George, startled.

"Certainly you muttered. You muttered, and you were exceedingly strange in your manner. So naturally Mullett, good zealous fellow, followed you to see that you came to no harm. He reports that you spend a large part of your leisure goggling at some girl in Seventy-Ninth Street, East."

George's pink face turned a shade pinker. A sullen look came into it.

"Well, what about it?"

"That's what I want to know—what about it?"

"Why shouldn't I goggle?"

"Why should you?"

"Because," said George Finch, looking like a stuffed frog, "I love her."

"Nonsense!"

"It isn't nonsense."

"Have you ever read my booklet on 'The Marriage Sane'?"

"No, I haven't."

"I show there that love is a reasoned emotion that springs from mutual knowledge, increasing over an extended period of time, and a community of tastes. How can you love a girl when you have never spoken to her and don't even know her name?"

"I do know her name."

"How?"

"I looked through the telephone directory till I found out who lived at Number 16 East Seventy-Ninth Street. It took me about a week, because . . ."

"Sixteen East Seventy-Ninth Street? You don't mean that this girl you've been staring at is little Molly Waddington?"

George started.

"Waddington is the name, certainly. That's why I was such an infernal time getting to it in the book. Waddington, Sigsbee H."

George choked emotionally, and gazed at his friend with awed eyes. "Hamilton! Hammy, old man! You—you don't mean to say you actually know her? Not positively know her?"

"Of course I know her Know her intimately. Many's the time I've seen her in her bath-tub."

George quivered from head to foot.

"It's a lie! A foul and contemptible . . ."

"When she was a child."

"Oh, when she was a child?" George became calmer. "Do you mean to say you've known her since she was a child? Why, then you must be in love with her yourself."

"Nothing of the kind."

"You stand there and tell me," said George incredulously, "that you have known this wonderful girl for many years and are not in love with her?"

"I do."

George regarded his friend with a gentle pity. He could only explain this extraordinary statement by supposing that there was some sort of a kink in Hamilton Beamish. Sad, for in so many ways he was such a fine fellow.

"The sight of her has never made you feel that, to win one smile, you could scale the skies and pluck out the stars and lay them at her feet?"

"Certainly not. Indeed, when you consider that the nearest star is several million . . ."

"All right," said George. "All right. Let it go. And now," he went on simply, "tell me all about her and her people and her house and her dog and what she was like as a child and when she first bobbed her hair and who is her favourite poet and where she went to school and what she likes for breakfast . . ."

Hamilton Beamish reflected.

"Well, I first knew Molly when her mother was alive."

"Her mother is alive. I've seen her. A woman who looks like Catherine of Russia."

"That's her stepmother. Sigsbee H. married again a couple of years ago."

"Tell me about Sigsbee H."

Hamilton Beamish twirled a dumb-bell thoughtfully.

"Sigsbee H. Waddington," he said. "is one of those men who must, I think, during the formative years of their boyhood have been kicked on the head by a mule. It has been well said of Sigsbee H. Waddington that, if men were dominoes, he would be the double-blank. One of the numerous things about him that rule him out of serious consideration by intelligent persons is the fact that he is a synthetic Westerner."

"A synthetic Westerner?"

"It is little known, but growing, sub-species akin to the synthetic Southerner,—with which curious type you are doubtless familiar."

"I don't think I am."

"Nonsense. Have you never been in a restaurant where the orchestra played Dixie?"

"Of course."

"Well, then, on such occasions you will have noted that the man who gives a rebel yell and springs on his chair and waves a napkin with flashing eyes is always a suit-and-cloak salesman named Rosenthal or Bechstein who was born in Passaic, New Jersey, and has never been farther South than Far Rockaway. That is the synthetic Southerner."

"I see."

"Sigsbee H. Waddington is a synthetic Westerner. His whole life, with the exception of one summer vacation when he went to Maine, has been spent in New York State: and yet, to listen to him, you would think he was an exiled cowboy. I fancy it must be the effect of seeing too many Westerns in the movies. Sigsbee Waddington has been a keen supporter of the motion-pictures from their inception: and was, I believe, one of the first men in this city to hiss the villain. Whether it was Tom Mix who caused the trouble, or whether his weak intellect was gradually sapped by seeing William S. Hart kiss his horse, I cannot say: but the fact remains that he now yearns for the great open spaces and, if you want to ingratiate yourself with him, all you have to do is to mention that you were born in Idaho,—a fact which I hope that, as a rule, you carefully conceal."

"I will," said George enthusiastically. "I can't tell you how grateful I am to you, Hamilton, for giving me this information."

"You needn't be. It will do you no good whatever. When Sigsbee Waddington married for the second time, he to all intents and purposes sold himself down the river. To call him a cipher in the home would be to give a too glowing picture of his importance. He does what his wife tells him—that and nothing more. She is the one with whom you want to ingratiate yourself."

"How can this be done?"

It can't be done. Mrs. Sigsbee Waddington is not an easy woman to conciliate."

"A tough baby?" inquired George anxiously.

Hamilton Beamish frowned.

"I dislike the expression. It is the sort of expression Mullett would use: and I know few things more calculated to make a thinking man shudder than Mullett's vocabulary. Nevertheless, in a certain crude horrible way it does describe Mrs. Waddington. There is an ancient belief in Tibet that mankind is descended from a demoness named Drasrinmo and a monkey. Both Sigsbee H. and Mrs. Waddington do much to bear out this theory. I am loath to speak ill of a woman, but it is no use trying to conceal the fact that Mrs. Waddington is a bounder and a snob and has a soul like the under-side of a flat stone. She worships wealth and importance. She likes only the rich and the titled. As a matter of fact, I happen to know that there is an English lord hanging about the place whom she wants Molly to marry."

"Over my dead body," said George.

"That could no doubt be arranged. My poor George," said Hamilton Beamish, laying a dumb-bell affectionately on his friend's head, "you are taking on too big a contract. You are going out of your class. It is not as if you were one of these dashing young Lochinvar fellows. You are mild and shy. You are diffident and timid. I class you among Nature's white mice. It would take a woman like Mrs. Sigsbee Waddington about two and a quarter minutes to knock you for a row of Portuguese ash-cans,—er, as Mullett would say," added Hamilton Beamish with a touch of confusion

"She couldn't eat me," said George valiantly.

"I don't know so much. She is not a vegetarian."

I was thinking," said George, "that you might take me round and introduce me."

"And have your blood on my head? No, no."

"What do you mean, my blood? You talk as if this woman were a syndicate of gunmen. I'm not afraid of her. To get to know Molly"—George gulped—"I would fight a mad bull."

Hamilton Beamish was touched. This great man was human.

"These are brave words, George. You extort my admiration. I disapprove of the reckless, unconsidered way you are approaching this matter, and I still think you would be well advised to read 'The Marriage Sane' and get a proper estimate of Love: but I cannot but like your spirit. If you really wish it, therefore, I will take you round and introduce you to Mrs. Sigsbee H. Waddington. And may the Lord have mercy on your soul."

"Hamilton! To-night?"

"Not to-night. I am lecturing to the West Orange Daughters of Minerva to-night on The Modern Drama. Some other time."

"Then to-night," said George, blushing faintly, "I think I may as well just stroll round Seventy-Ninth Street way and—er—well, just stroll round."

"What is the good of that?"

"Well, I can look at the house, can't I?"

"Young blood!" said Hamilton Beamish indulgently. "Young blood!"

He poised himself firmly on his No-Jars, and swung the dumb-bells in a forceful arc.

V

"Mullett," said George.

"Sir?"

"Have you pressed my dress clothes?"

"Yes, sir."

"And brushed them?"

"Yes, sir."

"My ties—are they laid out?"

"In a neat row, sir."

George coughed.

"Mullett!"

"Sir?"

"You recollect the little chat we were having just now?"

"Sir?"

"About the young lady I—er . . ."

"Oh, yes, sir."

"I understand you have seen her."

"Just a glimpse, sir."

George coughed again.

"Ah—rather attractive, Mullett, don't you think?"

"Extremely, sir. Very cuddly."

"The exact adjective I would have used myself, Mullett!"

"Indeed, sir?"

"Cuddly! A beautiful word."

"I think so, sir."

George coughed for the third time.

"A lozenge, sir?" said Mullett solicitously.

"No, thank you."

"Very good, sir."

"Mullett!"

"Sir?"

"I find that Mr. Beamish is an intimate friend of this young lady."

"Fancy that, sir!"

"He is going to introduce me."

"Very gratifying, I am sure, sir."

George sighed dreamily.

"Life is very sweet, Mullett."

"For those that like it, sir,—yes, sir."

"Lead me to the ties," said George.

# CHAPTER TWO

## I

At the hour of seven-thirty, just when George Finch was trying out his fifth tie, a woman stood pacing the floor in the Byzantine boudoir at Number 16 Seventy-Ninth Street, East.

At first sight this statement may seem contradictory. Is it possible, the captious critic may ask, for a person simultaneously to stand and pace the floor? The answer is Yes, if he or she is sufficiently agitated as to the soul. You do it by placing yourself on a given spot and scrabbling the feet alternately like a cat kneading a hearth-rug. It is sometimes the only method by which strong women can keep from having hysterics.

Mrs. Sigsbee H. Waddington was a strong woman. In fact, so commanding was her physique that a stranger might have supposed her to be one in the technical, or circus, sense. She was not tall, but she had bulged so generously in every possible direction that, when seen for the first time, she gave the impression of enormous size. No theatre, however little its programme had managed to attract the public, could be said to be 'sparsely filled' if Mrs. Waddington had dropped in to look at the show. Public speakers, when Mrs. Waddington was present, had the illusion that they were addressing most of the population of the United States. And when she went to Carlsbad or Aix-les-Bains to take the waters, the authorities huddled together nervously and wondered if there would be enough to go round.

Her growing bulk was a perpetual sorrow—one of the many—to her husband. When he had married her, she had been slim and *svelte*. But she had also been the relict of the late P. Homer Horlick, the Cheese King, and he had left her several million dollars. Most of the interest accruing from this fortune she had, so it sometimes seemed to Sigsbee H. Waddington, spent on starchy foods.

Mrs. Waddington stood and paced the floor, and presently the door opened.

"Lord Hunstanton," announced Ferris, the butler.

The standard of male looks presented up to the present in this story has not been high: but the man who now entered did much to raise the average. He was tall and slight and elegant, with frank blue eyes—one of them preceded by an eye-glass—and one of those clipped moustaches. His clothes had been cut by an inspired tailor and pressed by a genius. His tie was simply an ethereal white butterfly, straight from heaven, that hovered over the collar-stud as if it were sipping pollen from some exotic flower. (George Finch, now working away at number eight and having just got it creased in four places, would have screamed hoarsely with envy at the sight of that tie.)

"Well, here I am," said Lord Hunstanton. He paused for a moment, then added, "What, what!" as if he felt that it was expected of him.

"It was so kind of you to come," said Mrs. Waddington, pivoting on her axis and panting like a hart after the waterbrooks.

"Not at all."

"I knew I could rely on you."

"You have only to command."

"You are such a true friend, though I have known you only such a short time."

"Is anything wrong?" asked Lord Hunstanton.

He was more than a little surprised to find himself at seven-forty in a house where he had been invited to dine at half-past eight. His dressing had been interrupted by a telephone-call from Mrs. Waddington's butler, begging him to come round at once: and noting his hostess's agitation, he hoped that nothing had gone wonky with the dinner.

"Everything is wrong!"

Lord Hunstanton sighed inaudibly. Did this mean cold meat and a pickle?

"Sigsbee is having one of his spells!"

"You mean he has been taken ill?"

"Not ill. Fractious." Mrs. Waddington gulped. "It's so hard that this should have occurred on the night of an important dinner-party, after you have taken such trouble with his education. I have said a hundred times that, since you came, Sigsbee has been a different man. He knows all the forks now, and can even talk intelligently about *souffles*."

"I am only too glad if any little pointers I have been able to. . . ."

"And when I take him out for a run he always walks on the outside of the pavement. And here he must go, on the night of my biggest dinner-party, and have one of his spells."

"What is the trouble ? Is he violent ?"

"No, Sullen."

"What about ?"

Mrs. Waddington's mouth set in a hard line.

"Sigsbee is pining for the West again!"

"You don't say so ?"

"Yes, sir, he's pining for the great wide open spaces of the West. He says the East is effete and he wants to be out there among the silent canyons where men are men. If you want to know what I think, somebody's been feeding him Zane Grey."

"Can nothing be done ?"

"Yes—in time. I can get him right if I'm given time, by stopping his pocket money. But I need time, and here he is, an hour before my important dinner, with some of the most wealthy and exclusive people in New York expected at any moment, refusing to put on his dress clothes and saying that all a man that is a man needs is to shoot his bison and cut off a steak and cook it by the light of the western stars. And what I want to know is, what am I to do ?"

Lord Hunstanton twisted his moustache thoughtfully.

"Very perplexing."

"I thought if you went and had a word with him. . . ."

"I doubt if it would do any good. I suppose you couldn't dine without him ?"

"It would make us thirteen."

"I see." His lordship's face brightened. "I've got it! Send Miss Waddington to reason with him."

"Molly ? You think he would listen to her ?"

"He is very fond of her."

Mrs. Waddington reflected.

"It's worth trying. I'll go up and see if she is dressed. She is a dear girl, isn't she, Lord Hunstanton ?"

"Charming, charming."

"I'm sure I'm as fond of her as if she were my own daughter."

"No doubt."

"Though, of course, dearly as I love her, I am never foolishly indulgent. So many girls to-day are spoiled by foolish indulgence."

"True."

"My great wish, Lord Hunstanton, is one day to see her happily married to some good man."

His lordship closed the door behind Mrs. Waddington and stood for some moments in profound thought. He may have been wondering what was the earliest he could expect a cocktail, or he may have been musing on some deeper subject—if there is a deeper subject.

## II

Mrs. Waddington navigated upstairs, and paused before a door near the second landing.

"Molly!"

"Yes, mother?"

Mrs. Waddington was frowning as she entered the room. How often she had told the girl to call her 'mater'!

But this was a small point, and not worth mentioning at a time like the present. She sank into a chair with a creaking groan. Strong woman though she was, Mrs. Sigsbee Waddington, like the chair, was near to breaking down.

"Good heavens, mother! What's the matter?"

"Send her away," muttered Mrs. Waddington, nodding at her stepdaughter's maid.

"All right, mother. I shan't want you any more, Julie. I can manage now. Shall I get you a glasss of water, mother?"

Molly looked at her suffering stepparent with gentle concern, wishing that she had something stronger than water to offer. But her late mother had brought her up in that silly, stuffy way in which old-fashioned mothers used to bring up their daughters: and, incredible as it may seem in these enlightened days, Molly Waddington had reached the age of twenty without forming even a nodding acquaintance with alcohol. Now, no doubt, as she watched her stepmother gulping before her like a moose that has had trouble in the home, she regretted that she was not one of those sensible modern girls who always carry a couple of shots around with them in a jewelled flask.

But, though a defective upbringing kept her from being useful in this crisis, nobody could deny that, as she stood there half-dressed for dinner, Molly Waddington was extremely ornamental.

If George Finch could have seen her at that moment. . . . But then if George Finch had seen her at that moment, he would immediately have shut his eyes like a gentleman: for there was that about her costume, in its present stage of development, which was not for the male gaze.

Still, however quickly he had shut his eyes, he could not have shut them rapidly enough to keep from seeing that Mullett, in his recent remarks on the absorbing subject, had shown an even nicer instinct for the *mot juste* than he had supposed. Beyond all chance for evasion or doubt, Molly Waddington was cuddly. She was wearing primrose knickers, and her silk-stockinged legs, tapered away to little gold shoes. Her pink fingers were clutching at a blue dressing-jacket with swansdown trimming. Her bobbed hair hung about a round little face with a tip-tilted little nose. Her eyes were large, her teeth small and white and even. She had a little brown mole on the back of her neck and—in short, to sum the whole thing up, if George Finch could have caught even the briefest glimpse of her at this juncture, he must inevitably have fallen over sideways, yapping like a dog.

Mrs. Waddington's breathing had become easier, and she was sitting up in her chair with something like the old imperiousness.

"Molly," said Mrs. Waddington, "have you been giving your father Zane Grey?"

"Of course not."

"You're sure?"

"Quite. I don't think there's any Zane Grey in the house."

"Then he's been sneaking out and seeing Tom Mix again," said Mrs. Waddington.

"You don't mean . . . ?"

"Yes! He's got one of his spells."

"A bad one?"

"So bad that he refuses to dress for dinner. He says that if the boys"—Mrs. Waddington shuddered—"if the boys don't like him in a flannel shirt, he won't come in to dinner at all. And Lord Hunstanton suggested that I should send you to reason with him."

"Lord Hunstanton? Has he arrived already?"

"I telephoned for him. I am coming to rely on Lord Hunstanton more and more every day. What a dear fellow he is!"

"Yes," said Molly, a little dubiously. She was not fond of his lordship.

"So handsome."

"Yes."

"Such breeding."

"I suppose so."

"I should be very happy," said Mrs. Waddington, "if a man like Lord Hunstanton asked you to be his wife."

Molly fiddled with the trimming of her dressing-jacket. This was not the first time the subject had come up between her stepmother and herself. A remark like the one just recorded was Mrs. Waddington's idea of letting fall a quiet hint.

"Well . . ." said Molly.

"What do you mean, well?"

"Well, don't you think he's rather stiff."

"Stiff!"

"Don't you find him a little starchy?"

"If you mean that Lord Hunstanton's manners are perfect, I agree with you."

"I'm not sure that I like a man's manners to be too perfect," said Molly meditatively. "Don't you think a shy man can be rather attractive?" She scraped the toe of one gold shoe against the heel of the other. "The sort of man I think I should rather like." she said, a dreamy look in her eyes, "would be a sort of slimmish, smallish man with nice brown eyes and rather gold-y, chestnutty hair, who kind of looks at you from a distance because he's too shy to speak to you and, when he does get a chance to speak to you, sort of chokes and turns pink and twists his fingures and makes funny noises and trips over his feet and looks rather a lamb and . . ."

Mrs Waddington had risen from her chair like a storm-cloud brooding over a country-side.

"Molly!" she cried. "Who is this young man?"

"Why, nobody, of course! Just some one I sort of imagined."

"Oh!" said Mrs. Waddington, relieved. "You spoke as if you knew him."

"What a strange idea!"

"If any young man ever does look at you and make funny noises, you will ignore him."

"Of course."

Mrs. Waddington started.

"All this nonsense you have been talking has made me forget about your father. Put on your dress and go down to him at once. Reason with him! If he refuses to come in to dinner, we shall be thirteen, and my party will be ruined."

"I'll be ready in a couple of minutes. Where is he?"

"In the library."

"I'll be right down."

"And when you have seen him, go into the drawing-room and talk to Lord Hunstanton. He is all alone."

"Very well, mother."

"Mater."

"Mater," said Molly.

She was one of those nice, dutiful girls.

## III

In addition to being a nice, dutiful girl, Molly Waddington was also a persuasive, wheedling girl. Better proof of this statement can hardly be afforded than by the fact that, as the clocks were pointing to ten minutes past eight, a red-faced little man with stiff grey hair and a sulky face shambled down the stairs of Number 16 East Seventy-Ninth Street, and, pausing in the hall, subjected Ferris, the butler, to an offensive glare. It was Sigsbee H. Waddington, fully, if sloppily, dressed in the accepted mode of gentlemen of social standing about to dine.

The details of any record performance are always interesting, so it may be mentioned that Molly had reached the library at seven minutes to eight. She had started wheedling at exactly six minutes and forty-five seconds to the hour. At seven fifty-four Sigsbee Waddinton had begun to weaken. At seven fifty-seven he was fighting in the last ditch: and at seven fifty-nine, vowing he would ne'er consent, he consented.

Into the arguments used by Molly we need not enter fully. It is enough to say that, if a man loves his daughter dearly, and if she comes to him and says that she has been looking forward to a certain party and is wearing a new dress for that party, and if, finally, she adds that, should he absent himself from that party, the party and her pleasure will be ruined,—then, unless the man has a heart of stone, he will give in. Sigsbee Waddington had not a heart of stone. Many good judges considered that he had a head of concrete, but nobody had ever disparaged his heart. At eight precisely he was in his bedroom, shovelling on his dress clothes: and now, at ten minutes past, he stood in the hall and looked disparagingly at Ferris.

Sigsbee Waddington thought Ferris was an over-fed wart.

Ferris thought Sigsbee Waddington ought to be ashamed to appear in public in a tie like that.

But thoughts are not words. What Ferris actually said was: "A cocktail, sir?"

And what Sigsbee Waddington actually said was:

"Yup! Gimme!"

There was a pause. Mr. Waddington still unsoothed, continued to glower. Ferris, resuming his marmoreal calm, had begun to muse once more, as was his habit when in thought, on Brangmarley Hall, Little-Seeping-in-the-Wold, Salop, Eng., where he had spent the early, happy days of his butlerhood.

"Ferris!" said Mr. Waddington at length.

"Sir?"

"You ever been out West, Ferris?"

"No, sir."

"Ever want to go?"

"No, sir."

"Why not?" demanded Mr. Waddington belligerently.

"I understand that in the Western States of America, sir, there is a certain lack of comfort, and the social amenities are not rigorously observed."

"Gangway!" said Mr. Waddington, making for the front door,

He felt stifled. He wanted air. He yearned, if only for a few brief instants, to be alone with the silent stars.

It would be idle to deny that, at this particular moment, Sigsbee H. Waddington was in a dangerous mood. The history of nations shows that the wildest upheavals come from those peoples that have been most rigorously oppressed: and it is so with individuals. There is no man so terrible in his spasmodic fury as the hen-pecked husband during his short spasms of revolt. Even Mrs. Waddington recognized that, no matter how complete her control normally, Sigsbee H., when having one of his spells, practically amounted to a rogue elephant. Her policy was to keep out of his way till the fever passed, and then to discipline him severely.

As Sigsbee Waddington stood on the pavement outside his house, drinking in the dust-and-gasolene mixture which passes for air in New York and scanning the weak imitation stars which are the best the East provides, he was grim and squiggle-eyed and ripe for murders, stratagems and spoils. Molly's statement that there was no Zane Grey in the house had been very far from the truth. Sigsbee Waddington had his private store, locked away in a secret cupboard, and since early morning 'Riders of the Purple Sage' had hardly ever been out of his hand. During the afternoon, moreover, he had managed to steal away to a motion-picture house on Sixth Avenue where they were presenting Henderson Hoover and Sara Svelte in 'That L'il Gal From The Bar B Ranch.'

Sigsbee Waddington, as he stood on the pavement, was clad in dress clothes and looked like a stage waiter, but at heart he was wearing chaps and a Stetson hat and people spoke of him as Two-Gun Thomas.

A Rolls-Royce drew up at the kerb, and Mr. Waddington moved a step or two away. A fat man alighted and helped his fatter wife out. Mr. Waddington recognized them. B. and Mrs. Brewster Bodthorne. B. Brewster was the first vice-president of Amalgamated Tooth-Brushes, and rolled in money.

"Pah!" muttered Mr. Waddington, sickened to the core.

The pair vanished into the house, and presently another Rolls-Royce arrived, followed by a Hispano-Suiza. Consolidated Popcorn and wife emerged, and then United Beef and daughter. A consignment worth on the hoof between eighty and a hundred million.

"How long?" moaned Mr. Waddington. "How long?"

And then, as the door closed, he was aware of a young man behaving strangely on the pavement some few feet away from him.

IV

The reason why George Finch—for it was he—was behaving strangely was that he was a shy young man and consequently unable to govern his movements by the light of pure reason. The ordinary tough-skinned everyday young fellow with a face of brass and the placid gall of an Army mule would, of course, if he had decided to pay a call upon a girl in order to make inquiries about her dog, have gone right ahead and done it. He would have shot his cuffs and straightened his tie, and then trotted up the steps and punched the front-door bell. Not so the diffident George.

George's methods were different. Graceful and, in their way, pretty to watch, but different. First, he stood for some moments on one foot, staring at the house. Then, as if some friendly hand had dug three inches of a meat-skewer into the flesh of his leg, he shot forward in a spasmodic bound. Checking this as he reached the steps, he retreated a pace or two and once more became immobile. A few moments later, the meat-skewer had got to work again and he had sprung up the steps, only to leap backwards once more on to the sidewalk.

When Mr. Waddington first made up his mind to accost him, he had begun to walk round in little circles, mumbling to himself.

Sigsbee Waddington was in no mood for this sort of thing. It was the sort of thing, he felt bitterly, which could happen only in this degraded East. Out West, men are men and do not dance tangoes by themselves on front doorsteps. Venters, the hero of 'Riders of the Purple Sage,' he recalled, had been described by the author as standing 'tall and straight, his wide shoulders flung back, with the muscles of his arms rippling and a blue flame of defiance in his gaze.' How different, felt Mr. Waddington, from this imbecile young man who seemed content to waste life's springtime playing solitary round-games in the public streets.

"Hey!" he said sharply.

The exclamation took George amidships just as he had returned to the standing-on-one-leg position. It caused him to lose his balance, and if he had not adroitly clutched Mr. Waddington by the left ear, it is probable that he would have fallen.

"Sorry," said George, having sorted himself out.

"What's the use of being sorry?" growled the injured man, tenderly feeling his ear. "And what the devil are you doing any-way?"

"Just paying a call," explained George.

"Doing a what?"

"I'm paying a formal call at this house."

"Which house?"

"This one. Number sixteen. Waddington, Sigsbee H."

Mr. Waddington regarded him with unconcealed hostility.

"Oh, you are, are you? Well, it may interest you to learn that I am Sigsbee H. Waddington, and I don't know you from Adam. So now!"

George gasped

"You are Sigsbee H. Waddington?" he said reverently.

"I am."

George was gazing at Molly's father as at some beautiful work of art—a superb painting, let us say—the sort of thing which connoisseurs fight for and which finally gets knocked down to Dr. Rosenbach for three hundred thousand dollars. Which will give the reader a rough idea of what love can do: for, considered in a calm and unbiased spirit, Sigsbee Waddington was little, if anything, to look at.

"Mr. Waddington," said George, "I am proud to meet you."

"You're what?"

"Proud to meet you."

"What of it?" said Sigsbee Waddington churlishly.

"Mr. Waddington," said George, "I was born in Idaho."

Much has been written of the sedative effect of pouring oil on the raging waters of the ocean, and it is on record that the vision of the Holy Grail, sliding athwart a rainbow, was generally sufficient to still the most fiercely warring passions of young knights in the Middle Ages. But never since history began can there have been so sudden a change from red-eyed hostility to smiling benevolence as occurred now in Sigsbee H. Waddington. As George's words, like some magic spell, fell upon his ears, he forgot that one of those ears were smarting badly as the result of the impulsive clutch of this young man before him. Wrath melted from his soul like dew from a flower beneath the sun. He beamed on George. He pawed George's sleeve with a paternal hand.

"You really come from the West?" he cried.

"I do."

"From God's own country? From the great wonderful West with its wide open spaces where a red-blooded man can fill his lungs with the breath of freedom?"

It was not precisely the way George would have described East Gilead, which was a stuffy little hamlet with a poorish water-supply and one of the worst soda-fountains in Idaho, but he nodded amiably.

Mr. Waddington dashed a hand across his eyes.

"The West! Why, it's like a mother to me! I love every flower that blooms on the broad bosom of its sweeping plains, every sun-kissed peak of its everlasting hills."

George said he did, too.

"Its beautiful valleys, mystic in their transparent, luminous gloom, weird in the quivering, golden haze of the lightning that flickers over them."

"Ah!" said George.

"The dark spruces tipped with glimmering lights! The aspens bent low in the wind, like waves in a tempest at sea!"

"Can you beat them!" said George.

"The forest of oaks tossing wildly and shining with gleams of fire!"

"What could be sweeter?" said George.

"Say, listen," said Mr. Waddington, "you and I must see more of each other. Come and have a bite of dinner!"

"Now?"

"Right this very minute. We've got a few of these puny-souled Eastern millionaires putting on the nose-bag with us to-night, but you won't mind them. We'll just look at 'em and despise 'em. And after dinner you and I will slip off to my study and have a good chat."

"But won't Mrs. Waddington object to an unexpected guest at the last moment?"

Mr. Waddington expanded his chest, and tapped it spaciously.

"Say, listen—what's your name?—Finch?—Say, listen, Finch, do I look like the sort of man who's bossed by his wife?"

It was precisely the sort of man that George thought he did look like, but this was not the moment to say so.

"It's very kind of you," he said.

"Kind? Say, listen, if I was riding along those illimitable prairies and got storm-bound outside your ranch in Idaho, you wouldn't worry about whether you were being kind when you asked me in for a bite, would you? You'd say, 'Step right in, pardner! The place is yours.' Very well, then!"

Mr. Waddington produced a latch-key.

"Ferris," said Mr. Waddington in the hall, "tell those galoots down in the kitchen to set another place at table. A pard of mine from the West has happened in for a snack."

## CHAPTER THREE

### I

THE perfect hostess makes a point of never displaying discomposure. In moments of trial she aims at the easy repose of manner of a Red Indian at the stake. Nevertheless, there was a moment when, as she saw Sigsbee H. caracole into the drawing-room with George and heard him announce in a ringing voice that this fine young son of the western prairies had come to take pot-luck, Mrs. Waddington indisputably reeled.

She recovered herself. All the woman in her was urging her to take Sigsbee H. by his outstanding ears and shake him till he came unstuck, but she fought the emotion down. Gradually her glazed eye lost its dead-fishy look. Like Death in the poem, she 'grinned horrible a ghastly smile.' And it was with a well-assumed graciousness that she eventually extended to George the quivering right hand which, had she been a less highly civilized woman, would about now have been landing on the side of her husband's head, swung from the hip.

"Chahmed!" said Mrs. Waddington. "So very, very glad that you were able to come, Mr.——"

She paused, and George, eyeing her mistily, gathered that she wished to be informed of his name. He would have been glad to supply the information, but unfortunately at the moment he had forgotten it himself. He had a dim sort of idea that it began with an F or a G, but beyond that his mind was a blank.

The fact was that, in the act of shaking hands with his hostess, George Finch had caught sight of Molly, and the spectacle had been a little too much for him.

Molly was wearing the new evening dress of which she had spoken so feelingly to her father at their recent interview, and it seemed to George as if the scales had fallen from his eyes and he was seeing her for the first time. Before, in a vague way he had supposed that she possessed arms and shoulders and hair, but it was only at this moment that he perceived how truly those arms and those shoulders and that hair were arms and shoulders and hair in the deepest and holiest sense of the words. It was as if a goddess had thrown aside the veil. It was as if a statue had come to life. It was as if . . . well, the point we are trying to make is that George Finch was impressed. His eyes enlarged to the dimensions of saucers; the tip of his nose quivered like a rabbit's: and unseen hands began to pour iced water down his spine.

Mrs. Waddington, having given him a long, steady look that blistered his forehead, turned away and began to talk to a soda-water magnate. She had no real desire to ascertain George's name, though she would have read it with pleasure on a tombstone.

"Dinner is served," announced Ferris, the butler, appearing noiselessly like a Djinn summoned by the rubbing of a lamp.

George found himself swept up in the stampede of millionaires. He was still swallowing feebly.

There are few things more embarrassing to a shy and sensitive young man than to be present at a dinner-party where something seems to tell him he is not really wanted. The something that seemed to tell George Finch he was not really wanted at to-night's festive gathering was Mrs. Waddington's eye, which kept shooting down the table at intervals and reducing him to pulp at those very moments when he was beginning to feel that, if treated with gentle care and kindness, he might eventually recover.

It was an eye that, like a thermos flask, could be alternately extremely hot and intensely cold. When George met it during the soup course he had the feeling of having encountered a simoom while journeying across an African desert. When, on the other hand, it sniped him as he toyed with his fish, his sensations were those of a searcher for the Pole who unexpectedly bumps into a blizzard. But, whether it was cold or hot, there was always in Mrs. Waddington's gaze one constant factor—a sort of sick loathing which nothing that he could ever do, George felt, would have the power to allay. It was the kind of look which Sisera might have surprised in the eye of Jael the wife of Heber, had he chanced to catch it immediately before she began operations with the spike. George had made one new friend that night, but not two.

The consequence was that as regards George Finch's contribution to the feast of wit and flow of soul at that dinner-party we have nothing to report. He uttered no epigrams. He told no good stories. Indeed, the only time he spoke at all was when he said 'Sherry' to the footman when he meant 'Hock'.

Even, however, had the conditions been uniformly pleasant, it is to be doubted whether he would have really dominated the gathering. Mrs. Waddington, in her selection of guests, confined herself to the extremely wealthy: and, while the conversation of the extremely wealthy is fascinating in its way, it tends to be a little too technical for the average man.

With the soup, some one who looked like a cartoon of Capital in a Socialistic paper said he was glad to see that Westinghouse Common were buoyant again. A man who might have been his brother agreed that they had firmed up nicely at closing. Whereas Wabash Pref. A. falling to $73\frac{7}{8}$, caused shakings of the head. However, one rather liked the look of Royal Dutch Oil Ordinaries at $54\frac{3}{4}$.

With the fish, United Beef began to tell a neat, though rather long, story about the Bolivian Land Concession, the gist of which was that the Bolivian Oil and Land Syndicate, acquiring from the Bolivian Government the land and prospecting concessions of Bolivia, would be known as Bolivian Concessions, Ltd, and would have a capital of one million dollars in two hundred thousand five-dollar 'A' shares and two hundred thousand half-dollar 'B' shares, and that while no cash payment was to be made to the vendor syndicate the latter was being allotted the whole of the 'B' shares as consideration for the concession. And—this was where the raconteur made his point—the 'B' shares were to receive half the divisible profits and to rank equal with the 'A' shares in any distribution of assets.

The story went well, and conversation became general. There was a certain amount of good-natured chaff about the elasticity of the form of credit handled by the Commercial Banks, and once somebody raised a laugh with a sly retort about the Reserve against Circulation and Total Deposits. On the question of the collateral liability of shareholders, however, argument ran high, and it was rather a relief when, as tempers began to get a little heated, Mrs. Waddington gave the signal and the women left the table.

Coffee having been served and cigars lighted, the magnates drew together at the end of the table where Mr. Waddington sat. But Mr. Waddington, adroitly side-stepping, left them and came down to George.

"Out West," said Mr. Waddington in a rumbling undertone, malevolently eyeing Amalgamated Tooth-Brushes, who had begun to talk about the Mid-Continent Fiduciary Conference at St. Louis, "they would shoot at that fellow's feet."

George agreed that such behaviour could reflect nothing but credit on the West.

"These Easterners make me tired," said Mr. Waddington.

George confessed to a similar fatigue.

"When you think that at this very moment out in Utah and Arizona," said Mr. Waddington, "strong men are packing their saddle-bags and making them secure with their lassoes, you kind of don't know whether to laugh or cry, do you?"

That was the very problem, said George.

"Say, listen," said Mr. Waddington, "I'll just push these pot-bellied guys off upstairs, and then you and I will sneak off to my study and have a real talk."

II

Nothing spoils a *tête-à-tête* chat between two newly-made friends more than a disposition towards reticence on the part of the senior of the pair: and it was fortunate therefore, that, by the time he found himself seated opposite to George in his study, the heady influence of Zane Grey and the rather generous potations in which he had indulged during dinner had brought Sigsbee H. Waddington to quite a reasonably communicative mood. He had reached the stage when men talk disparagingly about their wives. He tapped George on the knee, informed him three times that he liked his face, and began.

"You married, Winch?"

"Finch," said George.

"How do you mean, Finch?" asked Mr. Waddington, puzzled.

"My name is Finch."

"What of it?"

"You called me Winch."

"Why ?"

"I think you thought it was my name."

"What was ?"

"Winch."

"You said just now it was Finch."

"Yes, it is. I was saying . . ."

Mr. Waddington tapped him on the knee once more.

"Young man," he said, "pull yourself together. If your name is Finch, why pretend that it is Winch ? I don't like this shiftiness. It does not come well from a Westerner. Leave this petty shilly-shallying to Easterners like that vile rabble of widow-and-orphan oppressors upstairs, all of whom have got incipient Bright's disease. If your name is Pinch, admit it like a man. Let your yea be yea and your nay be nay." said Mr. Waddington a little severely, holding a match to the fountain-pen which, as will happen to the best of us in moments of emotion, he had mistaken for his cigar.

"As a matter of fact, I'm not," said George.

"Not what ?"

"Married."

"I never said you were."

"You asked me if I was."

"Did I ?"

"Yes."

"You're sure of that ?" said Mr. Waddington keenly.

"Quite. Just after we sat down, you asked me if I was married."

"And your reply was . . . ?"

"No."

Mr. Waddington breathed a sigh of relief.

"Now we have got it straight at last," he said, "and why you beat about the bush like that, I cannot imagine. Well, what I say to you, Pinch—and I say it very seriously as an older, wiser, and better-looking man—is this." Mr. Waddington drew thoughtfully at the fountain-pen for a moment. "I say to you, Pinch, be very careful, when you marry, that you have money of your own. And, having money of your own, keep it. Never be dependent on your wife for the occasional little sums which even the most prudent man requires to see him through the day. Take my case. When I married, I was a wealthy man. I had money of my own. Lots of it. I was beloved by all, being generous to a fault. I bought my wife—I am speaking now of my first wife—a pearl necklace that cost fifty thousand dollars."

He cocked a bright eye at George, and George, feeling that comment was required, said that it did him credit.

"Not credit," said Mr. Waddington. "Cash. Cold cash. Fifty thousand dollars of it. And what happened? Shortly after I married again I lost all my money through unfortunate speculations on the Stock Exchange and became absolutely dependent on my second wife. And that is why you see me to-day, Winch, a broken man. I will tell you something, Pinch—something no one suspects and something which I have never told anybody else and wouldn't be telling you now if I didn't like your face. . . . I am not master in my own home!"

"No?"

"No. Not master in my own home. I want to live in the great, glorious West, and my second wife insists on remaining in the soul-destroying East. And I'll tell you something else." Mr. Waddington paused and scrutinized the fountain-pen with annoyance. "This darned cigar won't draw," he said petulantly.

"I think it's a fountain-pen," said George.

"A fountain pen?" Mr. Waddington, shutting one eye, tested this statement and found it correct. "There!" he said, with a certain moody satisfaction. "Isn't that typical of the East? You ask for cigars and they sell you fountain-pens. No honesty, no sense of fair trade."

"Miss Waddington was looking very charming at dinner, I thought," said George, timidly broaching the subject nearest his heart.

"Yes, Pinch," said Mr. Waddington, resuming his theme, "my wife oppresses me."

"How wonderfully that bobbed hair suits Miss Waddington."

"I don't know if you noticed a pie-faced fellow with an eye-glass and a toothbrush moustache at dinner? That was Lord Hunstanton. He keeps telling me things about etiquette."

"Very kind of him," hazarded George.

Mr. Waddington eyed him in a manner that convinced him that he had said the wrong thing.

"What do you mean, kind of him? It's officious and impertinent. He is a pest," said Mr. Waddington. "They wouldn't stand for him in Arizona. They would put hydrophobia skunks in his bed. What does a man need with etiquette? As long as a man is fearless and upstanding and can shoot straight and look the world in the eye, what does it matter if he uses the wrong fork?"

"Exactly."

"Or wears the wrong sort of hat?"

"I particularly admired the hat which Miss Waddington was wearing when I first saw her." said George. "It was of some soft material and of a light brown colour and . . ."

"My wife—I am still speaking of my second wife. My first, poor soul, is dead—sticks this Hunstanton guy on to me, and for financial reasons, darn it, I am unable to give him the good sock on the nose to which all my better instincts urge me. And guess what she's got into her head now."

"I can't imagine."

"She wants Molly to marry the fellow."

"I should not advise that," said George seriously. "No, no, I am strongly opposed to that. So many of these Anglo-American marriages turn out unhappily."

"I am a man of broad sympathies and a very acute sensibility," began Mr. Waddington, apropos, apparently, of nothing.

"Besides," said George, "I did not like the man's looks."

"What man ?"

"Lord Hunstanton."

"Don't talk of that guy! He gives me a pain in the neck."

"Me, too," said George. "And I was saying . . ."

"Shall I tell you something ?" said Mr. Waddington.

"What ?"

"My second wife—not my first—wants Molly to marry him Did you notice him at dinner ?"

"I did," said George patiently. "And I did not like his looks. He looked to me cold and sinister, the sort of man who might break the heart of an impulsive young girl. What Miss Waddington wants, I feel convinced, is a husband who would give up everything for her—a man who would sacrifice his heart's desire to bring one smile to her face—a man who would worship her, set her in a shrine, make it his only aim in life to bring her sunshine and happiness."

"My wife," said Mr. Waddington, "is much too stout."

"I beg your pardon ?"

"Much too stout."

"Miss Waddington, if I may say so, has a singularly beautiful figure."

"Too much starchy food, and no excercise—that's the trouble. What my wife needs is a year on a ranch, riding over the prairies in God's sunshine."

"I happened to catch sight of Miss Waddington the other day in riding costume. I thought it suited her admirably. So many girls look awkward in riding-breeches, but Miss Waddington was charming. The costume seemed to accentuate what I might describe as that strange boyish jauntiness of carriage which, to my mind, is one of Miss Waddington's chief . . ."

"And I'll have her doing it before long. As a married man, Winch—twice married, but my first wife, poor thing, passed away some years back—let me tell you something. To assert himself with his wife, to bend her to his will, if I may put it that way, a man needs complete financial independence. It is no use trying to bend your wife to your will when five minutes later you have got to try and wheedle twenty-five cents out of her for a cigar. Complete financial independence is essential, Pinch, and that is what I am on the eve of achieving. Some little time back, having raised a certain sum of money—we need not go into the methods which I employed to do so—I bought a large block of stock in a Hollywood Motion-Picture Company. Have you ever heard of the Finer and Better Motion Picture Company of Hollywood, Cal. ? Let me tell you that you will. It is going to be big, and I shall very shortly make an enormous fortune."

"Talking of the motion-pictures," said George, "I do not deny that many of the women engaged in that industry are superficially attractive, but what I do maintain is that they lack Miss Waddington's intense purity of expression. To me Miss Waddington seems like some . . ."

"I shall clean up big. It is only a question of time."

"The first thing anyone would notice on seeing Miss Waddington . . ."

"Thousands and thousands of dollars. And then . . ."

"A poet has spoken of a young girl as 'standing with reluctant feet where the brook and river meet. . . .' "

Mr. Waddington shook his head.

"It isn't only meat. What causes the real trouble is the puddings. It stands to reason that if a woman insists on cramming herself with rich stuff like what we were having to-night she is bound to put on weight. If I've said it once, I've said it a hundred times. . . ."

What Mr. Waddington was about to say for the hundred and first time must remain one of the historic mysteries. For, even as he drew in breath the better to say it, the door opened and a radiant vision appeared. Mr. Waddington stopped in mid-sentence, and George's heart did three back-somersaults and crashed against his front teeth.

"Mother sent me down to see what had become of you," said Molly.

Mr. Waddington got about half-way towards a look of dignity.

"I am not aware, my dear child," he said, "that anything has 'become of me.' I merely snatched the opportunity of having a quiet talk with this young friend of mine from the West."

"Well, you can't have quiet talks with your young friends when you've got a lot of important people to dinner."

"Important people!" Mr. Waddington snorted sternly. "A bunch of super-fatted bits of bad news! in God's country they would be lynched on sight."

"Mr. Brewster Bodthorne has been asking for you particularly. He wants to play checkers."

"Hell," said Mr. Waddington, with the air of quoting something out of Dante, "is full of Brewster Bodthornes."

Molly put her arms round her father's neck and kissed him fondly—a proceeding which drew from George a low, sharp howl of suffering like the bubbling cry of some strong swimmer in his agony. There is a limit to what the flesh can bear.

"Darling, you must be good. Up you go at once and be very nice to everybody. I'll stay here and entertain Mr.——"

"His name is Pinch," said Mr. Waddington, rising reluctantly and making for the door. "I met him out on the side-walk where men are men. Get him to tell you all about the West. I can't remember when I've ever heard a man talk so arrestingly. Mr. Winch has held me spell-bound. Positively spell-bound. And my name," he concluded, a little incoherently, groping for the door-handle, "is Sigsbee Horatio Waddington and I don't care who knows it."

III

The chief drawback to being a shy man is that in the actual crises of real life you are a very different person from the dashing and resourceful individual whom you have pictured in your solitary day-dreams. George Finch, finding himself in the position in which he had so often yearned to be—alone with the girl he loved, felt as if his true self had been suddenly withdrawn and an incompetent understudy substituted at the last moment.

The George with whom he was familiar in day-dreams was a splendid fellow—graceful, thoroughly at his ease, and full of the neatest sort of ingratiating conversation. He looked nice, and you could tell by the way he spoke that he was nice. Clever, beyond a doubt—you knew that at once by his epigrams—but not clever in that repellent, cold-hearted modern fashion: for, no matter how brilliantly his talk sparkled, it was plain all the while that his heart was in the right place and that, despite his wonderful gifts, there was not an atom of conceit in his composition. His eyes had an attractive twinkle: his mouth curved from time to time in an alluring smile: his hands were cool and artistic: and his shirt-front did not bulge. George, in short, as he had imagined himself in his day-dreams, was practically the answer to the Maiden's Prayer.

How different was this loathly changeling who now stood on one leg in the library of Number 16 Seventy-Ninth Street, East. In the first place, the fellow had obviously not brushed his hair for several days. Also, he had omitted to wash his hands, and something had caused them to swell up and turn scarlet. Furthermore, his trousers bagged at the knees: his tie was moving up towards his left ear: and his shirt-front protruded hideously like the chest of a pouter pigeon. A noisome sight.

Still, looks are not everything: and if this wretched creature had been able to talk one-tenth as well as the George of the day-dreams, something might yet have been saved out of the wreck. But the poor blister was inarticulate as well. All he seemed able to do was clear his throat. And what nice girl's heart has ever been won by a series of roopy coughs?

And he could not even achieve a reasonably satisfactory expression. When he tried to relax his features (such as they were) into a charming smile, he merely grinned weakly. When he forced himself not to grin, his face froze into a murderous scowl.

But it was his inability to speak that was searing George's soul. Actually, since the departure of Mr. Waddington, the silence had lasted for perhaps six seconds: but to George Finch it seemed like a good hour. He goaded himself to utterance.

"My name," said George, speaking in a low, husky voice, "is not Pinch."

"Isn't it?" said the girl. "How jolly!"

"Nor Winch."

"Better still"

"It is Finch  George Finch"

"Splendid!"

She seemed genuinely pleased. She beamed upon him as if he had brought her good news from a distant land.

"Your father," proceeded George, not having anything to add by way of development of the theme but unable to abandon it, "thought it was Pinch or Winch. But it is not. It is Finch."

His eye, roaming nervously about the room, caught hers for

an instant: and he was amazed to perceive that there was in it nothing of that stunned abhorrence which he felt his appearance and behaviour should rightly have aroused in any nice-minded girl. Astounding though it seemed, she appeared to be looking at him in a sort of pleased, maternal way, as if he were a child she was rather fond of. For the first time a faint far-off glimmer of light shone upon George's darkness. It would be too much to say that he was encouraged, but out of the night that covered him, black as the pit from pole to pole, there did seem to sparkle for an instant a solitary star.

"How did you come to know father?"

George could answer that. He was all right if you asked him questions. It was the having to invent topics of conversation that baffled him.

"I met him outside the house: and when he found that I came from the West he asked me in to dinner."

"Do you mean he rushed at you and grabbed you as you were walking by?"

"Oh, no. I wasn't walking by. I was·—er—sort of standing on the door-step. At least . . ."

"Standing on the door-step? Why?"

George's ears turned a riper red.

"Well, I was—er—coming, as it were, to pay a call."

"A call?"

"Yes."

"On mother?"

"On you."

The girl's eyes widened.

"On me?"

"To make inquiries."

"What about?"

"Your dog."

"I don't understand."

"Well, I thought—result of the excitement—and nerve-strain —I thought he might be upset."

"Because he ran away, do you mean?"

"Yes."

"You thought he would have a nervous break-down because he ran away?"

"Dangerous traffic," explained George. "Might have been run over. Reaction. Nervous collapse."

Woman's intuition is a wonderful thing. There was probably not an alienist in the land who, having listened so far, would not have sprung at George and held him down with one hand while with the other he signed the necessary certificate of lunacy. But Molly Waddington saw deeper into the matter. She was touched. As she realized that this young man thought so highly of her that, despite his painful shyness, he was prepared to try to worm his way into her house on an excuse which even he must have recognized as pure banana-oil, her heart warmed to him. More than ever, she became convinced that George was a lamb and that she wanted to stroke his head and straighten his tie and make cooing noises to him.

"How very sweet of you," she said.

"Fond of dogs," mumbled George.

"You must be fond of dogs."

"Are you fond of dogs?"

"Yes, I'm very fond of dogs."

"So am I. Very fond of dogs."

"Yes?"

"Yes. Very fond of dogs. Some people are not fond of dogs, but I am."

And suddenly eloquence descended upon George Finch. With gleaming eyes he broke out into a sort of Litany. He began to talk easily and fluently.

"I am fond of Airedales and wire-haired terriers and bull-dogs and Pekingese and Sealyhams and Alsatians and fox-terriers and greyhounds and Aberdeens and West Highlands and Cairns and Pomeranians and spaniels and schipperkes and pugs and Maltese and Yorkshires and borzois and bloodhounds and Bedlingtons and pointers and setters and mastiffs and Newfoundlands and St. Bernards and Great Danes and dachshunds and collies and chows and poodles and . . ."

"I see," said Molly. "You're fond of dogs."

"Yes," said George. "Very fond of dogs."

"So am I. There's something about dogs."

"Yes," said George. "Of course, there's something about cats, too."

"Yes, isn't there?"

"But, still cats aren't dogs."

"No, I've noticed that."

There was a pause. With a sinking of the heart, for the topic was one on which he felt he could rather spread himself, George perceived that the girl regarded the subject of dogs as fully threshed out. He stood for awhile licking his lips in thoughtful silence.

"So you come from the West?" said Molly.

"Yes."

"It must be nice out there."

"Yes."

"Prairies and all that sort of thing."

"Yes."

"You aren't a cowboy, are you?"

"No. I am an artist," said George proudly.

"An artist? Paint pictures, you mean?"

"Yes."

"Have you a studio?"

"Yes."

"Where?"

"Yes. I mean, near Washington Square. In a place called the Sheridan."

"The Sheridan? Really? Then perhaps you know Mr. Beamish?"

"Yes. Oh, Yes. Yes."

"He's a dear isn't he? I've known him all my life."

"Yes."

"It must be jolly to be an artist."

"Yes."

"I'd love to see some of your pictures."

Warm thrills permeated George's system.

"May I send you one of them?" he bleated.

"That's awfully sweet of you."

So uplifted was George Finch by this wholly unexpected development that there is no saying what heights of eloquence he might not now have reached, had he been given another ten minutes of the girl's uninterrupted society. The fact that she was prepared to accept one of his pictures seemed to bring them very close together. He had never yet met anybody who would. For the first time since their interview had begun he felt almost at his ease.

Unfortunately, at this moment the door opened: and like a sharp attack of poison-gas Mrs. Waddington floated into the room.

"What are you doing down here, Molly?" she said.

She gave George one of those looks of hers, and his newly-born sang-froid immediately turned blue at the roots.

"I've been talking to Mr. Finch, mother. Isn't it interesting—Mr. Finch is an artist. He paints pictures."

Mrs. Waddington did not reply: for she had been struck suddenly dumb by a hideous discovery. Until this moment she had not examined George with any real closeness. When she had looked at him before it had been merely with the almost impersonal horror and disgust with which any hostess looks at an excrescence who at the eleventh hour horns in on one of her carefully planned dinners. His face, though revolting, had had no personal message for her.

But now it was different. Suddenly this young man's foul features had become fraught with a dreadful significance. Subconsciously, Mrs. Waddington had been troubled ever since she had heard them by the words Molly had spoken in her bedroom: and now they shot to the surface of her mind like gruesome things from the dark depths of some sinister pool. 'The sort of man I think I should rather like,' Molly had said, 'would be a sort of slimmish, smallish man with nice brown eyes and rather gold-y, chestnutty hair.' She stared at George. Yes! He was slimmish. He was also smallish. His eyes, though far from nice, were brown: and his hair was undeniably of a chestnut hue.

'Who sort of chokes and turns pink and twists his fingers and makes funny noises and trips over his feet . . .' Thus had the description continued, and precisely thus was this young man before her now behaving. For her gaze had had the worst effect on George Finch, and seldom in his career had he choked more throatily, turned a brighter pink, twisted his fingers into a more intricate pattern, made funnier noises and tripped more heartily over his feet than he was doing now. Mrs. Waddington was convinced. It had been no mere imaginary figure that Molly had described, but a living, breathing pestilence—and this was he.

And he was an artist! Mrs. Waddington shuddered. Of all the myriad individuals that went to make up the kaleidoscopic life of New York, she disliked artists most. They never had any money. They were dissolute and feckless. They attended dances at Webster Hall in strange costumes, and frequently played the ukulele. And this man was one of them.

"I suppose," said Molly, "we had better go upstairs?"

Mrs. Waddington came out of her trance.

"*You* had better go upstairs," she said, emphasizing the pronoun in a manner that would have impressed itself upon the least sensitive of men. George got it nicely.

"I—er—think, perhaps," he mumbled, "as it is—er— getting late . . ."

"You aren't going?" said Molly, concerned.

"Certainly Mr. Finch is going," said Mrs. Waddington: and there was that in her demeanour which suggested that at any moment she might place one hand on the scruff of his neck and the other on the seat of his trousers and heave. "If Mr. Finch has appointments that call him elsewhere, we must not detain him. Good night, Mr. Finch."

"Good night. Thank you for a—er—very pleasant evening."

"It was most kay-eend of you to come." said Mrs. Waddington.

"Do come again," said Molly.

"Mr. Finch," said Mrs. Waddington, "is no doubt a very ba-husy man. Please go upstairs immediately, Molly. *Good* na'eet, Mr. Finch."

She continued to regard him in a manner hardly in keeping with the fine old traditions of American hospitality.

"Ferris," she said, as the door closed.

"Madam ?"

"On no pretext whatever, Ferris, is that person who has just left to be admitted to the house again."

"Very good, madam," said the butler.

IV

It was a fair sunny morning next day when George Finch trotted up the steps of Number 16 Seventy-Ninth Street East, and pressed the bell. He was wearing his dove-grey suit, and under his arm was an enormous canvas wrapped in brown paper. After much thought he had decided to present Molly with his favourite work, Hail, Jocund Spring!—a picture representing a young woman, scantily draped and obviously suffering from an advanced form of chorea, dancing with lambs in a flower-speckled field. At the moment which George had selected for her portrayal, she had—to judge from her expression—just stepped rather hard on a sharp stone. Still, she was George's masterpiece, and he intended to present her to Molly.

The door opened. Ferris, the butler, appeared.

"All goods," said Ferris, regarding George dispassionately, "must be delivered in the rear."

George blinked.

"I want ot see Miss Waddington "

"Miss Waddington is not at home "

"Can I see Mr. Waddington ?" asked George, accepting the second-best.

"Mr. Waddington is not at home."

George hesitated a moment before he spoke again. But love conquers all.

"Can I see Mrs. Waddington?"

"Mrs. Waddington is not at home."

As the butler spoke, there proceeded from the upper regions of the house a commanding female voice that inquired of an unseen Sigsbee how many times the speaker had told him not to smoke in the drawing-room.

"But I can hear her," George pointed out.

The butler shrugged his shoulders with an aloof gesture, as if disclaiming all desire to go into these mysteries. His look suggested that he thought George might possibly be psychic.

"Mrs. Waddington is not at home." he said once more.

There was a pause.

"Nice morning," said George.

"The weather appears to be clement," agreed Ferris.

George then tumbled backwards down the steps, and the interview concluded.

## CHAPTER FOUR

### I

TELL me all," said Hamilton Beamish.

George told him all. The unfortunate young man was still looking licked to a splinter. For several hours he had been wandering distractedly through the streets of New York, and now he had crawled into Hamilton Beamish's apartment in the hope that a keener mind than his own might be able to detect in the encompassing clouds a silver lining which he himself had missed altogether.

"Let me get this clear," said Hamilton Beamish. "You called at the house?"

"Yes."

"And the butler refused to admit you?"

"Yes."

Hamilton Beamish regarded his stricken friend compassionately.

"My poor cloth-headed George," he said, "you appear to have made a complete mess of things. By being impetuous you have ruined everything. Why could you not have waited and let me introduce you into this house in a normal and straightforward fashion, in my capacity of an old friend of the family? I would have started you right. As things are, you have allowed yourself to take on the semblance of an outcast."

"But when old Waddington invited me to dinner—actually invited me to dinner . . ."

"You should have kicked him in the eye and made good your escape," said Hamilton Beamish firmly "Surely, after all that I said to you about Sigsbee H Waddington, you were under no illusion that his patronage would make you popular in the home? Sigsbee H. Waddington is one of those men who have only to express a liking for anybody to cause their wives to look on him as something out of the Underworld. Sigsbee H. Waddington could not bring the Prince of Wales home to dinner and get away with it. And when he drags in and lays on the mat a specimen —I use the word in the kindliest spirit—like you, and does so, moreover, five minutes before the start of a formal dinner-party, thus upsetting the seating arrangements and leading to black thoughts in the kitchen, can you blame his wife for not fawning on you? And on top of that you pretend to be an artist."

"I am an artist," said George, with a flicker of spirit. It was a subject on which he held strong views.

"The point is a debatable one. And, anyhow, you should have concealed it from Mrs. Waddington. A woman of her type looks on artists as blots on the social scheme. I told you she judged her fellow-creatures entirely by their balance at the bank."

"I have plenty of money."

"How was she to know that? You tell her you are an artist, and she naturally imagines you . . ."

The telephone rang shrilly, interrupting Mr Beamish's flow of thought. There was an impatient frown on his face as he unhooked the receiver, but a moment later this had passed away and, when he spoke, it was in a kindly and indulgent tone.

"Ah, Molly, my child!"

"Molly!" cried George

Hamilton Beamish ignored the exclamation.

"Yes," he said. "He is a great friend of mine."

"Me?" said George.

Hamilton Beamish continued to accord to him that complete lack of attention characteristic of the efficient telephoner when addressed while at the instrument.

"Yes, he has been telling me about it. He's here now."

"Does she want me to speak to her?" quavered George.

"Certainly, I'll come at once."

Hamilton Beamish replaced the receiver, and stood for awhile in thought.

"What did she say?" asked George, deeply moved.

"This is interesting," said Hamilton Beamish.

"What did she say?"

"This causes me to revise my views to some extent."

"What did she say?"

"And yet I might have foreseen it."

"What did she say?"

Hamilton Beamish rubbed his chin meditatively.

"The mind of a girl works oddly."

"What did she say?"

"That was Molly Waddington," said Hamilton Beamish.

"What did she say?"

"I am by no means sure," said Mr. Beamish regarding George owlishly through his spectacles, "that, after all, everything has not happened for the best. I omitted to take into my calculations the fact that what has occurred would naturally give you in the eyes of a warm-hearted girl, surrounded normally by men with incomes in six figures, a certain romantic glamour. Any girl with nice instincts must inevitably be attracted to a penniless artist whom her mother forbids her to see "

"What did she say?"

"She asked me if you were a friend of mine."

"And then what did she say?"

"She told me that her stepmother had forbidden you the house and that she had been expressly ordered never to see you again."

"And what did she say after that?"

"She asked me to come up to the house and have a talk "

"About me?"

"So I imagine."

"You're going?"

"At once."

"Hamilton," said George in a quivering voice, "Hamilton, old man, pitch it strong!"

"You mean, speak enthusiastically on your behalf?"

"I mean just that. How well you put these things, Hamilton!"

Hamilton Beamish took up his hat and placed it on his head.

"It is strange," he said meditatively, "that I should be assisting you in this matter."

"It's your good heart," said George. "You have a heart of gold."

"You have fallen in love at first sight, and my views on love at first sight are well known."

"They're all wrong."

"My views are never wrong."

"I don't mean wrong exactly," said George with sycophantic haste. "I mean that in certain cases love at first sight is the only thing."

"Love should be a reasoned emotion."

"Not if you suddenly see a girl like Molly Waddington."

"When I marry," said Hamilton Beamish, "it will be the result of a carefully calculated process of thought. I shall first decide after cool reflection that I have reached the age at which it is best for me to marry. I shall then run over the list of my female friends till I have selected one whose mind and tastes are in harmony with mine. I shall then . . ."

"Aren't you going to change?" said George.

"Change what?"

"Your clothes  If you are going to see Her . . ."

"I shall then," proceeded Hamilton Beamish, "watch her carefully for a considerable length of time in order to assure myself that I have not allowed passion to blind me to any faults in her disposition. After that . . ."

"You can't possibly call on Miss Waddington in those trousers," said George. "And your shirt does not match your socks. You must . . ."

"After that, provided in the interval I have not observed any more suitable candidate for my affections, I shall go to her and in a few simple words ask her to be my wife. I shall point out that my income is sufficient for two, that my morals are above reproach, that . . ."

"Haven't you a really nice suit that's been properly pressed and brushed and a rather newer pair of shoes and a less floppy sort of hat and . . ."

". . . that my disposition is amiable and my habits regular. And she and I will settle down to the Marriage Sane."

"How about your cuffs?" said George.

"What about my cuffs?"

"Are you really going to see Miss Waddington in frayed cuffs?"

"I am."

George had nothing more to say. It was sacrilege, but there seemed no way of preventing it.

As Hamilton Beamish, some quarter of an hour later, climbed in a series of efficient movements up the stairs of the green omnibus which was waiting in Washington Square, the summer afternoon had reached its best and sweetest. A red-blooded, one hundred per cent American sun still shone warmly down from a sky of gleaming azure, but there had stolen into the air a hint of the cool of evening. It was the sort of day when Tin Pan Alley lyric-writers suddenly realize that 'love' rhymes with 'skies above,' and rush off, snorting, to turn out the song-hit of a lifetime. Sentimentality was abroad: and gradually, without his being aware of it, its seeds began to plant themselves in the stony and unpromising soil of Hamilton Beamish's bosom.

Yes, little by little, as the omnibus rolled on up the Avenue, there began to burgeon in Hamilton Beamish a mood of gentle tolerance for his species. He no longer blamed so whole-heartedly the disposition of his fellow-men to entertain towards the opposite sex on short acquaintance a warmth of emotion which could be scientifically justified only by a long and intimate knowledge of character. For the first time he began to debate within himself whether there was not something to be said for a man who, like George Finch, plunged headlong into love with a girl to whom he had never even spoken.

And it was at this precise moment—just, dramatically enough, when the bus was passing Twenty-Ninth Street with its pretty and suggestive glimpse of the Little Church Round The Corner—that he noticed for the first time the girl in the seat across the way.

She was a girl of *chic* and *elan*. One may go still further—a girl of *espiéglerie* and *je ne sais quoi*. She was dressed, as Hamilton Beamish's experienced eye noted in one swift glance, in a delightful two-piece suit composed of a smart coat in fine quality repp, lined throughout with crepe-de-chine, over a dainty long-sleeved frock of figured Marocain prettily pleated at the sides and finished at the neck with a small collar and kilted frill: a dress which, as every schoolboy knows, can be had in beige, grey, mid-grey, opal, snuff, powder, burnt wood, puce, brown, bottle, almond, navy, black, and dark Saxe. Her colour was dark Saxe.

Another glance enabled Hamilton Beamish to take in her hat. It was, he perceived, a becoming hat in Yedda Visca straw, trimmed and bound with silk petersham ribbon, individual without being conspicuous, artistic in line and exquisite in style: and from beneath it there strayed a single curl of about the colour of a good Pekingese dog. Judging the rest of her hair by the light of this curl, Hamilton Beamish deduced that, when combing and dressing it, she just moistened the brush with a little scalpoline, thus producing a gleamy mass, sparkling with life and possessing that incomparable softness, freshness and luxuriance, at the same time toning each single hair to grow thick, long and strong. No doubt she had read advertisements of the tonic in the papers and now, having bought a bottle was seeing how healthy and youthful her hair appeared after this delightful, refreshing dressing.

Her shoes were of black patent leather, her stockings of steel-grey. She had that schoolgirl complexion and the skin you love to touch.

All these things the trained eye of Hamilton Beamish noted, swivelling rapidly sideways and swivelling rapidly back again. But it was her face that he noted most particularly. It was just the sort of face which, if he had not had his policy of Sane Love all carefully mapped out, would have exercised the most disturbing effect on his emotions. Even as it was, this strong, competent man could not check, as he alighted from the bus at Seventy-Ninth Street, a twinge of that wistful melancholy which men feel when they are letting a good thing get away from them.

Sad, reflected Hamilton Beamish, as he stood upon the steps of Number 16 and prepared to ring the bell, that he would never see this girl again. Naturally, a man of his stamp was not in love at first sight, but nevertheless he did not conceal it from himself that nothing would suit him better than to make her acquaintance and, after careful study of her character and disposition, possibly discover in a year or two that it was she whom Nature had intended for his mate.

It was at this point in his reflection that he perceived her standing at his elbow.

There are moments when even the coolest-headed efficiency expert finds it hard to maintain his pose. Hamilton Beamish was definitely taken aback: and, had he been a lesser man, one would have said that he became for an instant definitely pop-eyed. Apart from the fact that he had been thinking of her and thinking of her tenderly, there was the embarrassment of standing side by side with a strange girl on a doorstep. In such a crisis it is very difficult for a man to know precisely how to behave. Should he endeavour to create the illusion that he is not aware of her presence? Or, should he make some chatty remark? And, if a chatty remark, what chatty remark?

Hamilton Beamish was still grappling with this problem, when the girl solved it for him. Suddenly screwing up a face which looked even more attractive at point-blank range than it had appeared in profile, she uttered the exclamation 'Oo!'

"Oo!" said this girl.

For a moment, all Hamilton Beamish felt was that almost ecstatic relief which comes over the man of sensibility when he finds that a pretty girl has an attractive voice. Too many times in his career he had admired girls from afar, only to discover, when they spoke, that they had voices like peacocks calling up the rain. The next instant however, he had recognized that his companion was suffering, and his heart was filled with a blend of compassion and zeal. Her pain aroused simultaneously the pity of the man and the efficiency of the efficiency expert.

"You have something in your eye?" he said.

"A bit of dust or something."

"Permit me," said Hamilton Beamish.

One of the most difficult tasks that can confront the ordinary man is the extraction of foreign bodies from the eye of a perfect stranger of the opposite sex. But Hamilton Beamish was not an ordinary man. Barely ten seconds later, he was replacing his handkerchief in his pocket and the girl was blinking at him gratefully.

"Thank you ever so much," she said.

"Not at all," said Hamilton Beamish.

"A doctor couldn't have done it more neatly."

"It's just a knack."

"Why is it," asked the girl, "that, when you get a speck of dust in your eye the size of a pin-point, it seems as big as all out-doors?"

Hamilton Beamish could answer that. The subject was one he had studied.

"The conjunctiva, a layer of mucous membrane which lines the back of the eyelids and is reflected on to the front of the globe, this reflection forming the fornix, is extremely sensitive. This is especially so at the point where the tarsal plates of fibrous tissue are attached to the orbital margin by the superior and inferior palpebral ligaments."

"I see," said the girl.

There was a pause.

"Are you calling on Mrs. Waddington?" asked the girl.

"On Miss Waddington."

"I've never met her."

"You don't know the whole family, then?"

"No. Only Mrs. Waddington. Would you mind ringing the bell?"

Hamilton Beamish pressed the button.

"I saw you on the omnibus," he said.

"Did you?"

"Yes. I was sitting in the next seat."

"How odd!"

"It's a lovely day, isn't it."

"Beautiful."

"The sun."

"Yes."

"The sky."

"Yes."

"I like the summer."

"So do I."

"When it's not too hot."

"Yes."

"Though, as a matter of fact," said Hamilton Beamish, "I always say that what one objects to is not the heat but the humidity."

Which simply goes to prove that even efficiency experts, when they fall in love at first sight, can babble like any man of inferior intellect in the same circumstances. Strange and violent emotions were racking Hamilton Beamish's bosom: and, casting away the principles of a lifetime, he recognized without a trace of shame that love had come to him at last—not creeping scientifically into his soul, as he had supposed it would, but elbowing its way in with the Berserk rush of a commuter charging into the five-fifteen. Yes, he was in love. And it is proof of the completeness with which passion had blunted his intellectual faculties that he was under the impression that in the recent exchange of remarks he had been talking rather well.

The door opened. Ferris appeared. He looked at the girl, not with the cold distaste which he had exhibited earlier in the day towards George Finch, but with a certain paternal affection. Ferris measured forty-six round the waist, but Beauty still had its appeal for him.

"Mrs. Waddington desired me to say, miss," he said, "that an appointment of an urgent nature has called her elsewhere, rendering it impossible for her to see you this afternoon."

"She might have phoned me," the girl complained.

Ferris allowed one eyebrow to flicker momentarily, conveying the idea, that, while he sympathized, a spirit of loyalty forbade him to join in criticism of his employer.

"Mrs. Waddington wished to know if it would be convenient to you, miss, if she called upon you to-morrow at five o'clock?"

"All right."

"Thank you, miss. Miss Waddington is expecting you, sir."

Hamilton Beamish continued to stare after the girl, who, with a friendly nod in his direction, had begun to walk light-heartedly out of his life along the street.

"Who is that young lady, Ferris?" he asked.

"I could not say, sir."

"Why couldn't you? You seemed to know her just now."

"No, sir. I had never seen the young lady before. Mrs. Waddington, however, had mentioned that she would be calling at this hour and instructed me to give the message which I delivered."

"Didn't Mrs. Waddington say who was calling?"

"Yes, sir. The young lady."

"Ass!" said Hamilton Beamish. But even he was not strong man enough to say it aloud. "I mean, didn't she tell you the young lady's name?"

"No, sir. If you will step this way, sir, I will conduct you to Miss Waddington, who is in the library."

"It seems funny that Mrs. Waddington did not tell you the young lady's name." brooded Hamilton Beamish.

"Very humorous, sir," agreed the butler indulgently.

III

"Oh, Jimmy, it was sweet of you to come," said Molly.

Hamilton Beamish patted her head absently. He was too preoccupied to notice the hateful name by which she had addressed him.

"I have had a wonderful experience," he said.

"So have I. I think I'm in love."

"I have given the matter as close attention as has been possible, in the limited time at my disposal," said Hamilton Beamish, "and I have reached the conclusion that I, too, am in love."

"I think I am in love with your friend George Finch."

"I am in love with . . ." Hamilton Beamish paused. "I don't know her name. She is a most charming girl. I met her coming up here on the bus, and we talked for awhile on the front door-steps. I took something out of her eye."

Molly stared incredulously.

"You have fallen in love with a girl and you don't know who she is? But I thought you always said that love was reasoned emotion and all that."

"One's views alter." said Hamilton Beamish. " A man's intellectual perceptions do not stand still. One develops."

"I was never so surprised in my life."

"It came as a complete surprise to me," said Hamilton Beamish. "It is excessively aggravating that I do not know her name nor where she lives nor anything about her except that she appears to be a friend—or at least an acquaintance—of your step-mother."

"Oh, she knows mother, does she?"

"Apparently. She was calling here by appointment."

"All sorts of people call on mother. She is honorary secretary to about a hundred societies."

"This girl was of medium height, with an extremely graceful figure and bright brown hair. She wore a two-piece suit with a coat of fine quality repp over a long-sleeved frock of figured Marocain pleated at the sides and finished at the neck with a small collar and kilted frill. Her hat was of Yedda Visca straw, trimmed and bound with silk-petersham ribbon. She had patent-leather shoes, silk stockings, and eyes of tender grey like the mists of sunrise floating over some magic pool of Fairyland. Does the description suggest anybody to you?"

"No, I don't think so—She sounds nice."

"She is nice. I gazed into those eyes only for a moment, but I shall never forget them. They were deeper than the depth of waters stilled at even."

"I could ask mother who she is."

"I shall be greatly obliged if you would do so," said Hamilton Beamish. "Mention that it is some one upon whom she is to call at five o'clock to-morrow, and telephone me the name and address. Oh, to seize her and hold her close to me and kiss her again and again and again! And now, child, tell me of yourself. I think you mentioned that you also were in love."

"Yes. With George Finch."

"A capital fellow."

"He's a lambkin," emended Molly warmly.

"A lambkin, if you prefer it."

"And I asked you to come here to-day to tell me what I ought to do. You see, mother doesn't like him."

"So I gathered."

"She has forbidden him the house."

"Yes."

"I suppose it's because he has no money."

Hamilton Beamish was on the point of mentioning that George had an almost indecent amount of money, but he checked himself. Who was he that he should destroy a young girl's dreams? It was as a romantic and penniless artist that George Finch had won this girl's heart. It would be cruel to reveal the fact that he was rich and the worst artist in New York.

"Your stepmother," he agreed, "is apt to see eye to eye with Bradstreet in her estimation of her fellows."

"I don't care if he hasn't any money," said Molly. "You know that, when I marry, I get that pearl necklace that father bought for mother. It's being held in trust for me. I can sell it and get thousands of dollars, so that we shall be as right as anything."

"Quite."

"But, of course, I don't want to make a runaway marriage if I can help it. I want to be married with bridesmaids and cake and presents and photographs in the rotogravure section and everything."

"Naturally."

"So the point is, mother must learn to love George. Now listen, Jimmy dear. Mother will be going to see her palmist, very soon— she's always going to palmists, you know."

Hamilton Beamish nodded. He had not been aware of this trait in Mrs. Waddington's character, but he could believe anything of her. Now that he came to consider the matter, he recognized that Mrs. Waddington was precisely the sort of woman who, in the intervals of sitting in the salons of beauty specialists with green mud on her face, would go to palmists.

"And what you must do is to go to this palmist before mother gets there and bribe her to say that my only happiness is bound up with a brown-haired artist whose name begins with a G."

"I scarcely think that even a palmist would make Mrs. Waddington believe that."

"She believes everything Madame Eulalie sees in the crystal."

"But hardly that."

"No perhaps you're right. Well, then, you must get Madame Eulalie at least to steer mother off Lord Hunstanton. Last night, she told me in so many words that she wanted me to marry him. He's always here, and it's awful."

"I could do that, of course."

"And you will?"

"Certainly."

"You're a darling. I should think she would do it for ten dollars."

"Twenty at the outside."

"Then that's settled. I knew I could rely on you. By the way, will you tell George something quite casually?"

"Anything you wish."

"Just mention to him that, if he happens to be strolling in Central Park to-morrow afternoon near the Zoo, we might run into each other."

"Very well."

"And now," said Molly, "tell me all about George and how you came to know one another and what you thought of him when you first saw him and what he likes for breakfast and what he talks about and what he said about me."

IV

It might have been expected that the passage of time, giving opportunity for quiet reflection on the subject of the illogical nature of the infatuation in which he had allowed himself to become involved, would have brought remorse to so clear and ruthless a thinker as Hamilton Beamish. It was not so, but far otherwise. As Hamilton Beamish sat in the ante-chamber of Madame Eulalie's office next day, he gloried in his folly: and when his better self endeavoured to point out to him that what had happened was that he had allowed himself to be ensnared by a girl's face—that is to say, by a purely fortuitous arrangement of certain albuminoids and fatty molecules, all Hamilton Beamish did was to tell his better self to put its head in a bag. He was in love, and he liked it. He was in love, and proud of it. His only really coherent thought as he waited in the ante-room was a resolve to withdraw the booklet on 'The Marriage Sane' from circulation and try his hand at writing a poem or two.

"Madame Eulalie will see you now, sir," announced the maid, breaking in upon his reverie.

Hamilton Beamish entered the inner room. And, having entered it, stopped dead.

"You!" he exclaimed.

The girl gave that fleeting pat at her hair which is always Woman's reaction to the unexpected situation. And Hamilton Beamish, looking at that hair emotionally, perceived that he had been right in his yesterday's surmise. It was, as he had suspected, a gleamy mass, sparkling with life and possessing that incomparable softness, freshness and luxuriance.

"Why, how do you do?" said the girl.

"I'm fine," said Hamilton Beamish.

"We seem fated to meet."

"And I'm not quarrelling with fate."

"No?"

"No," said Hamilton Beamish. "Fancy it being you!"

"Fancy who being me?"

"Fancy you being you." It occurred to him that he was not making himself quite clear. "I mean, I was sent here with a message for Madame Eulalie, and she turns out to be you."

"A message? Who from?"

"From whom?" corrected Hamilton Beamish. Even in the grip of love, a specialist on Pure English remains a specialist on Pure English.

"That's what I said—Who from?"

Hamilton Beamish smiled an indulgent smile. These little mistakes could always be corrected later—possibly on the honeymoon.

"From Molly Waddington. She asked me to . . ."

"Oh, then you don't want me to read your hand?"

"There is nothing I want more in this world," said Hamilton Beamish warmly, "than to have you read my hand."

"I don't have to read it to tell your character, of course," said the girl. "I can see that at a glance."

"You can?"

"Oh, certainly. You have a strong, dominating nature and a keen incisive mind. You have great breadth of vision, iron determination, and marvellous insight. Yet with it all you are at heart gentle, kind and lovable; deeply altruistic and generous to a fault. You have it in you to be a leader of men. You remind me of Julius Caesar, Shakespeare and Napoleon Bonaparte."

"Tell me more," said Hamilton Beamish.

"If you ever fell in love . . ."

"If I ever fell in love . . ."

"If you ever fell in love," said the girl, raising her eyes to his and drawing a step closer, "you would . . ."

"Mr. Delancy Cabot," announced the maid.

"Oh, darn it!" said Madame Eulalie. "I forgot I had an appointment. Send him in."

"May I wait?" breathed Hamilton Beamish devoutly.

"Please do. I shan't be long." She turned to the door. "Come in, Mr. Cabot."

Hamilton Beamish wheeled round. A long, stringy person was walking daintily into the room. He was richly, even superbly, dressed in the conventional costume of the popular clubman and pet of Society. He wore lavender gloves and a carnation in his buttonhole, and a vast expanse of snowy collar encircled a neck which suggested that he might be a throw-back to some giraffe ancestor. A pleasing feature of this neck was an Adam's apple that could have belonged to only one man of Hamilton Beamish's acquaintance.

"Garroway!" cried Hamilton Beamish. "What are you doing here? And what the devil does this masquerade mean?"

The policeman seemed taken aback. His face became as red as his wrists. But for the collar, which held him in a grip of iron, his jaw would no doubt have fallen.

"I didn't expect to find you here, Mr. Beamish," he said apologetically.

"I didn't expect to find you here, calling yourself De Courcy Bellville."

"Delancy Cabot, sir."

"Delancy Cabot, then."

"I like the name," urged the policeman. "I saw it in a book."

The girl was breathing hard.

"Is this man a policeman?" she cried.

"Yes, he is," said Hamilton Beamish. "His name is Garroway, and I am teaching him to write poetry. And what I want to know," he thundered, turning on the unhappy man, whose Adam's apple was now leaping like a young lamb in the spring time, "is what are you doing here, interrupting a—interrupting a—in short, interrupting, when you ought either to be about your constabulary duties or else sitting quietly at home studying John Drinkwater. That," said Hamilton Beamish, "is what I want to know."

Officer Garroway coughed.

"The fact is, Mr. Beamish, I did not know that Madame Eulalie was a friend of yours."

"Never mind whose friend she is."

"But it makes all the difference, Mr. Beamish. I can now go back to headquarters and report that Madame Eulalie is above suspicion You see, sir, I was sent here by my superior officers to effect a cop."

"What do you mean, effect a cop?"

"To make an arrest, Mr Beamish."

"Then do not say 'effect a cop.' Purge yourself of these vulgarisms, Garroway."

"Yes, sir. I will indeed, sir."

"Aim at the English Pure."

"Yes, sir. Most certainly, Mr. Beamish."

"And what on earth do you mean by saying that you were sent here to arrest this lady?"

"It has been called to the attention of my superior officers, Mr. Beamish, that Madame Eulalie is in the habit of telling fortunes for a monetary consideration. Against the law, sir."

Hamilton Beamish snorted.

"Ridiculous! If that's the law, alter it."

"I will do my best, sir."

"I have had the privilege of watching Madame Eulalie engaged upon her art, and she reveals nothing but the most limpid truth. So go back to your superior officers and tell them to jump off the Brooklyn Bridge."

"Yes, sir. I will, sir."

"And now leave us. We would be alone."

"Yes, Mr. Beamish," said Officer Garroway humbly. "At once, Mr. Beamish."

For some moments after the door had closed, the girl stood staring at Hamilton Beamish with wondering eyes.

"Was that man really a policeman?"

"He was."

"And you handled him like that, and he said 'Yes, sir!' and 'No, sir!' and crawled out on all fours." She drew a deep breath. "It seems to me that you are just the sort of friend a lonely girl needs in this great city."

"I am only too delighted that I was able to be of service."

"Service is right! Mr. Beamish . . ."

"My first name is Hamilton."

She looked at him, amazed.

"You are not *the* Hamilton Beamish? Not the man who wrote the Booklets?"

"I have written a few booklets."

"Why, you're my favourite author! If it hadn't been for you, I would still be mouldering in a little one-horse town where there wasn't even a good soda-fountain. But I got hold of a couple of your Are You In A Groove? things, and I packed up my grip and came right along to New York to lead the larger life. If I'd known yesterday that you were Hamilton Beamish, I'd have kissed you on the doorstep!"

It was Hamilton Beamish's intention to point out that a curtained room with a closed door was an even more suitable place for such a demonstration, but, even as he tried to speak, there gripped him for the first time in his life a strange, almost George Finch-like, shyness. One deprecates the modern practice of exposing the great, but candour compels one to speak out and say that at this juncture Hamilton Beamish emitted a simpering giggle and began to twiddle his fingers.

The strange weakness passed, and he was himself again. He adjusted his glasses firmly.

"Would you," he asked, "could you possibly . . . Do you think you could manage to come and lunch somewhere to-morrow?"

The girl uttered an exclamation of annoyance.

"Isn't that too bad!" she said. "I can't."

"The day after?"

"I'm sorry. I'm afraid I shall be off the map for three weeks. I've got to jump on a train to-morrow and go visit the old folks back in East Gilead. It's pop's birthday on Saturday, and I never miss it."

"East Gilead?"

"Idaho. You wouldn't have heard of the place, but it's there."

"But I have heard of it. A great friend of mine comes from East Gilead."

"You don't say! Who?"

"A man named George Finch."

She laughed amusedly.

"You don't actually mean to tell me you know George Finch?"

"He is my most intimate friend."

"Then I trust for your sake," said the girl, "that he is not such a yap as he used to be."

Hamilton Beamish reflected. Was George Finch a yap? How precisely did one estimate the yaphood of one's friends?

"By the word 'yap' you mean . . ."

"I mean a yap. The sort of fellow who couldn't say Bo to a goose."

Hamilton Beamish had never seen George Finch in conversation with a goose, but he thought he was a good enough judge of character to be able to credit him with the ability to perform the very trivial deed of daring indicated.

"I fancy New York has changed George," he replied, after reflection. "In fact, now that I remember, it was on more or less that very subject that I called to see you in your professional capacity. The fact is, George Finch has fallen violently in love with Molly Waddington, the step-daughter of your client, Mrs. Waddington."

"You don't say! And I suppose he's too shy to come within a mile of her."

"On the contrary. The night before last he seems to have forced his way into the house—you might say, practically forced his way—and now Mrs. Waddington has forbidden him to see Molly again, fearing that he will spoil her plan of marrying the poor child to a certain Lord Hunstanton."

The girl stared.

"You're right! George must have altered."

"And we were wondering—Molly and I—if we could possibly induce you to stoop to a—shall I say a benevolent little ruse. Mrs. Waddington is coming to see you to-day at five, and it was Molly's suggestion that I should sound you as to whether you would consent to take a look in the crystal and tell Mrs. Waddington that you see danger threatening Molly from a dark man with an eyeglass."

"Of course."

"You will?"

"It isn't much to do in return for all you have done for me."

"Thank you, thank you," said Hamilton Beamish. "I knew, the moment I set eyes on you, that you were a woman in a million. I wonder,—could you possibly come to lunch one day after you return?"

"I'd love it."

"I'll leave you my telephone number."

"Thanks. Give George my regards. I'd like to see him when I get back."

"You shall. Good-bye."

"Good-bye, Mr. Beamish."

"Hamilton."

Her face wore a doubtful look.

"I don't like that name Hamilton. It's kind of stiff."

Hamilton Beamish had a brief struggle with himself.

"My name is also James. At one time in my life many people used to call me Jimmy." He shuddered a little, but repeated the word bravely. "Jimmy."

"Put me on the list," said the girl. "I like that much better. Good-bye, Jimmy."

"Good-by" said Hamilton Beamish.

So ended the first spasm of a great man's love-story. A few moments later, Hamilton Beamish was walking in a sort of dance-measure down the street. Near Washington Square he gave a small boy a dollar and asked him if he was going to be President some day.

V

"George," said Hamilton Beamish "I met some one to-day who knew you back in East Gilead. A girl."

"What was her name? Did Molly give you any message for me?"

"Madame Eulalie."

"I don't remember anyone called that. Did Molly give you any message for me?"

"She is slim and graceful and has tender grey eyes like mists floating over some pool in Fairyland."

"I certainly don't remember anyone in East Gilead like that. Did Molly give you any message for me?"

"No."

"She didn't?" George flung himself despairingly into a chair. "This is the end!"

"Oh yes, she did," said Hamilton Beamish. "I was forgetting. She told me to tell you that, if you happened to be in Central Park to-morrow afternoon near the Zoo, you might meet her."

"This is the maddest, merriest day of all the glad New Year." said George Finch.

# CHAPTER FIVE

I

MADAME EULALIE peered into the crystal that was cupped between her shapely hands. The face that had caused Hamilton Beamish to jettison the principles of a lifetime was concentrated and serious.

"The mists begin to clear away!" she murmured.

"Ah!" said Mrs. Waddington. She had been hoping they would.

"There is some one very near to you . . ."

"A spirit?" said Mrs. Waddington nervously, casting an apprehensive glance over her shoulder. She was never quite sure that something of the sort might not pop out at any moment from a corner of this dim-lit, incense-scented room.

"You misunderstand me," said Madame Eulalie gravely. "I mean that that which is taking shape in the crystal concerns some one very near to you, some near relative."

"Not my husband?" said Mrs. Waddington in a flat voice. A woman careful with her money, she did not relish the idea of handing over ten dollars for visions about Sigsbee H.

"Does your husband's name begin with an M.?"

"No," said Mrs. Waddington, relieved.

"The letter M. seems to be forming itself among the mists."

"I have a step-daughter, Molly."

"Is she tall and dark?"

"No. Small and fair."

"Then it is she!" said Madame Eulalie. "I see her in her wedding-dress, walking up an aisle. Her hand is on the arm of a dark man with an eyeglass Do you know such a person?"

"Lord Hunstanton!"

"I do seem to sense the letter H."

"Lord Hunstanton is a great friend of mine, and devoted to Molly. Do you really see her marrying him?"

"I see her walking up the aisle."

"It's the same thing."

"No! For she never reaches the altar."

"Why not?" asked Mrs. Waddington, justly annoyed.

"From the crowd a woman springs forth. She bars the way. She seems to be speaking rapidly, with great emotion. And the man with the eyeglass is shrinking back, his face working horribly. His expression is very villainous. He raises a hand. He strikes the woman. She reels back. She draws out a revolver. And then . . ."

"Yes?" cried Mrs. Waddington. "Yes?"

"The vision fades," said Madame Eulalie, rising briskly with the air of one who has given a good ten dollars' worth.

"But it can't be! It's incredible."

"The crystal never deceives."

"But Lord Hunstanton is a most delightful man."

"No doubt the woman with the revolver found him so—to her cost."

"But you may have been mistaken. Many men are dark and wear an eyeglass. What did this man look like?"

"What does Lord Hunstanton look like?"

"He is tall and beautfully proportioned, with clear blue eyes and a small moustache, which he twists between the finger and thumb of his right hand."

"It was he!"

"What shall I do?"

"Well, obviously it would seem criminal to allow Miss Waddington to associate with this man."

"But he's coming to dinner to-night."

Madame Eulalie, whose impulses sometimes ran away with her, was about to say 'Poison his soup': but contrived in time to substitute for this remark a sober shrug of the shoulders.

"I must leave it to you, Mrs. Waddington," she said, "to decide on the best course of action. I cannot advise. I only warn. If you want change for a large bill, I think I can manage it for you," she added, striking the business note.

All the way home to Seventy-Ninth Street, Mrs. Waddington pondered deeply. And, as she was not a woman who, as a rule, exercised her brain to any great extent by the time she reached the house she was experiencing some of the sensations of one who has been hit on the head by a sand-bag. What she felt that she needed above all things in the world was complete solitude: and it was consequently with a jaundiced eye that she looked upon her husband, Sigsbee Horatio, when, a few moments after her return, he shuffled into the room where she had planted herself down for further intensive meditation.

"Well, Sigsbee?" said Mrs. Waddington, wearily.

"Oh, there you are," said Sigsbee H.

"Do you want anything?"

"Well, yes and no," said Sigsbee.

Mrs. Waddington was exasperated to perceive at this point that her grave matrimonial blunder was slithering about the parquet floor in the manner of one trying out new dance-steps.

"Stand still!" she cried.

"I can't," said Sigsbee H. "I'm too nervous."

Mrs. Waddington pressed a hand to her throbbing brow.

"Then sit down!"

"I'll try," said Sigsbee doubtfully. He tested a chair, and sprang up instantly as if the seat had been charged with electricity. "I can't," he said. "I'm all of a twitter."

"What in the world do you mean?"

"I've got something to tell you and I don't know how to begin."

"What do you wish to tell me?"

"I don't wish to tell you it at all," said Sigsbee frankly. "But I promised Molly I would. She came in a moment ago."

"Well?"

"I was in the library. She found me there and told me this."

"Do kindly get to the point, Sigsbee!"

"I promised her I would break it gently."

"Break what gently? You are driving me mad."

"Do you remember," asked Sigsbee, "a splendid young Westerner named Pinch who dropped in to dinner the night before last? A fine breezy . . ."

"I am not likely to forget the person you mention. I have given strict instructions that he is never again to be admitted to the house."

"Well, this splendid young Pinch . . ."

"I am not interested in Mr. Finch,—which is, I believe, his correct name."

"Pinch, I thought."

"Finch! And what does his name matter, anyway?"

"Well," said Sigsbee, "it matters this much, that Molly seems to want to make it hers. What I'm driving at, if you see what I mean, is that Molly came in a moment ago and told me that she and this young fellow Finch have just gone and got engaged to be married!"

## II

Having uttered these words, Sigsbee Horatio stood gazing at his wife with something of the spell-bound horror of a man who has bored a hole in a dam and sees the water trickling through and knows that it is too late to stop it. He had had a sort of idea all along that the news might affect her rather powerfully, and his guess was coming true. Nothing could make a woman of Mrs. Waddington's physique 'leap from her chair': but she had begun to rise slowly like a balloon half-filled with gas, and her face had become so contorted and her eyes so bulging that any competent medical man of sporting tastes would have laid seven to four on a fit of apoplexy in the next few minutes.

But by some miracle this disaster—if you could call it that—did not occur. For quite a considerable time the sufferer had trouble with her vocal chords and could emit nothing but guttural croaks. Then, mastering herself with a strong effort, she spoke.

"What did you say?"

"You heard," said Sigsbee H. sullenly, twisting his fingers and wishing that he was out in Utah, rustling cattle.

Mrs. Waddington moistened her lips.

"Did I understand you to say that Molly was engaged to be married to that Finch?"

"Yes, I did. And," added Sigsbee H., giving battle in the first line of trenches, "it's no good saying it was all my fault, because I had nothing to do with it."

"It was you who brought this man into the house."

"Well, yes." Sigsbee had overlooked that weak spot in his defences. "Well, yes."

There came upon Mrs. Waddington a ghastly calm like that which comes upon the surface of molten lava in the crater of a volcano just before the stuff shoots out and starts doing the local villagers a bit of no good.

"Ring the bell," she said.

Sigsbee H. rang the bell.

"Ferris," said Mrs. Waddington, "ask Miss Molly to come here."

"Very good, madam."

In the interval which elapsed between the departure of the butler and the arrival of the erring daughter, no conversation brilliant enough to be worth reporting took place in the room. Once Sigsbee said 'Er——' and in reply Mrs. Waddington said 'Be quiet!' but that completed the dialogue. When Molly entered, Mrs. Waddington was looking straight in front of her and heaving gently, and Sigsbee H. had just succeeded in breaking a valuable china figure which he had taken from an occasional table and was trying in a preoccupied manner to balance on the end of a paper-knife.

"Ferris says you want to see me, mother," said Molly, floating brightly in.

She stood there, looking at the two with shining eyes. Her cheeks were delightfully flushed: and there was about her so radiant an air of sweet, innocent, girlish gaiety that it was all Mrs. Waddington could do to refrain from hurling a bust of Edgar Allan Poe at her head.

"I do want to see you," said Mrs. Waddington. "Pray tell me instantly what is all this nonsense I hear about you and . . ." She choked. " . . . and Mr. Finch."

"To settle a bet," said Sigsbee H., "is his name Finch or Pinch?"

"Finch, of course."

"I'm bad at names," said Sigsbee. "I was in college with a fellow called Follansbee and do you think I could get it out of my nut that that guy's name was Ferguson? Not in a million years! I . ."

"Sigsbee!"

"Hello?"

"Be quiet." Mrs. Waddington concentrated her attention on Molly once more. "Your father says that you told him some absurd story about being . . ."

"Engaged to George?" said Molly. "Yes, it's quite true I am. By a most extraordinary chance we met this afternoon in Central Park near the Zoo . . ."

"A place," said Sigsbee H., "I've meant to go to a hundred times and never seen yet."

"Sigsbee!"

"All right, all right! I was only saying . . ."

"We were both tremendously surprised, of course," said Molly. "I said 'Fancy meeting you here!' and he said . . ."

"I have no wish to hear what Mr. Finch said."

"Well, anyway, we walked round for awhile, looking at the animals, and suddenly he asked me to marry him outside the cage of the Siberian yak."

"No, sir!" exclaimed Sigsbee H. with a sudden strange firmness, the indulgent father who for once in his life asserts himself. "When you get married, you'll be married in St. Thomas's like any other nice girl."

"I mean it was outside the cage of the Siberian yak that he asked me to marry him."

"Oh, ah!" said Sigsbee H.

A dreamy look had crept into Molly's eyes. Her lips were curved in a tender smile, as if she were re-living that wonderful moment in a girl's life when the man she loves beckons to her to follow him into Paradise.

"You ought to have seen his ears!" she said. "They were absolutely crimson."

"You don't say!" chuckled Sigsbee H.

"Scarlet! And when he tried to speak, he gargled"

"The poor simp!"

"How dare you call my dear darling Georgie a simp?"

"How dare you call that simp your dear darling Georgie?" demanded Mrs. Waddington.

"Because he is my dear darling Georgie. I love him with all my heart, the precious lamb, and I'm going to marry him."

"You are going to do nothing of the kind!" Mrs. Waddington quivered with outraged indignation. "Do you imagine I intend to allow you to ruin your life by marrying a despicable fortune-hunter?"

"He isn't a despicable fortune-hunter."

"He is a penniless artist."

"Well, I'm sure he is frightfully clever and will be able to sell his pictures for ever so much."

"Tchah!"

"Besides," said Molly defiantly, "when I marry I get that pearl necklace which father gave mother. I can sell that, and it will keep us going for years."

Mrs. Waddington was about to reply—and there is little reason to doubt that that reply would have been about as red-hot a come-back as any hundred and eighty pound woman had ever spoken—when she was checked by a sudden exclamation of agony that proceeded from the lips of her husband.

"Whatever is the matter, Sigsbee?" she said, annoyed.

Sigsbee H. seemed to be wrestling with acute mental agitation. He was staring at his daughter with protruding eyes.

"Did you say you were going to sell that necklace?" he stammered.

"Oh, be quiet, Sigsbee!" said Mrs. Waddington. "What does it matter whether she sells the necklace or not? It has nothing to do with the argument. The point is that this misguided girl is proposing to throw herself away on a miserable, paint-daubing, ukulele-playing artist . . ."

"He doesn't play the ukulele. He told me so."

" . . . when she might, if she chose, marry a delightful man with a fine old English title who would . . ."

Mrs. Waddington broke off. There had come back to her the memory of that scene in Madame Eulalie's office.

Molly seized the opportunity afforded by her unexpected silence to make a counter-attack.

"I wouldn't marry Lord Hunstanton if he were the last man in the world."

"Honey," said Sigsbee H. in a low, pleading voice, "I don't think I'd sell that necklace if I were you."

"Of course I shall sell it. We shall need the money when we are married."

"You are not going to be married," said Mrs. Waddington, recovering. "I should have thought any right-minded girl would have despised this wretched Finch. Why, the man appears to be so poor-spirited that he didn't even dare to come here and tell me this awful news. He left it to you . . ."

"George was not able to come here. The poor pet has been arrested by a policeman."

"Ha!" cried Mrs. Waddington triumphantly. "And that is the sort of man you propose to marry! A gaol-bird!"

"Well, I think it shows what a sweet nature he has. He was so happy at being engaged that he suddenly stopped at Fifty-Ninth Street and Fifth Avenue and started giving away dollar-bills to everybody who came by. In about twenty minutes there was a crowd stretching right across to Madison Avenue, and the traffic was blocked for miles, and they called out the police-reserves, and George was taken away in a patrol-wagon, and I telephoned to Hamilton Beamish to go and bail him out and bring him along here. They ought to arrive at any moment."

"Mr. Hamilton Beamish and Mr. George Finch," said Ferris in the doorway. And the nicely graduated way in which he spoke the two names would have conveyed at once to any intelligent listener that Hamilton Beamish was an honoured guest but that he had been forced to admit George Finch—against all the promptings of his better nature—because Mr. Beamish had told him to and he had been quelled by the man's cold, spectacled eye.

"Here we are," said Hamilton Beamish heartily. "Just in time, I perceive, to join in a jolly family discussion."

Mrs. Waddington looked bleachingly at George, who was trying to hide behind a gate-leg table. For George Finch was conscious of not looking his best. Nothing so disorders the outer man as the process of being arrested and hauled to the coop by a *posse* of New York gendarmes. George's collar was hanging loose from its stud: his waistcoat lacked three buttons: and his right eye was oddly discoloured where a high-minded officer, piqued by the fact that he should have collected crowds by scattering dollar-bills and even more incensed by the discovery that he had scattered all he possessed and had none left, had given him a hearty buffet during the ride in the patrol-wagon.

"There is no discussion," said Mrs. Waddington. "You do not suppose I am going to allow my daughter to marry a man like that."

"Tut-tut!" said Hamilton Beamish. "George is not looking his best just now, but a wash and brush-up will do wonders. . . . What is your objection to George?"

Mrs. Waddington was at a momentary loss for a reply. Anybody, suddenly questioned as to why he disliked a slug or a snake or a black-beetle, might find it difficult on the spur of the moment to analyse and dissect his prejudice. Mrs. Waddington looked on her antipathy to George Finch as one of those deep, natural, fundamental impulses which the sensible person takes for granted. Broadly speaking, she objected to George because he was George.

It was, as it were, his essential Georgeness that offended her. But, seeing that she was expected to be analytical, she forced her mind to the task.

"He is an artist."

"So was Michael Angelo."

"I never met him."

"He was a very great man."

Mrs. Waddington raised her eyebrows.

"I completely fail to understand, Mr. Beamish, why, when we are discussing this young man here with the black eye and the dirty collar, you should persist in diverting the conversation to the subject of a perfect stranger like this Mr. Angelo."

"I merely wished to point out," said Hamilton Beamish stiffly, "that the fact that he is an artist does not necessarily damn a man."

"There is no need," retorted Mrs. Waddington with even greater stiffness, "to use bad language."

"Besides, George is a rotten artist."

"Rotten to the core, no doubt."

"I mean," said Hamilton Beamish, flushing slightly at the lapse from the English Pure into which emotion had led him. "he paints so badly that you can hardly call him an artist at all."

"Is that so?" said George, speaking for the first time and speaking nastily

"I am sure George is one of the cleverest artists living." cried Molly.

"He is not," thundered Hamilton Beamish. "He is an incompetent amateur."

"Exactly!" said Mrs. Waddington. "And consequently can never hope to make money."

Hamilton Beamish's eyes lit up behind their spectacles.

"Is that your chief objection?" he asked.

"Is what my chief objection?"

"That George has no money?"

"But . . ." began George.

"Shut up!" said Hamilton Beamish. "I ask you, Mrs. Waddington, would you give your consent to this marriage if my friend George Finch were a wealthy man?"

"It is a waste of time to discuss such . . ."

"Would you?"

"Possibly I would."

"Then allow me to inform you," said Hamilton Beamish, triumphantly, "that George Finch is an exceedingly wealthy man.

His uncle Thomas, whose entire fortune he inherited two years ago, was Finch, Finch, Finch, Butterfield and Finch, the well-known Corporation Law firm. George, my boy, let me congratulate you. All is well. Mrs. Waddington has withdrawn her objections."

Mrs. Waddington snorted, but it was the snort of a beaten woman, out-generalled by a superior intelligence.

"But . . ."

"No." Hamilton Beamish raised his hand. "You cannot go back on what you said. You stated in distinct terms that, if George had money, you would consent to the marriage."

"And, anyway, I don't know what all the fuss is about," said Molly. "Because I am going to marry him, no matter what anybody says."

Mrs. Waddington capitulated.

"Very well! I am nobody, I see. What I say does not matter in the slightest."

"Mother!" said George reproachfully.

"Mother?" echoed Mrs. Waddington, starting violently.

"Now that everything is so happily settled, of course I regard you in that light."

"Oh, do you?" said Mrs. Waddington.

"Oh, I do," said George.

Mrs. Waddington sniffed unpleasantly.

"I have been overwhelmed and forced into consenting to a marriage of which I strongly disapprove," she said, "but I may be permitted to say one word. I have a feeling that this wedding will never take place."

"What do you mean?" said Molly. "Of course it will take place. Why shouldn't it?"

Mrs. Waddington sniffed again.

"Mr. Finch," she said, "though a very incompetent artist, has lived for a considerable time in the heart of Greenwich Village and mingled daily with Bohemians of both sexes and questionable morals. . . ."

"What are you hinting?" demanded Molly.

"I am not hinting," replied Mrs. Waddington with dignity. "I am saying. And what I am saying is this. Do not come to *me* for sympathy if this Finch of yours turns out to have the sort of moral code which you might expect in one who deliberately and of his own free will goes and lives near Washington Square. I say again, that I have a presentiment that this marriage will never take place. I had a similar presentiment regarding the wedding of my sister-in-law and a young man named John Porter. I said, 'I feel that this wedding will never take place.' And events proved me right. John Porter, at the very moment when he was about to enter the church, was arrested on a charge of bigamy."

George uttered protesting noises.

"But my morals are above reproach."

"So you say."

"I assure you that, as far as women are concerned, I can scarcely tell one from another."

"Precisely," replied Mrs. Waddington, "what John Porter said when they asked him why he had married six different girls."

Hamilton Beamish looked at his watch.

"Well, now that everything is satisfactorily settled . . ."

"For the moment," said Mrs. Waddington.

"Now that everything is satisfactorily settled," proceeded Hamilton Beamish, "I will be leaving you. I have to get back and dress. I am speaking at a dinner of the Great Neck Social and Literary Society to-night."

The silence that followed his departure was followed by a question from Sigsbee H. Waddington.

"Molly, my dear," said Sigsbee H., "touching on that necklace. Now that this splendid young fellow turns out to be very rich, you will not want to sell it, of course?"

Molly reflected.

"Yes, I think I will. I never liked it much. It's too showy. I shall sell it and buy something very nice with the money for George. A lot of diamond pins or watches or motor-cars or something. And, whenever we look at them we will think of you, daddy dear."

"Thanks," said Mr. Waddington huskily. "Thanks."

"Seldom in my life," observed Mrs. Waddington, coming abruptly out of the brooding coma into which she had sunk, "have I ever had a stronger presentiment than the one to which I alluded just now."

"Oh, mother!" said George.

Hamilton Beamish, gathering up his hat in the hall, became aware that somehting was pawing at his sleeve. He looked down and perceived Sigsbee H. Waddington.

"Say!" said Sigsbee H. in a hushed undertone. "Say, listen!"

"Is anything the matter?"

"You bet your tortoiseshell-rimmed spectacles something's the matter," whispered Sigsbee H. urgently. "Say, listen. Can I have a word with you? I want your advice."

"I'm in a hurry."

"How long will you be before you start out for this Hoboken Clam-Bake of yours?"

"The dinner of the Great Neck Social and Literary Society, to which I imagine you to allude, is at eight o'clock. I shall motor down, leaving my apartment at twenty minutes past seven."

"Then it's no good trying to see you to-night. Say, listen. Will you be home to-morrow?"

"Yes."

"Right!" said Sigsbee H.


# CHAPTER SIX

## I

"Say, listen!" said Sigsbee H. Waddington.

"Proceed," said Hamilton Beamish.

"Say, listen!"

"I am all attention."

Say, listen!" said Mr. Waddington.

Hamilton Beamish glanced at his watch impatiently. Even at its normal level of imbecility, the conversation of Sigsbee H. Waddington was apt to jar upon his critical mind, and now, it seemed to him, the other was plumbing depths which even he had never reached before.

"I can give you seven minutes," he said. "At the end of that period of time I must leave you. I am speaking at a luncheon of the Young Women Writers of America. You came here, I gather, to make a communication to me. Make it."

"Say, listen!" said Sigsbee H.

Hamilton Beamish compressed his lips sternly. He had heard parrots with a more intelligent flow of conversation. He was conscious of a strange desire to beat this man over the head with a piece of lead-piping.

"Say, listen!" said Sigsbee H. "I've gone and got myself into the devil of a jam."

"A position of embarrassment?"

"You said it!"

"State nature of same," said Hamilton Beamish, looking at his watch again.

Mr. Waddington glanced quickly and nervously over his shoulder.

"It's like this. You heard Molly say yesterday she was going to sell those pearls."

"I did."

"Well, say, listen!" said Mr. Waddington, lowering his voice and looking apprehensively about him once more. "They aren't pearls!"

"What are they then?"

"Fakes!"

Hamilton Beamish winced.

"You mean imitation stones?"

"That's just what I do mean. What am I going to do about it?"

"Perfectly simple. Bring an action against the jeweller who sold them to you as genuine."

"But they were genuine then. You don't seem to get the position."

"I do not."

Sigsbee H. Waddington moistened his lips.

"Have you ever heard of the Finer and Better Motion Picture Company of Hollywood, Cal.?"

"Kindly keep to the point. My time is limited."

"This is the point. Some time ago a guy who said he was a friend of mine tipped me off that this company was a wow."

"A what?"

"A winner. He said it was going to be big and advised me to come in on the ground floor. The chance of a lifetime he said it was."

"Well?"

"Well, I hadn't any money,—not a cent. Still, I didn't want to miss a good thing like that, so I sat down and thought. I thought and thought and thought. And then suddenly something seemed to say to me 'Why not?' That pearl necklace, I mean. There it was, you get me, just sitting and doing nothing and I only needed the money for a few weeks till this Company started to clean up and . . . well, to cut a long story short, I sneaked the necklace away, had the fake stones put in, sold the others, bought the stock, and there I was, so I thought, all hotsy-totsy."

"All—what?"

"Hotsy-totsy. It seemed to me I was absolutely hotsy-totsy."

"And what has caused you to revise this opion?"

"Why, I met a man the other day who said these shares weren't worth a bean. I've got 'em here. Take a look at them."

Hamilton Beamish scrutinized the documents with distaste.

"The man was right," he said. "When you first mentioned the name of the company, it seemed familiar. I now recall why. Mrs. Henrietta Byng Masterson, the president of the Great Neck Social and Literary Society, was speaking to me of it last night. She also had bought shares and mentioned the fact with regret. I should say at a venture that these of yours are worth possibly ten dollars."

"I gave fifty thousand for them."

"Then your books will show a loss of forty-nine thousand nine hundred and ninety. I am sorry."

"But what am I to do?"

"Write it off to experience."

"But hell's bells! Don't you understand? What's going to happen when Molly tries to sell that necklace and it comes out that it's a fake?"

Hamilton Beamish shook his head. With most of the ordinary problems of life he was prepared to cope, but this, he frankly admitted, was beyond him.

"My wife'll murder me."

"I'm sorry."

"I came here, thinking that you would be able to suggest something."

"Short of stealing the necklace and dropping it in the Hudson River, I fear I can think of no solution."

"You used to be a brainy sort of gink," said Mr. Waddington reproachfully.

"No human brain could devise a way out of this impasse. You can but wait events and trust to Time the great healer eventually to mend matters."

"That's a lot of help."

Hamilton Beamish shrugged his shoulders. Sigsbee H. Waddington regarded the stock-certificates malevolently.

"If the stuff's no good," he said, "what do they want to put all those dollar-signs on the back for? Misleading people! And look at that seal. And all those signatures."

"I am sorry," said Hamilton Beamish. He moved to the window and leaned out, sniffing the summer air "What a glorious day."

"No, it isn't," said Mr. Waddington.

"Have you ever by any chance met Madame Eulalie, Mrs. Waddington's palmist?" asked Hamilton Beamish dreamily.

"Darn all palmists!" said Sigsbee H. Waddington. "What am I going to do about this stock?"

"I have already told you that there is nothing that you can do, short of stealing the necklace."

"There must be something. What would you do if you were me?"

"Run away to Europe."

"But I can't run away to Europe. I haven't any money."

"Then shoot yourself . . . stand in front of a train . . . anything, anything," said Hamilton Beamish impatiently. "And now I must really go. Good-bye."

"Good-bye. Thanks for being such a help."

"Not at all," said Hamilton Beamish. "Don't mention it. I am always delighted to be of any assistance, always."

He gave a last soulful glance at the photograph on the mantel-piece and left the room. Mr. Waddington could hear him singing an old French love-song as he waited for the elevator, and the sound seemed to set the seal upon his gloom and despair.

"You big stiff!" said Mr. Waddington morosely.

He flung himself into a chair and gave himself up to melancholy meditation. For awhile, all he could think of was how much he disliked Hamilton Beamish. There was a man who went about the place pretending to be clever, and yet the moment you came to him with a childishly simple problem which he ought to have been able to solve in half a dozen different ways in five minutes, he could do nothing but say he was sorry and advise a fellow to stand in front of trains and shoot himself. What on earth was the use of trying to be optimistic about a world which contained people like Hamilton Beamish?

And that idiotic suggestion of his about stealing the necklace! How could he possibly . . . ?

Sigsbee H. Waddington sat up in his chair. There was a gleam in his eyes. He snorted. Was it such an idiotic suggestion, after all?

He gazed into the future. At the moment the necklace was in safe custody at the bank, but, if Molly was going to marry this young Pinch, it would presumably be taken from there and placed on exhibition among the other wedding-presents. So that ere long there would undeniably be a time—say, the best part of a day—when a resolute man with a nimble set of fingers might . . .

Mr. Waddington sank back in his chair again. The light died out of his eyes. Philosophers tell us that no man really knows himself: but Sigsbee H. Waddington knew himself well enough to be aware that he fell short by several miles of the nerve necessary for such an action. Stealing necklaces is no job for an amateur.

You cannot suddenly take to it in middle life without any previous preparation. Every successful stealer of necklaces has to undergo a rigorous and intensive training from early boyhood, starting with milk-cans and bags at railway stations and working his way up. What was needed for this very delicate operation was a seasoned professional.

And there, felt Sigsbee H. Waddington bitterly, you had in a nutshell the thing that made life so difficult to live—the tragic problem of how to put your hand on the right specialist at the exact moment when you required him. All these reference-books like the Classified Telephone Directory omitted the vital trades, —the trades whose members were of assistance in the real crises of life. They told you where to find a Glass Beveller, as if anyone knew what to do with a Glass Beveller when they had got him. They gave you the address of Yeast Producers and Designers of Quilts: but what was the good of a producer of yeast when you wanted some one who would produce a jemmy and break into a house, or a designer of quilts when what you required was a man who could design a satisfactory scheme for stealing an imitation-pearl necklace?

Mr. Waddington groaned in sheer bitterness of spirit. The irony of things afflicted him sorely. Every day the papers talked about the Crime Wave: every day a thousand happy crooks were making off in automobiles with a thousand bundles of swag: and yet here he was, in urgent need of one of these crooks, and he didn't know where to look for him.

A deprecating tap sounded on the door.

"Come in!" shouted Mr. Waddington irritably.

He looked up and perceived about seventy-five inches of bony policeman shambling over the threshold.

II

"I beg your pardon, sir, if I seem to intrude," said the policeman, beginning to recede. "I came to see Mr. Beamish. I should have made an appointment."

"Hey! Don't go." Said Mr. Waddington.

The policeman paused doubtfully at the door.

"But as Mr. Beamish is not at home . . ."

"Come right in and have a chat. Sit down and take the weight off your feet. My name is Waddington."

"Mine is Garroway," replied the officer, bowing courteously. "Pleased to meet you."

"Happy to meet you, sir."

"Have a good cigar."

"I should enjoy it above all things."

"I wonder where Mr. Beamish keeps them," said Sigsbee H., rising and routing about the room. "Ah, here we are. Match?"

"I have a match, thank you."

"Capital!"

Sigsbee H. Waddington resumed his seat and regarded the other affectionately. An instant before, he had been bemoaning the fact that he did not know where to lay his hands on a crook, and here, sent from heaven, was a man who was probably a walking directory of malefactors.

"I like policemen," said Mr. Waddington affably.

"That is very gratifying, sir."

"Always have. Shows how honest I am, ha ha! If I were a crook, I suppose I'd be scared stiff, sitting here talking to you." Mr. Waddington drew bluffly at his cigar. "I guess you come across a lot of criminals, eh?"

"It is the great drawback to the policeman's life," assented Officer Garroway, sighing. "One meets them on all sides. Only last night, when I was searching for a vital adjective, I was called upon to arrest an uncouth person who had been drinking home-brewed hootch. He soaked me on the jaw, and inspiration left me."

"Wouldn't that give you a soft-pine finish!" said Mr. Waddington sympathetically. "But what I was referring to was real crooks. Fellows who get into houses and steal pearl necklaces. Ever meet any of them?"

"I meet a great number. In the pursuance of his duty, a policeman is forced against his will to mix with all sorts of questionable people. It may be that my profession biases me, but I have a hearty dislike for thieves."

"Still, if there were no thieves, there would be no policemen."

"Very true, sir."

"Supply and demand."

"Precisely."

Mr. Waddington blew a cloud of smoke.

"I'm kind of interested in crooks." he said, "I'd like to meet a few."

"I assure you that you would not find the experience enjoyable," said Officer Garroway, shaking his head. "They are unpleasant, illiterate men with little or no desire to develop their souls. I make an exception, I should mention, however, in the case of Mr. Mullett, who seemed a nice sort of fellow. I wish I could have seen more of him."

"Mullett? Who's he?"

"He is an ex-convict, sir, who works for Mr. Finch in the apartment upstairs."

"You don't say! An ex-convict and works for Mr. Finch? What was his line?"

"Inside burglary jobs, sir. I understand, however, that he has reformed and is now a respectable member of society."

"Still, he was a burglar once?"

"Yes, sir."

"Well, well!"

There was a silence. Officer Garroway, who was trying to find a good synonym for one of the adjectives in the poem on which he was occupied, stared thoughtfully at the ceiling. Mr. Waddington chewed his cigar intensely.

"Say, listen!" said Mr. Waddington.

"Sir?" said the policeman, coming out of his reverie with a start.

"Suppose," said Mr. Waddington, "suppose, just for the sake of argument, that a wicked person wanted a crook to do a horrible, nefarious job for him, would he have to pay him?"

"Undoubtedly, sir. These men are very mercenary."

"Pay him much?"

"I imagine a few hundred dollars. It would depend on the magnitude of the crime contemplated, no doubt."

"A few hundred dollars!"

"Two, perhaps, or three."

Silence fell once more. Officer Garroway resumed his inspection of the ceiling. What he wanted was something signifying the aspect of the streets of New York, and he had used 'sordid' in line two. 'Scabrous!' That was the word. He was rolling it over his tongue when he became aware that his companion was addressing him.

"I beg your pardon, sir?"

Mr. Waddington's eyes were glittering in a peculiar way. He leaned forward and tapped Officer Garroway on the knee.

"Say, listen! I like your face, Larrabee."

"My name is Garroway."

"Never mind about your name. It's your face I like. Say, listen, do you want to make a pile of money?"

"Yes, sir."

"Well, I don't mind telling you that I've taken a fancy to you, and I'm going to do something for you that I wouldn't do for many people. Have you ever heard of the Finer and Better Motion Picture Company of Hollywood, Cal. ?"

"No, sir."

"That's the wonderful thing," said Mr. Waddington in a sort of ecstacy. "Nobody's ever heard of it. It isn't one of those worn-out propositions like the Famous Players that everybody's sick and tired of. It's new. And do you know what I'm going to do ? I'm going to let you have a block of stock in it for a quite nominal figure. It would be insulting you to give it you for nothing, which is what I'd like to do, of course. But it amounts to the same thing. This stock here is worth thousands and thousands of dollars, and you shall have it for three hundred. Have you got three hundred ?" asked Mr. Waddington, anxiously.

"Yes, sir, I have that sum, but . . ."

Mr. Waddington waved his cigar.

"Don't use that word 'but'! I know what you're trying to say. You're trying to tell me I'm robbing myself. I know I am, and what of it ? What's money to me ? The way I look at is that, when a man has made his pile, like me, and has got enough to keep his wife and family in luxury, the least he can do as a lover of humanity is to let the rest go to folks who'll appreciate it. Now you probably need money as much as the rest of them, eh ?"

"I certainly do, sir."

"Then here you are," said Mr. Waddington, brandishing the bundle of stock certificates. "This is where you get it. You can take it from me that the Finer and Better Motion Picture Company is the biggest thing since Marconi invented the victrola."

Officer Garroway took the stock and fondled it thoughtfully.

"It's certainly very nicely engraved," he said.

"You bet it is ! And look at those dollar-signs on the back. Look at that seal. Cast your eye over those signatures. Those mean something. And you know what the motion-pictures are. A bigger industry than the beef business. And the Finer and Better is the greatest proposition of them all. It isn't like the other companies. For one thing, it hasn't been paying out all its money in dividends."

"No ?"

"No, sir ! Not wasted a cent that way."

"It's all still there ?"

"All still there. And, what's more, it hasn't released a single picture."

"All still there ?"

"All still there. Lying on the shelves,—dozens of them. And then take the matter of overhead expenses,—the thing that cripples all these other film companies. Big studios . . . expensive directors . . . high-salaried stars . . ."

"All still there ?"

"No, sir ! That's the point. They're not there. The Finer and Better Motion Picture Company hasn't any of these D. W. Griffiths and Gloria Swansons eating away its capital. It hasn't even a studio."

"Not even a studio ?"

"No, sir. Nothing but a company. I tell you it's big !"

Officer Garroway's mild blue eyes widened.

"It sounds like the opportunity of a lifetime," he agreed.

"The opportunity of a dozen lifetimes," said Mr. Waddington. "And that's the way to get on in the world—by grabbing your opportunities. Why, what's Big Ben but a wrist-watch that saw its chance and made good ?" Mr. Waddington paused. His forehead wrinkled. He snatched the bundle of stock from his companion's grasp and made a movement towards his pocket. "No !" he said, "No ! I can't do it. I can't let you have it, after all !"

"Oh, sir !"

"No. It's too big."

"Oh, but, Mr. Waddington . . ."

Sigsbee H. Waddington seemed to come out of a trance. He shook himself and stared at the policeman as if he were saying 'Where am I ?' He heaved a deep, remorseful sigh.

"Isn't money the devil !" he said. "Isn't it terrible the way it saps all a fellow's principles and good resolutions ! Sheer greed, that was what was the matter with me, when I said I wouldn't let you have this stock. Sheer, grasping greed. Here am I, with millions in the bank, and the first thing you know I'm trying to resist a generous impulse to do a fellow human-being, whose face I like, a kindly act. It's horrible !" He wrenched the bundle from his pocket and threw it to the policeman. "Here, take it before I weaken again. Give me the three hundred quick and let me get away."

"I don't know how to thank you, sir."

"Don't thank me, don't thank me. One—two—three," said Mr. Waddington, counting the bills. "Don't thank me at all. It's a pleasure."

Upstairs, while the conversation just recorded was in progress, Frederick Mullett was entertaining his fiancée, Fanny Welch, to a light collation in the kitchen of George Finch's apartment. It is difficult for a man to look devotional while his mouth is full of cold beef and chutney,—but not impossible, for Mullett was doing it now. He gazed at Fanny very much as George Finch had gazed at Molly Waddington, Hamilton Beamish at Madame Eulalie, and as a million other young men in New York and its outskirts were or would shortly be gazing at a million other young women. Love had come rather late to Frederick Mullett, for his had been a busy life, but it had come to stay.

Externally, Fanny Welch appeared not unworthy of his devotion. She was a pretty little thing with snapping black eyes and a small face. The thing you noticed about her first was the slim shapeliness of her hands, with their long sensitive fingers. One of the great advantages of being a pickpocket is that you do have nice hands.

"I like this place," said Fanny, looking about her.

"Do you, honey?" said Mullett tenderly. "I was hoping you would. Because I've got a secret for you."

"What's that?"

"This is the place where you and me are going to spend our honeymoon!'

"What, in this kitchen?"

"Of course not. We'll have the run of the whole apartment, with the roof thrown in."

"What'll Mr. Finch have to say to that?"

"He won't know, pettie. You see, Mr. Finch has just gone and got engaged to be married himself, and he'll be off on his honeymoon-trip, so the whole place'll be ours for ever so long. What do you think of that?"

"Sounds good to me."

"I'll take and show you the place in a minute or two. It's the best studio-apartment for miles around. There's a nice large sitting-room that looks on to the roof, with French windows so that you can stroll out and take the air when you like. And there's a sleeping-porch on the roof, in case the weather's warm. And a bath H. and C., with shower. It's the snuggest place you'll ever want to find, and you and I can stay perched up here like two little birds in a nest. And, when we've finished honeymooning, we'll go down to Long Island and buy a little duck-farm and live happy ever after."

Fanny looked doubtful.

"Can you see me on a duck-farm, Freddy?"

"Can I?" Mullet's eyes beamed adoration. "You bet I can see you there,—standing in a gingham apron on the old brick path between the hollyhocks, watching little Frederick romping under the apple-tree."

"Little *who*?"

"Little Frederick."

"Oh? and did you notice little Fanny clinging to my skirts?"

"So she is. And William John in his cradle on the porch."

"I think we'd better stop looking for awhile," said Fanny. "Our family's growing too fast."

Mullett sighed ecstatically.

"Doesn't it sound quiet and peaceful after the stormy lives we've led. The quacking of the ducks. . . . The droning of the bees. . . . Put back that spoon, dearie. You know it doesn't belong to you."

Fanny removed the spoon from the secret places of her dress and eyed it with a certain surprise.

"Now, how did that get there?" she said.

"You snitched it up, sweetness," said Mullett gently. "Your little fingers just hovered for a moment like little bees over a flower, and the next minute the thing was gone. It was beautiful to watch, dearie, but put it back. You've done with all that sort of thing now, you know."

"I guess I have," said Fanny wistfully.

"You don't guess you have, precious," corrected her husband-to-be. "You know you have. Same as I've done."

"Are you really on the level now, Freddy?"

"I'm as honest as the day is long."

"Work at nights, eh? Mullett, the human moth. Goes through his master's clothes like a jealous wife."

Mullett laughed indulgently.

"The same little Fanny. How you do love to tease. Yes, precious, I'm through with the game for good. I wouldn't steal a bone collar-stud now, not if my mother came and begged me on her bended knee. All I want is my little wife and my little home in the country."

Fanny frowned pensively.

"You don't think it'll be kind of quiet down on that duck-farm? Kind of slow?"

"Slow?" said Mullett, shocked.

"Well, maybe not. But we're retiring from business awful young, Freddy."

A look of concern came into Mullett's face.

"You don't mean you still have a hankering for the old game?"

"Well, what if I do?" said Fanny defiantly. "You do, too, if you'd only come clean and admit it."

The look of concern changed to one of dignity.

"Nothing of the kind," said Mullett. "I give you my word, Fanny, that there isn't the job on earth that could tempt me now. And I do wish you would bring yourself to feel the same, honey."

"Oh, I'm not saying I would bother with anything that wasn't really big. But, honest to goodness, Freddy, it would be a crime to side-step anything worth-while, if it came along. It isn't as if we had all the money in the world. I've picked up some nice little things at the stores and I suppose you've kept some of the stuff you got away with, but outside of that we've nothing but the bit of cash we've managed to save. We've got to be practical."

"But, sweetie, think of the awful chances you'd be taking of getting pinched."

"I'm not afraid. If they ever do nab me, I've got a yarn about my poor old mother . . ."

"You haven't got a mother."

"Who said I had? . . . a yarn about my poor old mother that would draw tears from the Woolworth Building. Listen! 'Don't turn me over to the police, mister, I only did it for ma's sake. If you was out of work for weeks and starvin' and you had to sit and watch your poor old ma bendin' over the wash-tub . . .' "

"Don't, Fanny, please! I can't bear it even though I know it's just a game. I . . . Hello! Somebody at the front door. Probably only a model wanting to know if Mr. Finch has a job for her. You wait here, honey. I'll get rid of her and be back in half a minute."

IV

More than twenty times that period had, however, elapsed before Frederick Mullett returned to the kitchen. He found his bride-to-be in a considerably less amiable mood than that in which he had left her. She was standing with folded arms, and the temperature of the room had gone down a number of degrees.

"Pretty girl?" she inquired frostily, as Mullett crossed the threshold.

"Eh?"

"You said you were going to send that model away in half a minute, and I've been waiting here nearer a quarter of an hour," said Fanny, verifying this statement by a glance at the wristwatch, the absence of which from their stock was still an unsolved mystery to a prosperous firm of jewellers on Fifth Avenue.

Mullett clasped her in his arms. It was a matter of some difficulty, for she was not responsive, but he did it.

"It was not a model, darling. It was a man. A guy with grey hair and a red face."

"Oh? What did he want?"

Mullett's already somewhat portly frame seemed to expand, as if with some deep emotion.

"He came to tempt me, Fanny."

"To tempt you?"

"That's what he did. Wanted to know if my name was Mullett, and two seconds after I had said it was he offered me three hundred dollars to perpetrate a crime."

"He did? What crime?"

"I didn't wait for him to tell me. I spurned his offer and came away. That'll show you if I've reformed or not. A nice, easy, simple job he said it was, that I could do in a couple of minutes."

"And you spurned him, eh?"

"I certainly spurned him. I spurned him good and plenty."

"And then you came away?"

"Came right away."

"Then listen here," said Fanny in a steely voice, "it don't seem to me that your times add up right. You say he made you this offer two seconds after he heard your name. Well, why did it take you a quarter of an hour to get back to this kitchen? If you want to know what I think, it wasn't a red-faced man with grey hair at all—it was one of those Washington Square vamps and you were flirting with her."

"Fanny!"

"Well, I've read Gingery Stories, and I know what it's like down here in Bohemia with all these artists and models and everything."

Mullett drew himself up.

"Your suspicions pain me, Fanny. If you care to step out on to the roof, you can peek in at the sitting-room window and see him for yourself. He's waiting there for me to bring him a drink. The reason I was so long coming back was that it took him ten minutes before he asked my name. Up till then he just sat and spluttered."

"All right. Take me out on the roof."

"There!" said Mullett, a moment later. "Now perhaps you'll believe me."

Through the French windows of the sitting-room there was undeniably visible a man of precisely the appearance described. Fanny was remorseful.

"Did I wrong my poor little Freddy, then?" she said.

"Yes, you did."

"I'm sorry. There!"

She kissed him. Mullett melted immediately.

"I must go back and get that drink," he said.

"And I must be getting along."

"Oh, not yet," begged Mullett.

"Yes I must. I've got to look in at one or two of the stores."

"Fanny!"

"Well, a girl's got to have her trousseau, hasn't she?"

Mullett sighed.

"You'll be very careful precious?" he said anxiously.

"I'm always careful. Don't you worry about me."

Mullett retired, and Fanny, blowing a parting kiss from her pretty fingers, passed through the door leading to the stairs.

It was perhaps five minutes later, while Mullett sat dreaming golden dreams in the kitchen and Sigsbee H. Waddington sat sipping his whisky-and-soda in the sitting-room, that a sudden tap on the French window caused the latter to give a convulsive leap and spill most of the liquid down the front of his waistcoat.

He looked up. A girl was standing outside the window, and from her gestures he gathered that she was requesting him to open it.

v

It was some time before Sigsbee H. Waddington could bring himself to do so. There exist, no doubt, married men of the baser sort who would have enjoyed the prospect of a *tête-à-tête* chat with a girl with snapping black eyes who gesticulated at them through windows: but Sigsbee Waddington was not one of them. By nature and training he was circumspect to a degree. So for awhile he merely stood and stared at Fanny. It was not until her eyes became so imperative as to be practically hypnotic that he brought himself to undo the latch.

"And about time, too," said Fanny, with annoyance, stepping softly into the room.

"What do you want?"

"I want a little talk with you. What's all this I hear about you asking people to perpetrate crimes for you?"

Sigsbee Waddington's conscience was in such a feverish condition by now that this speech affected him as deeply as the explosion of a pound of dynamite would have done. His vivid imagination leaped immediately to the supposition that this girl who seemed so intimate with his private affairs was one of those Secret Service investigation agents who do so much to mar the comfort of the amateur in crime.

"I don't know what you're talking about," he croaked.

"Oh, shucks!" said Fanny impatiently. She was a business girl and disliked this beating about the bush. "Freddy Mullett told me all about it. You want someone to do a job for you and he turned you down. Well, take a look at the understudy. I'm here, and, if the job's in my line, lead me to it."

Mr. Waddington continued to eye her warily. He had now decided that she was trying to trap him into a damaging admission. He said nothing, but breathed stertorously.

Fanny, a sensitive girl, misunderstood his silence. She interpreted the look in his eyes to indicate distrust of the ability of a woman worker to deputize for the male.

"If it's anything Freddy Mullett could do, I can do it," she said. She seemed to Mr. Waddington to flicker for a moment. "See here!" she said.

Before Mr. Waddington's fascinated gaze she held up between her delicate fingers a watch and chain.

"What's that?" he gasped.

"What does it look like?"

Mr. Waddington knew exactly what it looked like. He felt his waistcoat dazedly.

"I didn't see you take it."

"Nobody don't ever see me take it," said Fanny proudly, stating a profound truth. "Well, then, now you've witnessed the demonstration, perhaps you'll believe me when I say that I'm not so worse. If Freddy can do it, I can do it."

A cool, healing wave of relief poured over Sigsbee H. Waddington's harassed soul. He perceived that he had wronged his visitor. She was not a detective, after all, but a sweet, womanly woman who went about lifting things out of people's pockets so deftly that they never saw them go. Just the sort of girl he had been wanting to meet.

"I am sure you can," he said fervently.

"Well, what's the job?"

"I want some one to steal a pearl necklace."

"Where is it?"

"In the strong-room at the bank."

Fanny's mobile features expressed disappointment and annoyance.

"Then what's the use of talking about it? I'm not a safe-smasher. I'm a delicately nurtured girl that never used an oxy-acetylene blowpipe in her life."

"Ah, but you don't understand," said Mr. Waddington hastily. "When I say that the necklace is in the strong-room, I mean that it is there just now. Eventually it will be taken out and placed among the other wedding-presents."

"This begins to look more like it."

"I can mention no names, of course . . ."

"I don't expect you to."

"Then I will simply say that A, to whom the necklace belongs, is shortly about to be married to B."

"I might have known it. Doing all those bridge problems together, they kind of got fond of one another."

"I have my reasons for thinking that the wedding will take place down at Hempstead on Long Island, where C, A's step-mother, has her summer house."

"Why? Why not in New York?"

"Because," said Mr. Waddington simply. "I expressed a wish that it should take place in New York."

"What have you got to do with it?"

"I am D, C's husband."

"Oh, the fellow who could fill a tank with water in six hours fifteen minutes while C was filling another in five hours forty-five? Pleased to meet you."

"I am now strongly in favour of the Hempstead idea," said Mr. Waddington. "In New York it might be difficult to introduce you into the house, whereas down at Hempstead you can remain concealed in the garden till the suitable moment arrives. Down at Hempstead the presents will be on view in the dining-room, which has French windows opening on to a lawn flanked with shrubberies."

"Easy!"

"Just what I thought. I will, therefore, make a point to-night of insisting that the wedding take place in New York, and the thing will be definitely settled."

Fanny eyed him reflectively.

"It all seems kind of funny to me. If you're D and you're married to C and C is A's step-mother, you must be A's father. What do you want to go stealing your daughter's necklace for?"

"Say, listen," said Mr. Waddington urgently, "the first thing you've got to get into your head is that you're not to ask questions."

"Only my girlish curiosity."

"Tie a can to it," begged Mr. Waddington. "This is a delicate business, and the last thing I want is anybody snooping into motives and first causes. Just you go ahead, like a nice girl, and get that necklace and pass it over to me when nobody's looking, and then put the whole matter out of your pretty little head and forget about it."

"Just as you say. And now, coming down to it, what is there in it for me?"

"Three hundred dollars."

"Not nearly enough."

"It's all I've got."

Fanny meditated. Three hundred dollars, though a meagre sum, was three hundred dollars. You could always use three hundred dollars when you were furnishing, and the job, as outlined, seemed simple.

"All right," she said.

"You'll do it?"

"I'm on."

"Good girl," said Mr. Waddington. "Where can I find you when I want you?"

"Here's my address."

"I'll send you a line. You've got the thing clear?"

"Sure. I hang about in the bushes till there's nobody around, and then I slip into the room and snitch the necklace . . ."

" . . . and hand it over to me."

"Sure."

"I'll be waiting in the garden just outside, and I'll meet you the moment you come out. The very moment. Thus," said Mr. Waddington with a quiet, meaning look at his young friend, "avoiding any rannygazoo."

"What do you mean by rannygazoo?" said Fanny warmly.

"Nothing, nothing," said Mr. Waddington, with a deprecating wave of the hand. "Just rannygazoo."

# CHAPTER SEVEN

THERE are, as everybody knows, many ways of measuring time:
and right through the ages learned men have argued heatedly in
favour of their different systems. Hipparchus of Rhodes sneered
every time anybody mentioned Marinus of Tyre to him: and the
views of Ahmed Ibn Abadallah of Baghdad gave Purbach and
Regiomontanus the laugh of their lives. Purbach in his bluff way
said the man must be a perfect ass: and when Regiomontanus,
whose motto was Live and let live, urged that Ahmed Ibn was just
a young fellow trying to get along and ought not to be treated too
harshly, Purbach said Was that so? and Regiomontanus said
Yes, that was so, and Purbach said that Regiomontanus made him
sick. It was their first quarrel.

Tycho Brahe measured time by means of altitudes, quadrants,
azimuths, cross-staves, armillary spheres and parallactic rules:
and, as he often said to his wife when winding up the azimuth and
putting the cat out for the night, nothing could be fairer than that.
And then in 1863 along came Dollen with his *Die Zeitbesttimmung
vermitteslt des tragbaren Durchgangsinstrument in Verticale des
Polarstens* (a best seller in its day, subsequently filmed under the
title Purple Sins), and proved that Tycho, by mistaking an armillary sphere for a quadrant one night after a bump-supper at
Copenhagen University, had got his calculations all wrong.

The truth is that time cannot be measured. To George Finch,
basking in the society of Molly Waddington, the next three weeks
seemed but a flash. Whereas to Hamilton Beamish, with the girl
he loved miles away in East Gilead, Idaho, it appeared incredible
that any sensible person could suppose that a day contained only
twenty-four hours. There were moments when Hamilton Beamish
thought that something must have happened to the sidereal moon
and that time was standing still.

But now the three weeks were up, and at any minute he might
hear that she was back in the metropolis. All day long he had been
going about with a happy smile on his face, and it was with a
heart that leaped and sang from pure exuberance that he now
turned to greet Officer Garroway, who had just presented himself at his apartment.

"Ah, Garroway!" said Hamilton Beamish. "How goes it?
What brings you here?"

"I understood you to say, sir," replied the policeman, "that I was to bring you my poem when I had completed it."

"Of course, of course. I had forgotten all about it. Something seems to have happened eh to my memory these days. So you have written your first poem eh ? All about love and youth and springtime, I suppose ? . . . Excuse me."

The telephone bell had rung: and Hamilton Beamish, though the instrument had disappointed him over and over again in the past few days, leaped excitedly to snatch up the receiver.

"Hello ?"

This time there was no disappointment. The voice that spoke was the voice he had heard so often in his dreams.

"Mr. Beamish. I mean, Jimmy ?"

Hamilton Beamish drew a deep breath. And so overcome was he with sudden joy that for the first time since he had reached years of discretion he drew it through the mouth.

"At last!" he cried.

"What did you say ?"

"I said 'At last!' Since you went away every minute has seemed an hour."

"So it has to me."

"Do you mean that ?" breathed Hamilton Beamish fervently.

"Yes. That's the way minutes do seem in East Gilead."

"Oh, ah, yes," said Mr. Beamish, a little damped. "When did you get back ?"

"A quarter of an hour ago."

Hamilton Beamish's spirits soared once more.

"And you called me up at once!" he said emotionally.

"Yes. I wanted to know Mrs. Waddington's telephone number at Hempstead."

"Was that the only reason ?"

"Of course not. I wanted to hear how you were . . ."

"Did you ? Did you ?"

" . . . and if you had missed me."

"Missed you!"

"Did you ?"

"Did I!"

"How sweet of you. I should have thought you would have forgotten my very existence."

"Guk!" said Hamilton Beamish, completely overcome.

"Well, shall I tell you something ? I missed you, too."

Hamilton Beamish drew another completely unscientific deep breath, and was about to pour out his whole soul into the instrument in a manner that would probably have fused the wire, when a breezy masculine voice suddenly smote his ear-drum.

"Is that Ed. ?" inquired the voice.

"No," thundered Hamilton Beamish.

"This is Charley, Ed. Is it all right for Friday ?"

"It is not!" boomed Hamilton Beamish. "Get off the wire, you blot! Go away, curse you!"

"Certainly, if you want me to," said a sweet, feminine voice. "But . . ."

"I beg your pardon! I am sorry, sorry, sorry. A fiend in human shape got on the wire," explained Mr. Beamish hastily.

"Oh! Well, what were we saying ?"

"I was just going to . . ."

"I remember. Mrs. Waddington's telephone number. I was looking through my mail just now, and I found an invitation from Miss Waddington to her wedding. I see it's to-morrow. Fancy that!"

Hamilton Beamish would have preferred to speak of other things than trivialities like George Finch's wedding, but he found it difficult to change the subject.

"Yes. It is to take place at Hempstead to-morrow. George is staying down there at the inn."

"It's going to be a quiet country wedding, then ?"

"Yes. I think Mrs. Waddington wants to hush George up as much as possible."

"Poor George!"

"I am going down by the one-thirty train. Couldn't we travel together ?"

"I'm not sure that I shall be able to go. I have an awful lot of things to see to here, after being away so long. Shall we leave it open ?"

"Very well," said Hamilton Beamish resignedly. "But, in any case, can you dine with me to-morrow night ?"

"I should love it."

Hamilton Beamish's eyes closed, and he snuffled for awhile.

"And what is Mrs. Waddington's number ?"

"Hempstead 4076."

"Thanks."

"We'll dine at the Purple Chicken, shall we ?"

"Splendid."

"You can always get it there, if they know you."

"Do they know you ?"

"Intimately."

"Fine! Well, good-bye."

Hamilton Beamish stood for a few moments in deep thought: then, turning away from the instrument was astonished to perceive Officer Garroway.

"I'd forgotten all about you," he said. "Let me see, what did you say you had come for?"

"To read you my poem, sir."

"Ah yes, of course."

The policeman coughed modestly.

"It's just a little thing, Mr. Beamish—sort of study, you might say, of the streets of New York as they appear to a policeman on his beat. I would like to read it to you, if you will permit me."

Officer Garroway shifted his Adam's apple up and down once or twice: and, closing his eyes, began to recite in the special voice which he as a rule reserved for giving evidence before magistrates.

'Streets!'

"That is the title, eh?"

"Yes, sir, And also the first line."

Hamilton Beamish started.

"Is it *vers libre*?"

"Sir?"

"Doesn't it rhyme?"

"No, sir. I understood you to say that rhymes were an outworn convention."

"Did I really say that?"

"You did, indeed, sir. And a great convenience I found it. It seems to make poetry quite easy."

Hamilton Beamish looked at him perplexedly. He supposed he must have spoken the words which the other had quoted, and yet, that he should deliberately have wished to exclude a fellow-creature from the pure joy of rhyming 'heart' with 'Cupid's dart' seemed to him in his present uplifted state inconceivable.

"Odd!" he said. "Very odd. However, go on."

Officer Garroway went once more through the motions of swallowing something large and sharp, and shut his eyes again.

> 'Streets!
> Grim, relentless, sordid streets!
> Miles of poignant streets,
> East, West, North,
> And stretching starkly South;
> Sad, hopeless, dismal, cheerless, chilling
> Streets!'

Hamilton Beamish raised his eyebrows.

> 'I pace the mournful streets
> With aching heart.'

"Why?" asked Hamilton Beamish.

"It is part of my duties, sir. Each patrolman is assigned a certain portion of the city as a beat."

"I mean, why do you pace with aching heart?"

"Because it is bleeding, sir."

"Bleeding? You mean your heart?"

"Yes, sir. My heart is bleeding. I look at all the sordid gloom and sorrow and my heart bleeds."

"Well, go on. It all seems very peculiar to me, but go on."

> 'I watch grey men slink past
> With shifty, sidelong eyes
> That gleam with murderous hate;
> Lepers that prowl the streets.'

Hamilton Beamish seemed about to speak, but checked himself.

> 'Men who once were men,
> Women that once were women,
> Children like wizened apes,
> And dogs that snarl and snap and growl and hate.
> Streets!
> Loathsome, festering streets!
> I pace the scabrous streets
> And long for death.'

Officer Garroway stopped, and opened his eyes: and Hamilton Beamish, crossing the room to where he stood, slapped him briskly on the shoulder.

"I see it all," he said. "What's wrong with you is liver. Tell me, have you any local pain and tenderness?"

"No, sir."

"High temperature accompanied by shiverings and occasional rigors?"

"No, sir."

"Then you have not a hepatic abscess. All that is the matter, I imagine, is a slight sluggishness in the aesophageal groove, which can be set right with calomel. My dear Garroway, it surely must be obvious to you that this poem of yours is all wrong. It is absurd for you to pretend that you do not see a number of pleasant and attractive people on your beat. The streets of New York are full of the most delightful persons. I have noticed them on all sides. The trouble is that you have been looking on them with a bilious eye."

"But I thought you told me to be stark and poignant, Mr. Beamish."

"Nothing of the kind. You must have misunderstood me. Starkness is quite out of place in poetry. A poem should be a thing of beauty and charm and sentiment, and have as its theme the sweetest and divinest of all human emotions—Love. Only Love can inspire the genuine bard. Love, Garroway, is a fire that glows and enlarges, until it warms and beams upon multitudes, upon the universal heart of all, and so lights up the whole world and all nature with its generous flames. Shakespeare speaks of the ecstasy of love and Shakespeare knew what he was talking about. Ah, better to live in the lowliest cot, Garroway, than pine in a palace alone. In peace, Love tunes the shepherd's reed: in war he mounts the warrior's steed. In halls, in gay attire is seen; in hamlets, dances on the green. Love rules the court, the camp, the grove, and men below and saints above; for love is heaven and heaven is love. Get these simple facts into your silly fat head, Garroway, and you may turn out a poem worth reading. If, however, you are going to take this absurd attitude about festering streets and scabrous dogs and the rest of it, you are simply wasting your time and would be better employed writing sub-titles for the motion-pictures."

Officer Garroway was not a man of forceful character. He bowed his head meekly before the storm.

"I see what you mean, Mr. Beamish."

"I should hope you did. I have put it plainly enough. I dislike intensely this modern tendency on the part of young writers to concentrate on corpses and sewers and despair. They should be writing about Love. I tell thee Love is nature's second sun, Garroway, causing a spring of virtues where he shines. All love is sweet, given or returned. Common as light is love, and its familiar voice wearies not ever. True love's the gift which God has given to man alone beneath the heaven. It is not—mark this, Garroway!—it is not fantasy's hot fire, whose wishes soon as granted die. It liveth not in fierce desire, with fierce desire it does not die. It is the secret sympathy, the silver link, the silken tie, which heart to heart and mind to mind in body and in soul can bind."

"Yes, sir. Exactly, Mr. Beamish. I quite see that."

"Then go away and rewrite your poem on the lines I have indicated."

"Yes, Mr. Beamish." The policeman paused. "Before I go, there is just one other thing . . ."

"There is no other thing in the world that matters except love."

"Well, sir, there are the motion-pictures, to which you made a brief allusion just now, and . . ."

"Garroway," said Hamilton Beamish, "I trust that you are not going to tell me that, after all I have done to try to make you a poet, you wish to sink to writing motion-picture scenarios ?"

"No, sir. No, indeed. But some little time ago I happened to purchase a block of stock in a picture company, and so far all my efforts to dispose of it have proved fruitless. I have begun to entertain misgivings as to the value of these shares, and I thought that, while I was here, I would ask you if you knew anything about them."

"What is the company ?"

"The Finer and Better Motion Picture Company of Hollywood, California, Mr. Beamish."

"How many shares did you buy ?"

"Fifty thousand dollars worth."

"How much did you pay ?"

"Three hundred dollars."

"You were stung," said Hamilton Beamish. "The stock is so much waste paper. Who sold it to you ?"

"I have unfortunately forgotten his name. He was a man with a red face and grey hair. And if I'd got him here now," said Officer Garroway with honest warmth, "I'd soak him so hard it would jolt his grand-children. The smooth, salve-slinging crocodile !"

"It is a curious thing," said Hamilton Beamish musingly, "there seems to be floating at the back of my consciousness a sort of nebulous memory having to do with this very stock you mention. I seem to recall somebody at some time and place consulting me about it. No, it's no good, it won't come back. I have been much preoccupied of late, and things slip my mind. Well, run along, Garroway, and set about re-writing that poem of yours."

The policeman's brow was dark. There was a rebellious look in his usually mild eyes.

"Re-write it nothing! It's the goods."

"Garroway!"

"I said New York was full of lepers, and so it is. Nasty, oily, lop-eared lepers that creep up to a fellow and sell him scabrous stock that's not worth the paper it's printed on. That poem is right, and I don't alter a word of it. No, sir!"

Hamilton Beamish shook his head.

"One of these days, Garroway, love will awaken in your heart and you will change your views."

"One of these days," replied the policeman frigidly, "I shall meet that red-faced guy again, and I'll change his face. It won't be only my heart that'll be aching by the time I've finished with him."

## CHAPTER EIGHT

GEORGE FINCH'S wedding-day dawned fair and bright. The sun beamed down as if George by getting married were doing it a personal favour. The breezes, playing about him, brought with them a faint but well-defined scent of orange-blossom. And from the moment when they had finished the practical business of getting outside their early worm, all the birds for miles around had done nothing but stand in the trees singing Mendelsohnn's Wedding March. It was the sort of day to make a man throw out his chest and say 'Tra-la!': and George did so.

Delightful, he reflected, as he walked up from the inn after lunch, to think that in a few short hours he and Molly would be bowling away together in a magic train, each revolution of its wheels taking them nearer to the Islands of the Blest and—what was almost more agreeable—farther away from Mrs. Waddington.

It would be idle to deny that in the past three weeks George Finch had found his future mother-in-law something of a trial. Her consistent failure to hide the pain which the mere sight of him so obviously caused her was damping to an impressionable young man. George was not vain, and if Molly's stepmother had been content to look at him simply as if she thought he was some-thing the cat had dragged out of the dust-bin, he could have borne up. But Mrs. Waddington went further. Her whole attitude betrayed her belief that the cat, on inspecting George, had been disappointed. Seeing what it had got, her manner suggested, it had given him the look of chagrin which cats give when conscious of effort wasted and had gone elsewhere to try again. A lover, counting the days until the only girl in the world shall be his, will see sweetness and light in practically everything: but George Finch, despite his most earnest endeavours, had been compelled to draw the line at Mrs. Waddington.

However, these little annoyances were, after all, the merest trifles: and the thought, as he approached the house, that inside it there sat a suffering woman who, thinking of him, mourned and would not be comforted, did nothing to diminish his mood of overflowing happiness. He entered the grounds, humming lightly: and, starting to pass up the drive, came upon Hamilton Beamish, smoking a thoughtful cigarette.

"Hullo," said George. "So you've got here?"

"Correct," said Hamilton Beamish.

"How do you think Molly is looking?"

"Charming. But I only caught a glimpse of her as she was hurrying off."

"Hurrying off?"

"Yes. There has been a slight hitch in the proceedings. Didn't you know?"

"My God! Tell me!" said George, clutching his friend's arm.

"Ouch!" said Hamilton Beamish, releasing the arm and rubbing it. "It is nothing to get excited about. All that has happened is that the clergyman who was to have married you has met with an accident. His wife telephoned just now to say that, while standing on a chair and trying to reach down a volume of devotional thought from an upper shelf, he fell and sprained his ankle."

"The poor fish!" said George warmly. "What does he want to go doing that sort of thing for, at a time like this? A man ought to decide once and for all at the outset of his career whether he is a clergyman or an acrobat and never deviate from his chosen path. This is awful news, Hamilton. I must rush about and try to find a substitute. Good heavens! An hour or so before the wedding, and no clergyman!"

"Calm yourself, George. The necessary steps are being taken. I think Mrs. Waddington would have been just as pleased to let the whole thing drop, but Molly became very active. She telephoned in all directions, and eventually succeeded in locating a disengaged minister in the neighbourhood of Flushing. She and Mrs. Waddington have gone off together in the car to fetch him. They will be back in about an hour and a half."

"You mean to tell me," demanded George, paling "that I shall not see Molly for an hour and a half?"

"Absence makes the heart grow fonder. I quote Thomas Haynes Bayly. And Frederick William Thomas, a poet of the early nineteenth century, amplifies this thought in the lines:

'Tis said that absence conquers love:
But oh, believe it not:
I've tried, alas, its power to prove,
But thou art not forgot.'

Be a man, George. Clench your hands and try to endure."

"It's sickening."

"Be brave," said Hamilton Beamish. "I know just how you feel. I, also, am going through the torment of being parted from the one woman."

"Absolutely sickening! A clergyman, and not able to stand on a chair without falling off!" A sudden, gruesome thought struck him. "Hamilton! What's it a sign of when a clergyman falls off a chair and sprains his ankle on the morning of the wedding?"

"How do you mean, what is it a sign of?"

"I mean, is it bad luck?"

"For the clergyman, undoubtedly."

"You don't think it means that anything is going to go wrong with the wedding?"

"I have never heard of any such superstition. You must endeavour to control these fancies, George. You are allowing yourself to get into a thoroughly overwrought condition."

"Well, what sort of a condition do you expect a fellow to be in on his wedding morning, with clergymen falling off chairs wherever he looks?"

Hamilton smiled tolerantly.

"I suppose nerves are inevitable on such an occasion. I notice that even Sigsbee H., who can scarcely consider himself a principal in this affair, is thoroughly jumpy. He was walking on the lawn some little time ago, and when I came up behind him and laid a hand on his shoulder, he leaped like a startled roe. If Sigsbee H. Waddington possessed a mind, I would say that there was something on it. No doubt he is brooding on the West again."

The sun was still shining brightly, but somehow the day seemed to George to have grown overcast and chill. A grey foreboding had come upon him.

"I wish this hadn't happened."

"Exactly what the clergyman said."

"It isn't fair that a delicate, highly-strung girl like Molly should be upset like this at such a time."

"I think you exaggerate the effects of the occurrence on Molly. She seemed to me to be bearing it with equanimity."

"She wasn't pale?"

"Not in the least."

"Or agitated?"

"She seemed quite her normal self."

"Thank God!" said George.

"In fact, the last thing she said to Ferris, as the car drove away, was. . . ."

"What?"

Hamilton Beamish had broken off. He was frowning.

"My memory is terrible. It is the effect, of course, of love. I have just remembered . . ."

"What did Molly say?"

"I have forgotten. But I have just remembered what it was that I was told to tell you as soon as you arrived. It is curious how often the mention of a name will, as it were, strike a chord. I spoke of Ferris, and it has just come back to me that Ferris gave me a message for you."

"Oh, darn Ferris!"

"He asked me when I saw you, to say that a female of some kind was calling you up on the telephone earlier in the morning. He told her that you were at the inn, and advised her to get you there, but she said it didn't matter, as she was coming down here immediately. She said she had known you in East Gilead."

"Oh?" said George indifferently.

"And her name, if I remember rightly, was Dubbs or Tubbs or Jubbs or—no, I have it. My memory is better than I supposed It was May Stubbs. Does it convey anything to you?"

## CHAPTER NINE

IT chanced that as he spoke these light and casual words Hamilton Beamish, glancing down, noted that his shoe-lace had come untied. Stooping to attend to this, he missed seeing George's face. Nor— for he was a man who concentrated even on the lightest task the full attention of a great mind—did he hear the other's sudden whistling gasp of astonishment and horror. A moment later, however, he obsvered out of the corner of his eye something moving: and, looking, perceived that George's legs were wobbling strangely.

Hamilton Beamish straightened himself. He was now in a position to see George steadily and see him whole: and the spectacle convinced him at once that something in the message he had just delivered must have got right in among his friend's ganglions. George Finch's agreeable features seemed to be picked out in a delicate Nile-green. His eyes were staring. His lower jaw had fallen. Nobody who had ever seen a motion-picture could have had the least doubt as to what he was registering. It was dismay.

"My dear George!" said Hamilton Beamish, concerned.

"Wok . . . Wuk . . . Wok . . ." George swallowed desperately. "Wok name did you say?"

"May Stubbs." Hamilton Beamish's expression grew graver, and he looked at his friend with a sudden suspicion. "Tell me all, George. It is idle to pretend that the name is strange to you. Obviously it has awakened deep and unpleasant memories. I trust, George, that this is not some poor girl with whose happiness you have toyed in the past, some broken blossom that you have culled and left to perish by the wayside?"

George Finch was staring before him in a sort of stupor.

"All is over!" he said dully.

Hamilton Beamish softened.

"Confide in me. We are friends. I will not judge you harshly, George."

A sudden fury melted the ice of George's torpor.

"It's all that parson's fault!" he cried vehemently. "I knew all along it meant bad luck. Gosh, what a Paradise this world would be if only clergymen could stand on chairs without spraining their ankles! I'm done for."

"Who is this May Stubbs?"

"I knew her in East Gilead," said George hopelessly. "We were sort of engaged."

Hamilton Beamish pursed his lips.

"Apart from the slovenly English of the phrase, which is perhaps excusable in the circumstances, I cannot see how you can have been 'sort of' engaged. A man is either engaged or he is not."

"Not where I come from. In East Gilead they have what they call understandings."

"And there was an understanding between you and this Miss Stubbs?"

"Yes. Just one of those boy and girl affairs. You know. You see a girl home once or twice from church, and you take her to one or two picnics, and people kid you about her, and . . . well, there you are. I suppose she thought we were engaged. And now she's read in the papers about my wedding, and has come to make herself unpleasant."

"Did you and this girl quarrel before you separated?"

"No. We sort of drifted apart. I took it for granted that the thing was over and done with. And when I saw Molly . . ."

Hamilton Beamish laid a hand upon his arm.

"George," he said, "I want you to give me your full attention: for we have arrived now at the very core of the matter. Were there any letters?"

"Dozens. And of course she has kept them. She used to sleep with them under her pillow."

"Bad!" said Hamilton Beamish, shaking his head. "Very bad!"

"And I remember her saying once that she believed in breach of promise suits."

Hamilton Beamish frowned. He seemed to be deploring the get-rich-quick spirit of the modern girl, who is not content to sit down and wait for her alimony.

"You think it certain that she is coming here with the intention of making trouble?"

"What other reason could she have?"

"Yes, I fancy you are right. I must think. I must think. Let me think."

And, so saying, Hamilton Beamish turned sharply to the left and began to walk slowly round in a circle, his hands behind his back and his face bent and thoughtful. His eyes searched the ground as if to wrest inspiration from it.

Few sights in this world are more inspiring than that of a great thinker actually engaged in thought: and yet George Finch, watching his friend, chafed. He had a perhaps forgivable craving for quick results: and Hamilton Beamish, though impressive, did not seem to be getting anywhere.

"Have you thought of anything?" he asked, as the other came round for the third time.

Hamilton Beamish held up a hand in silent reproof, and resumed his pacing. Presently he stopped.

"Yes?" said George.

"With regard to this engagement . . ."

"It wasn't an engagement. It was an understanding."

"With regard to this understanding or engagement, the weak spot in your line of defence is undoubtedly the fact that it was you who broke it off."

"But I didn't break it off."

"I used the wrong expression. I should have said that it was you who took the initiative. You left East Gilead and came to New York. Therefore, technically, you deserted this girl."

"I wish you wouldn't say things like that. Can't you understand that it was just one of those boy and girl affairs which come to an end of themselves?"

"I was looking at the thing from a lawyer's view-point. And may I point out that the affair appears not to have come to an end. What I am trying to make clear is this: that, if you had wished it to come to an end, you should, before you left East Gilead, have arranged somehow that this Miss Stubbs broke off the engagement."

"Understanding."

"The engagement or understanding. That would have cleaned the slate. You should have done something that would have made her disgusted with you."

"How could I? I'm not the sort of fellow who can do things like that."

"Even now, it seems to me, if you could do something that would revolt this Miss Stubbs . . . make her recoil from you with loathing . . ."

"Well, what?"

"I must think," said Hamilton Beamish.

He did four more laps.

"Suppose you had committed some sort of crime?" he said, returning to the fixed point. "Suppose she were to find out you were a thief? She wouldn't want to marry you if you were on your way to Sing-Sing."

"No. And neither would Molly."

"True. I must think again."

It was some moments later that George, eyeing his friend with the growing dislike which those of superior brain-power engender in us when they fail to deliver the goods in our times of crisis, observed him give a sudden start.

"I think I have it." said Hamilton Beamish.

"Well?"

"This Miss Stubbs. Tell me, is she strait-laced? Prudish? Most of those village girls are."

George reflected.

"I don't remember ever having noticed. I never did anything to make her prudish about."

"I think we may assume that, having lived all her life in a spot like East Gilead, she is. The solution of this difficulty, then, is obviously to lead her to suppose that you have become a reprobate."

"A what?"

"A Don Juan. A Lothario. A libertine. It should be perfectly easy. She has seen motion-pictures of life in New York, and will not be hard to convince that you have deteriorated since you came to live there. Our plan of action now becomes straightforward and simple. All we have to do is to get some girl to come along and say that you have no right to marry anybody but her."

"What!"

"I can see the scene now. This Miss Stubbs is sitting beside you, a dowdy figure in her home-made village gown. You are talking of the old days. You are stroking her hand. Suddenly you look up and start. The door has opened and a girl, all in black with a white face, is entering. Her eyes are haggard, her hair disordered. In her arms she clasps a little bundle."

"No, no! Not that!"

"Very well, we will dispense with the bundle. She stretches out her arms to you. She totters. You rush to support her. The scene is similar to one in Haddon Chambers' 'Passers-By.' "

"What happened in that?"

"What could happen? The fiancée saw the ruined girl had the greater claim, so she joined their hands together and crept silently from the room."

George laughed mirthlessly.

"There's just one thing you're overlooking. Where are we going to get the white-faced girl?"

Hamilton Beamish stroked his chin.

"There is that difficulty. I must think."

"And while you're thinking," said George coldly. "I'll do the only practical thing there is to be done, and go down to the station and meet her, and have a talk with her and try to get her to be sensible."

"Perhaps that would be as well. But I still feel that my scheme would be the ideal one, if only we could find the girl. It is too bad that you have not a dark past."

"My dark past," said George bitterly, "is now all ahead of me."

He turned and hurried down the drive. Hamilton Beamish, still meditating, made his way towards the house.

He had reached the lawn, when, as he stopped to light a cigarette to assist his thoughts, he saw a sight that made him drop the match and draw back smartly into the shelter of a tree.

Hamilton Beamish stopped, looked and listened. A girl had emerged from a clump of rhododendrons, and was stealing softly round the lawn towards the dining-room window.

Girlhood is the season of dreams. To Fanny Welch, musing over the position of affairs after Sigsbee H. Waddington had given her final instructions, there had come a quaint, fantastic thought, creeping into her mind like a bee into a flower—the thought that if she got to the house an hour earlier than the time he had mentioned, it might be possible for her to steal the necklace and keep it for herself.

The flaw in the scheme, as originally outlined, had seemed to her all along to lie in the fact that Mr. Waddington was to preside over the enterprise and take the loot from her the moment she had got it. The revised plan appeared immeasurably more attractive, and she proceeded to put it into action.

Luck seemed to be with her. Nobody was about, the window was ajar, and there on the table lay that which she had now come to look on in the light of a present for a good girl. She crept out of her hiding-place, stole round the edge of the lawn, entered the room, and had just grasped the case in her hand, when it was borne sharply in upon her that luck was not with her so much as she had supposed. A heavy hand was placed upon her shoulder: and, twisting round, she perceived a majestic-looking man with a square chin and horn-rimmed spectacles.

"Well, young lady!" said this person.

Fanny breathed hard. These little contretemps are the risk of the profession, but that makes them none the easier to bear philosophically.

"Put down that jewel-case."

Fanny did so. There was a pause. Hamilton Beamish moved to the window, blocking it up.

"Well?" said Fanny.

Hamilton Beamish adjusted his spectacles.

"Well, you've got me. What are you going to do?"

"What do you expect me to do?"

"Turn me over to the police?"

The figure in the window nodded curtly. Fanny clasped her hands together. Her eyes filled with tears.

"Don't turn me over to the bulls, mister! I only did it for ma's sake . . ."

"All wrong!"

"If you was out of work and starvin' and you had to sit and watch your poor old ma bendin' over the wash-tub . . ."

"All wrong!" repeated Hamilton Beamish forcefully.

"What do you mean, all wrong?"

"Mere crude Broadway melodrama. That stuff might deceive some people, but not me."

Fanny shrugged her shoulders.

"Well, I thought it was worth trying," she said.

Hamilton Beamish was regarding her keenly. That busy brain was never still, and now it had begun to work with even more than its normal intensity.

"Are you an actress?"

"Me? I should say not. My folks are awful particular."

"Well, you have considerable dramatic ability. There was a ring of sincerity in that drivel you just recited which would have convinced most men. I think I could use you in a little drama which I have been planning. I'll make a bargain with you. I have no wish to send you to prison."

"Spoken like a man."

"I ought to, of course."

"Yes, but it's a lot better fun doing things that you oughtn't, isn't it?"

"Well, the point is, I have a friend who is in a difficulty, and it occurs to me that you can get him out."

"Always glad to oblige."

"My friend is going to be married to-day, and he has just heard that a previous fiancée of his, whom in the excitement inseparable from falling in love with the girl who is to be his bride he had unfortunately overlooked, is on her way here."

"To make trouble?"

"Precisely."

"Well, what can I do about it?"

"Just this. For five minutes I want you to play the role of my friend's discarded victim."

"I don't get it."

"I will put it more plainly. In a short while this girl will arrive, probably in company with my friend, who has gone to meet her at the station. You will be waiting outside here. At an appropriate moment you will rush into the room, hold out your arms to my friend and cry 'George! George! Why did you desert me? You don't belong to that girl there. You belong to me—the woman you have wronged!' "

"Not on your life!"

"What!"

Fanny drew herself up haughtily.

"Not on your life!" she said. "Suppose my husband got to hear of it!"

"Are you married?"

"Married this morning at the Little Church Round The Corner."

"And you come here and try to steal on your wedding-day!"

"Why not? You know as well as I do what it costs nowadays to set up house."

"Surely it would be a severe shock to your husband to find that you had been sent to prison? I think you had better be reasonable."

Fanny scraped the floor with her shoe.

"Would this thing you want me to do get into the papers?"

"Good heavans, no!"

"And there's another thing. Suppose I did come in and pull that spiel, who would believe it?"

"The girl would. She is very simple."

"She must be."

"Just an ignorant village girl. The sort who would naturally recoil from a man in the circumstances I have outlined."

"Suppose they ask me questions?"

"They won't."

"But suppose they do? Suppose the girl says, Where did you meet him and when did all this happen and what the hell and all like that, what do I say?"

Hamilton Beamish considered the point.

"I think the best plan would be for you to pretend, immediately after you have spoken the words I have indicated, that emotion has made you feel faint. Yes, that is best. Having said those words, exclaim, 'Air! Air! I want air!' and rush out."

"Now you're talking. I like that bit about rushing out. I'll go so quick, they won't see me."

"Then you are prepared to do this thing?"

"Looks as if I'd got to."

"Good. Kindly run through your opening speech. I must see that you are letter-perfect."

"George! George! . . ."

"Pause before the second George and take in breath. Remember that the intensity or loudness of the voice depends on the amplitude of the movements of the vocal chords, while pitch depends on the number of vibrations per second. Tone is strengthened by the resonance of the air on the air-passages and in the pharyngeal and oral cavities. Once more, please."

"George! George! Why did you desert me ? . . ."

"Arms extended."

"You don't belong to that girl there."

"Pause. Breath."

"You belong to me—the woman you have wronged!"

Hamilton Beamish nodded with restrained approval.

"Not bad. Not at all bad. I should have liked, if it had been possible, to have an expert examine your thyroarytenoid ligaments: and I wish there had been time for you to study my booklet on 'Voice Production' . . . . However, I think it will do. Now back and hide in the rhododendrons. This girl may be arriving at any moment."

## CHAPTER TEN

HAMILTON BEAMISH strolled out into the hall. Something attempted, something done, had earned a cigarette. He was just lighting one, when there was a grinding of wheels on the gravel, and through the open door he saw Madame Eulalie alighting from a red two seater car. He skipped joyously to meet her.

"So you managed to come after all!"

Madame Eulalie shook his hand with that brisk amiability which was one of her main charms.

"Yes. But I've got to turn right round and go back again. I've three appointments this afternoon. I suppose you're staying on for the wedding ?"

"I had intended to. I promised George I would be his best man."

"That's a pity. I could have driven you back."

"Oh, I can easily cancel the thing," said Hamilton Beamish quickly. "In fact, I will, directly George returns. He can get dozens of best men—dozens."

"Returns ? Where has he gone ?"

"To the station."

"What a nuisance. I came specially to see him. Still, it doesn't matter. I had better see Miss Waddington for a moment, I suppose."

"She is out."

Madame Eulalie raised her eyebrows.

"Doesn't anybody stay in the house in these parts when there's going to be a wedding?"

"There has been a slight accident," explained Hamilton Beamish. "The clergyman sprained his ankle, and Mrs. Waddington and Molly have gone to Flushing to pick up an understudy. And George has gone to the station . . ."

"Yes, why has George gone to the station?"

Hamilton Beamish hesitated. Then, revolted by the thought that he should be hiding anything from this girl, he spoke.

"Can you keep a secret?"

"I don't know. I've never tried."

"Well, this is something quite between ourselves. Poor George is in trouble."

"Any worse trouble than most bridegrooms?"

"I wish you would not speak like that," said Hamilton Beamish, pained. "You seem to mock at Love."

"Oh, I've nothing against Love."

"Thank you, thank you!"

"Don't mention it."

"Love is the only thing worth while in the world. In peace, Love tunes the shepherd's reed, in war he mounts the warrior's steed. . . ."

"Yes, doesn't he. You were going to tell me what George is in trouble about."

Hamilton Beamish lowered his voice.

"Well, the fact is, on the eve of his wedding an old acquaintance of his has suddenly appeared."

"Female?"

"Female."

"I begin to see."

"George wrote her letters. She still has them."

"Worse and worse."

"And if she makes trouble it will stop the wedding. Mrs. Waddington is only waiting for an excuse to forbid it. Already, she has stated in so many words that she is suspicious of George's morals."

"How absurd! George is like the driven snow."

"Exactly. A thoroughly fine-minded man. Why, I remember him once leaving the table at a bachelor dinner because some one told an improper story."

"How splendid of him! What was the story?"

"I don't remember. Still, Mrs. Waddington has this opinion of him, so there it is."

"All this sounds very interesting. What are you going to do about it?"

"Well, George has gone to the station to try to intercept this Miss Stubbs and reason with her."

"Miss Stubbs?"

"That is her name. By the way, she comes from your home-town, East Gilead. Perhaps you know her?"

"I seem to recollect the name. So George has gone to reason with her?"

"Yes. But, of course, she will insist on coming here."

"That's bad."

Hamilton Beamish smiled.

"Not quite so bad as you think," he said. "You see, I have been giving the matter some little thought, and I may say I have the situation well in hand. I have arranged everything."

"You have?"

"Everything."

"You must be terribly clever."

"Oh, well!" said Hamilton Beamish modestly.

"But of course, I knew you were, the moment I read your Booklets. Have you a cigarette?"

"I beg your pardon."

Madame Eulalie selected a cigarette from his case and lit it. Hamilton Beamish, taking the match from her fingers, blew it out and placed reverently in his left top waistcoat-pocket.

"Go on," said Madame Eulalie.

"Ah, yes," said Hamilton Beamish, coming out of his thoughts. "We were speaking about George. It appears that George, before he left East Gilead, had what he calls an understanding, but which seems to me to have differed in no respect from a definite engagement, with a girl named May Stubbs. Unpleasant name!"

"Horrible. Just the sort of name I would want to change."

"He then came into money, left for New York, and forgot all about her."

"But she didn't forget all about him?"

"Apparently not. I picture her as a poor, dowdy little thing— you know what these village girls are—without any likelihood of getting another husband. So she has clung to her one chance. I suppose she thinks that by coming here at this time she will force George to marry her."

"But you are going to be too clever to let anything like that happen?"

"Precisely."

"Aren't you wonderful!"

"It is extremely kind of you to say so," said Hamilton Beamish, pulling down his waistcoat.

"What have you arranged?"

"Well, the whole difficulty is that at present George is in the position of having broken the engagement. So, when this May Stubbs arrives, I am going to get her to throw him over of her own free-will."

"And how do you propose to do that?"

"Quite simply. You see, we may take it for granted that she is a prude. I have, therefore, constructed a little drama, by means of which George will appear an abandoned libertine."

"George!"

"She will be shocked and revolted and will at once break off all relations with him."

"I see. Did you think all this out by yourself?"

"Entirely by myself."

"You're too clever for one man. You ought to incorporate."

It seemed to Hamilton Beamish that the moment had arrived to speak out frankly and without subterfuge, to reveal in the neatest phrases at his disposal the love which had been swelling in his heart like some yeasty ferment ever since he had first taken a speck of dust out of this girl's eye on the doorstep of Number Sixteen East Seventy-Ninth Street. And he was about to begin doing so, when she looked past him and uttered a pleased laugh.

"Why, George Finch!"

Hamilton Beamish turned, justly exasperated. Every time he endeavoured to speak his love, it seemed that something had to happen to prevent him. Yesterday it had been the loathsome Charley on the telephone, and now it was George Finch. George was standing in the doorway, flushed as if he had been walking quickly. He was staring at the girl in a manner which Hamilton Beamish resented. To express his resentment he coughed sharply.

George paid no attention. He continued to stare.

"And how is Georgie? You have interrupted a most interesting story, George."

"May!" George Finch placed a finger inside his collar, as if trying to loosen it. "May! I—I've just been down to the station to meet you."

"I came by car."

"May?" exclaimed Hamilton Beamish, a horrid light breaking upon him.

Madame Eulalie turned to him brightly.

"Yes, I'm the dowdy little thing."

"But you're not a dowdy little thing," said Hamilton Beamish, finding thought difficult but concentrating on the one uncontrovertible fact.

"I was when George knew me."

"And your name is Madame Eulalie."

"My professional name. Didn't we agree that anyone who had a name like May Stubbs would want to change it as quickly as possible."

"You are really May Stubbs?"

"I am."

Hamilton Beamish bit his lip. He regarded his friend coldly.

"I congratulate you, George. You are engaged to two of the prettiest girls I have ever seen."

"How very charming of you, Jimmy!" said Madame Eulalie. George Finch's face worked convulsively.

"But, May, honestly. . . . Have a heart! . . . You don't really look on me as engaged to you?"

"Why not?"

"But . . . but . . . I thought you had forgotten all about me."

"What after all those beautiful letters you wrote!"

"Boy and girl affair," babbled George.

"Was it, indeed!"

"But, May! . . ."

Hamilton Beamish had been listening to these exchanges with a rapidly rising temperature. His heart was pounding feverishly in his bosom. There is no one who becomes so primitive, when gripped by love, as the man who all his life has dwelt in the cool empyrean of the intellect. For twenty years and more, Hamilton Beamish had supposed that he was above the crude passions of the ordinary man, and when love had got him it got him good. And now, standing there and listening to these two, he was conscious of a jealousy so keen that he could no longer keep silent. Hamilton Beamish, the thinker, had ceased to be: and there stood in his place Hamilton Beamish, the descendant of ancestors who had conducted their love affairs with stout clubs and who, on seeing a rival, wasted no time in calm reflection but jumped on him like a ton of bricks and did their best to bite his head off. If you had given him a bearskin and taken away his spectacles, Hamilton Beamish at this moment would have been Prehistoric Man.

"Hey!" said Hamilton Beamish.

"But May, you know you don't love me. . . ."

"Hey!" said Hamilton Beamish again in a nasty, snarling voice. And silence fell.

The cave-man adjusted his spectacles, and glared at his erst-while friend with venomous dislike. His fingers twitched, as if searching for a club.

"Listen to me, you," said Hamilton Beamish, "and get me right! See? That'll be about all from you about this girl loving you, unless you want me to step across and bust you on the beezer. I love her, see? And she's going to marry me, see? And nobody else, see? And anyone who says different had better notify his friends where he wants his body sent, see? Love you, indeed? A swell chance! I'm the little guy she's going to marry, see? Me!"

And, folding his arms, the thinker paused for a reply.

It did not come immediately. George Finch unused to primi-tive emotions from this particular quarter, remained completely dumb. It was left for Madame Eulalie to supply comment.

"Jimmy!" she said faintly.

Hamilton Beamish caught her masterfully about the waist. He kissed her eleven times.

"So that's that!" said Hamilton Beamish.

"Yes, Jimmy."

"We'll get married to-morrow."

"Yes, Jimmy."

"You are my mate!"

"Yes, Jimmy."

"All right, then," said Hamilton Beamish.

George came to life like a clockwork toy.

"Hamilton, I congratulate you!"

"Thanks, thanks."

Mr. Beamish spoke a little dazedly. He blinked. Already the ferment had begun to subside, and Beamish the cave-man was fast giving place to Beamish of the Booklets. He was dimly cons-cious of having expressed himself a little too warmly and in language which in a calmer moment he would never have selected. Then he caught the girl's eyes, fixed on him adoringly, and he had no regrets.

"Thanks," he said again.

"May is a splendid girl," said George. "You will be very happy.

I speak as one who knows her. How sympathetic you always were in the old days, May."

"Was I?"

"You certainly were. Don't you remember how I used to bring my troubles to you, and we would sit together on the sofa in front of your parlour fire?"

"We were always afraid that some one was listening at the door."

"If they had been, the only thing they'd have found out would have been the lamp."

"Hey!" said Hamilton Beamish abruptly.

"Those were happy days," said Madame Eulalie.

"And do you remember how your little brother used to call me April Showers?"

"He did, did he?" said Mr. Beamish, snorting a little. "Why?"

"Because I brought May flowers."

"That's quite enough," said Hamilton Beamish, not without reason. "I should like to remind you, Finch, that this lady is engaged to me."

"Oh, quite," said George.

"Endeavour not to forget it," said Hamilton Beamish curtly. "And, later on, should you ever come to share a meal at our little home, be sparing of your reminiscences of the dear old days. You get—you take my meaning?"

"Oh, quite."

"Then we will be getting along. May has to return to New York immediately, and I am going with her. You must look elsewhere for a best man at your wedding. You are very lucky to be having a wedding at all. Goodbye, George. Come, darling."

The two-seater was moving down the drive, when Hamilton Beamish clapped a hand to his forehead.

"I had quite forgotten," he exclaimed.

"What have you forgotten, Jimmy dear?"

"Just something I wanted to say to George, sweetheart. Wait here for me."

"George," said Hamilton Beamish, returning to the hall, "I have just remembered something. Ring for Ferris and tell him to stay in the room with the wedding-presents and not leave it for a moment. They aren't safe, lying loose like that. You should have had a detective."

"We intended to, but Mr. Waddington insisted on it so strongly that Mrs. Waddington said the idea was absurd. I'll go and tell Ferris immediately."

"Do so," said Hamilton Beamish.

He passed out on to the lawn: and reaching the rhododendron bushes, whistled softly.

"Now what?" said Fanny, pushing out an inquiring head.

"Oh, there you are."

"Yes, here I am. When does the show start?"

"It doesn't," said Hamilton Beamish. "Events have occurred which render our little ruse unnecessary. So you can return to your home and husband as soon as you please."

"Oh?" said Fanny.

She plucked a rhododendron leaf and crushed it reflectively.

"I don't know as I'm in any hurry," she said. "I kind of like it out here. The air and the sun and the birds and everything. I guess I'll stick around for awhile."

Hamilton Beamish regarded her with a quiet smile.

"Certainly, if you wish it," he said. "I should mention, however, that if you were contemplating another attempt on those jewels, you would do well to abandon the idea. From now on a large butler will be stationed in the room, watching over it, and there might be unpleasantness."

"Oh?" said Fanny meditatively.

"Yes."

"You think of everything, don't you?"

"I thank you for the compliment," said Hamilton Beamish.


## CHAPTER ELEVEN

GEORGE did not delay. Always sound, Hamilton Beamish's advice appeared to him now even sounder than usual. He rang the bell for Ferris.

"Oh, Ferris," said George, "Mr. Beamish thinks you had better stay in the room with the wedding-presents and keep an eye on them."

"Very good, sir."

"In case somebody tries to steal them, you know."

"Just so, sir."

Relief, as it always does, had given George a craving for conversation. He wanted to buttonhole some fellow-creature and babble. He would have preferred this fellow-creature to have been anyone but Ferris, for he had not forgotten the early passages of their acquaintanceship and seemed still to sense in the butler's manner a lingering antipathy. But Ferrrs was there, so he babbled to him.

"Nice day, Ferris."

"Yes, sir."

"Nice weather."

"Yes, sir."

"Nice country round here."

"No, sir."

George was somewhat taken aback.

"Did you say, No, sir?"

"Yes, sir."

"Oh, Yes, sir? I thought you said No, sir."

"Yes, sir. No, sir."

"You mean you don't like the country round here?"

"No, sir."

"Why not?"

"I disapprove of it, sir."

"Why?"

"It is not the sort of country to which I have been accustomed, sir. It is not like the country round Little-Seeping-in-the-Wold."

"Where's that?"

"In England, sir."

"I suppose the English country's nice?"

"I believe it gives uniform satisfaction, sir."

George felt damped. In his mood of relief he had hoped that Ferris might have brought himself to sink the butler in the friend.

"What don't you like about the country round here?"

"I disapprove of the mosquitoes, sir."

"But there are only a few."

"I disapprove of even one mosquito, sir."

George tried again.

"I suppose everybody downstairs is very excited about the wedding, Ferris?"

"By 'everybody downstairs' you allude to . . ?"

"The—er—the domestic staff."

"I have not canvassed their opinions, sir. I mix very little with my colleagues."

"I suppose you disapprove of them?" said George, nettled.

"Yes, sir."

"Why?"

The butler raised his eyebrows. He preferred the lower middle classes not to be inquisitive. However, he stooped to explain.

"Many of them are Swedes, sir, and the rest are Irish."

"You disapprove of Swedes?"

"Yes, sir."

"Why?"

"Their heads are too square, sir."

"And you disapprove of the Irish?"

"Yes, sir."

"Why?"

"Because they are Irish, sir."

George shifted his feet uncomfortably.

"I hope you don't disapprove of weddings, Ferris?"

"Yes, sir."

"Why?"

"They seem to me melancholy occasions, sir."

"Are you married, Ferris?"

"A widower, sir."

"Well, weren't you happy when you got married?"

"No, sir."

"Was Mrs. Ferris?"

"She appeared to take a certain girlish pleasure in the ceremony, sir, but it soon blew over."

"How do you account for that?"

"I could not say, sir."

"I'm sorry weddings depress you, Ferris. Surely when two people love each other and mean to go on loving each other . . ."

"Marriage is not a process for prolonging the life of love, sir. It merely mummifies its corpse."

"But, Ferris, if there were no marriages, what would become of posterity?"

"I see no necessity for posterity, sir."

"You disapprove of it?"

"Yes, sir."

George walked pensively out on to the drive in front of the house. He was conscious of a diminution of the exuberant happiness which had led him to engage the butler in conversation. He saw clearly now that, Ferris's conversation being what it was, a bridegroom who engaged him in it on his wedding-day was making a blunder. A suitable, even an ideal, companion for a funeral, Ferris seemed out of harmony when the joy-bells were ringing.

He looked out upon the pleasant garden with sobered gaze: and, looking, was aware of Sigsbee H. Waddington approaching. Sigsbee's manner was agitated. He conveyed the impression of having heard bad news or of having made some discovery which disconcerted him.

"Say, listen!" said Sigsbee H. "What's that infernal butler doing in the room with the wedding presents ?"

"Keeping guard over them."

"Who told him to ?"

"I did."

"Hell's bells!" said Sigsbee H.

He gave George a peculiar look and shimmered off. If George had been more in the frame of mind to analyse the looks of his future father-in-law, he might have seen in this one a sort of shuddering loathing. But he was not in the frame of mind. Besides, Sigsbee H. Waddington was not the kind of man whose looks one analysed. He was one of those negligible men whom one pushes out of sight and forgets about. George proceeded to forget about him almost immediately. He was still forgetting about him, when an automobile appeared round the bend of the drive and, stopping beside him, discharged Mrs. Waddington, Molly, and a man with a face like a horse, whom, from his clerical costume, George took correctly to be the deputy from Flushing.

"Molly!" cried George.

"Here we are, angel," said Molly.

"And mother!" said George, with less heartiness.

"Mother!" said Mrs. Waddington, with still less heartiness than George.

"This is the Reverend Gideon Voules," said Molly, "He's going to marry us."

"This," said Mrs. Waddington, turning to the clergyman and speaking in a voice which seemed to George's sensitive ear to contain too strong a note of apology, "is the bridegroom."

The Reverend Gideon Voules looked at George with a dull and poached-egg-like eye. He did not seem to the latter to be a frightfully cheery sort of person: but, after all, when you're married, you're married, no matter how like a poached egg the presiding minister may look.

"How do you do ?" said the Rev. Gideon.

"I'm fine," said George. "How are you ?"

"I am in robust health, I thank you."

"Splendid! Nothing wrong with the ankles, eh ?"

The Rev. Gideon glanced down at them and seemed satisfied

with this section of his lower limbs, even though they were draped in white socks.

"Nothing, thank you."

"So many clergymen nowadays," explained George, "are falling off chairs and spraining them."

"I never fall off chairs."

"Then you're just the fellow I've been scouring the country for," said George. "If all clergymen were like you . . ."

Mrs. Waddington came to life.

"Would you care for a glass of milk?"

"No, thank you, mother," said George.

"I was not addressing you," said Mrs. Waddington. "I was speaking to Mr. Voules. He has had a long drive and no doubt requires refreshment."

"Of course, of course," said George. "What am I thinking about? Yes, you must certainly stoke up and preserve your strength. We don't want you fainting halfway through the ceremony."

"He would have every excuse," said Mrs. Waddington.

She led the way into the dining-room where light refreshments were laid out on a side-table—a side-table brightly decorated by the presence of Sigsbee H. Waddington, who was sipping a small gin and tonic and watching with lowering gaze the massive imperturbability of Ferris, the butler. Ferris, though he obviously disapproved of wedding-presents, was keeping a loyal eye on them.

"What are you doing here, Ferris?" asked Mrs. Waddington.

The butler raised the loyal eye.

"Guarding the gifts, madam."

"Who told you to?"

"Mr. Finch, madam."

Mrs. Waddington shot a look of disgust at George.

"There is no necessity whatever."

"Very good, madam."

"Only an imbecile would have suggested such a thing."

"Precisely, madam."

The butler retired. Sigsbee Horatio, watching him go, sighed unhappily. What was the good of him going now? felt Sigsbee. From now on the room would be full. Already automobiles were beginning to arrive, and a swarm of wedding-guests had begun to settle upon the refreshments on the side-table.

The Rev. Gideon Voules, thoughtfully lowering a milk and ham-sandwich into the abyss, had drawn George into a corner and was endeavouring to make his better acquaintance.

"I always like to have a little chat with the bridegroom before the ceremony," he said. "It is agreeable to be able to feel that he is, in a sense, a personal friend."

"Very nice of you," said George, touched.

"I married a young fellow in Flushing named Miglett the other day—Claude R. Miglett. Perhaps you recall the name?"

"No."

"Ah! I thought you might have seen it in the papers. They were full of the affair. I always feel that, if I had not made a point of establishing personal relations with him before the ceremony, I should not have been in a position to comfort him as I did after the accident occurred."

"Accident?"

"Yes. The bride was most unfortunately killed by a motor-lorry as they were leaving the church."

"Good heavens!"

"I have always thought it singularly unfortunate. But then it almost seems as if there were some fatality about the weddings at which I officiate. Only a week before, I had married a charming young couple, and both were dead before the month was out. A girder fell on them as they were passing a building which was under construction. In the case of another pair whom I married earlier in the year, the bridegroom contracted some form of low fever. A fine young fellow. He came out in pink spots. We were all most distressed about it." He turned to Mrs. Waddington, whom an inrush of guests had driven into the corner. "I was telling our young friend here of a rather singular coincidence. In each of the last two weddings at which I officiated the bridegroom died within a few days of the ceremony."

A wistful look came into Mrs. Waddington's face. She seemed to be feeling that luck like that could not hold.

"I, personally," she said, "have had a presentiment right from the beginning that this marriage would never take place."

"Now, that is very curious," said the Rev. Gideon. "I am a strong believer in presentiments."

"So am I."

"I think they are sent to warn us—to help us to prepare ourselves for disaster."

"In the present instance," said Mrs. Waddington, "the word disaster is not the one I would have selected."

George tottered away. Once more there was creeping over him that grey foreboding which had come to him earlier in the day. So reduced was his nervous system that he actually sought comfort in the society of Sigsbee Horatio. After all, he thought, whatever Sigsbee's shortcomings as a man, he at least was a friend. A philosopher with the future of the race at heart might sigh as he looked upon Sigsbee H. Waddington, but in a bleak world George could not pick and choose his chums.

A moment later there was forced upon him the unpleasing discovery that in supposing that Mr. Waddington liked him he had been altogether too optimistic. The look which his future father-in-law bestowed upon him as he sidled up was not one of affection. It was the sort of look which, had he been Sheriff of Gory Gulch, Arizona, the elder man might have bestowed upon a horse-thief.

"Darned officious!" rumbled Sigsbee H., in a querulous under-tone. "Officious and meddling."

"Eh?" said George.

"Telling that butler to come in here and watch the presents."

"But, good heavens, don't you realize that, if I hadn't told him, some one might have sneaked in and stolen something?"

Mr. Waddington's expression was now that of a cowboy who, leaping into bed, discovers too late that a frolicsome friend has placed a cactus between the sheets: and George at the lowest ebb, was about to pass on to the refreshment-table and see if a little potato-salad might not act as a restorative, when there stepped from the crowd gathered round the food a large and ornately dressed person chewing the remains of a slab of caviare on toast. George had a dim recollection of having seen him among the guests at that first dinner-party at Number Sixteen East Seventy-Ninth Street. His memory had not erred. The new-comer was no less a man than United Beef.

"Hello there, Waddington," said United Beef.

"Ur," said Sigsbee Horatio. He did not like the other, who had once refused to lend him money and—what was more—had gone to the mean length of quoting Shakespeare to support his refusal.

"Say, Waddington," proceeded United Beef, "don't I seem to remember you coming to me sometime ago and asking about that motion-picture company, the Finer and Better? You were think-ing of putting some money in, if I recollect."

An expression of acute alarm shot into Mr. Waddington's face. He gulped painfully.

"Not me," he said hastily. "Not me. Get it out of your nut that it was I who wanted to buy the stuff. I just thought that if the stock was any good my dear wife might be interested."

"Same thing."

"It is not at all the same thing."

"Do you happen to know if your wife bought any?"

"No, she didn't. I heard later that the company was no good, so I did not mention it to her."

"Too bad," said United Beef. "Too bad."

"What do you mean, too bad?"

"Well, a rather remarkable thing has happened. Quite a romance in its way. As a motion-picture company the thing was, as you say, no good. Couldn't seem to do anything right. But yesterday, when a workman started to dig a hole on the lot to put up a 'For Sale' sign, I'm darned if he didn't strike oil."

The solid outline of United Beef shimmered uncertainly before Mr. Waddington's horrified eyes.

"Oil?" he gurgled.

"Yes, sir. Oil. What looks like turning out the biggest gusher in the south-west."

"But—but—do you mean to say, then, that the shares are—are really worth something?"

"Only millions, that's all. Merely millions. It's a pity you didn't buy some. This caviare," said United Beef, champing meditatively, "is good. That's what it is. Waddington—good. I think I'll have another slice."

It is difficult to arrest the progress of a millionaire who is starting off in the direction of caviare, but Mr. Waddington, with a frenzied clutch at the other's coat-sleeve, succeeded in doing so for a brief instant.

"When did you hear this?"

"Just as I was starting out this morning."

"Do you think anybody else knows about it?"

"Everybody down-town, I should say."

"But, listen," said Mr. Waddington urgently. "Say, listen!" He clung to the caviare-maddened man's sleeve with a desperate grip. "What I am getting at is, I know a guy—nothing to do with business—who has a block of that stock. Do you think there's any chance of him not having heard about this?"

"Quite likely. But, if you're thinking of getting it off him, you'd better hurry. The story is probably in the evening papers by now."

The words acted on Sigsbee H. Waddington like an electric shock. He released the other's sleeve, and United Beef shot off towards the refreshment-table like a homing pigeon. Mr. Waddington felt in his hip-pocket to make sure that he still possessed the three hundred dollars which he had hoped that day to hand over to Fanny Welch, and bounded out of the room, out of the house, and out of the front gate; and, after bounding along the broad highway to the station, leaped into a train which might have been meeting him there by appointment. Never in his life before had Sigsbee H. Waddington caught a train so expeditiously: and the fact seemed to him a happy omen. He looked forward with a cheery confidence to the interview with that policeman fellow to whom he had—in a moment of mistaken generosity—parted with his precious stock. The policeman had seemed a simple sort of soul, just the sort of man with whom it is so nice to do business. Mr. Waddington began to rehearse the opening speeches of the interview.

"Say, listen," he would say. "Say, listen, my dear . . ."

He sat up in his seat with a jerk. He had completely forgotten the policeman's name.

## CHAPTER TWELVE

SEVERAL hours later, when the stars had begun to peep out and the birds were rustling sleepily in the trees, a solitary figure might have been observed moving slowly up the drive towards the front door of the Waddington summer-residence at Hempstead, Long Island. It was Sigsbee H., returning from his travels.

He walked apprehensively, like a cat that expects a half-brick. Oh, sings the poet, to be home again, home again, home again: but Sigsbee H. Waddington could not bring himself to share that sunny view-point. With the opportunity for quiet reflection there had come to him the numbing realization that beneath the roof before him trouble waited. On other occasions while serving his second sentence as a married man he had done things of which his wife had disapproved—and of which she had expressed her disapproval in a manner that was frank and unrestrained: but never before had he committed such a domestic crime as the one beneath the burden of which he was staggering now. He had actually absented himself from the wedding of his only child after having been specifically instructed to give her away at the altar: and if on a theme like this his wife did not extend herself in a fashion calculated to stagger Humanity—well, all Sigsbee H.

could say was that past form meant nothing, and could be ruled out as a guide completely.

He sighed drearily. He felt depressed and battered, in no mood to listen to home-truths about himself. All he wanted was to be alone on a sofa with his shoes off and something to drink at his elbow. For he had had a trying time in the great city.

Sigsbee H. Waddington, as has perhaps been sufficiently indicated in this narrative, was not a man who could think deeply without getting a headache: but even at the expense of an aching head he had been compelled to do some very deep thinking as he journeyed to New York in the train. From somewhere in the muddy depths of his sub-consciousness it was imperative that he should bring to the surface the name of the policeman to whom he had sold that stock. He started the dredging operations immediately, and by the time the train had reached the Pennsylvania Station had succeeded in narrowing the search down to this extent—that he felt sure the man was called either Mulcahy or Garrity.

Now, a man who goes about New York looking for a policeman named Mulcahy has quite an afternoon's work in hand. So has the man who seeks a Garrity. For one who pursues both there is not a dull moment. Flitting hither and thither about the city and questioning the various officers he encountered, Sigsbee H. Waddington soon began to cover ground. The policeman on point duty in Times Square said that there was a Mulcahy up near Grant's Tomb and a choice of Garritys at Columbus Circle and Irving Place. The Grant's Tomb Mulcahy, expressing regret that he could not himself supply the happy ending, recommended the Hundred-and-Twenty-Fifth Street Mulcahy or—alternately—the one down on Third Avenue and Sixteenth. The Garrity at Columbus Circle spoke highly of a Garrity near the Battery, and the Garrity at Irving Place seemed to think his cousin up in the Bronx might fill the long-felt want. By the time the clocks were striking five, Mr. Waddington had come definitely to the decision that what the world wanted to make it a place fit for heroes to live in was fewer and better Mulcahys. At five-thirty, returning from the Bronx, he would have supported any amendment to the Constitution which Congress might have cared to introduce, totally prohibiting Garritys. At six sharp, he became suddenly convinced that the name of the man he sought was Murphy.

He was passing through Madison Square at the moment, having just flushed Fourteenth Street for another Mulcahy: and so deeply did this new idea affect him that he tottered to one of the benches and, sitting down, groaned heavily. It was the breaking-point. Mr. Waddington decided to give it up and go home. His head was aching, his feet were aching, and the small of his back was aching. The first fine careless rapture with which he had started his quest had ebbed away to nothing. In short, if there was one man in New York utterly incapable of going about the place looking for Murphys, that man was Sigsbee H. Waddington. He limped to the Pennsylvania Station and took the next train home, and here he was, approaching journey's end.

The house, as he drew near, seemed very silent. And, of course, it had every right to be. Long since, the wedding must have taken place and the happy pair departed on their honeymoon. Long since, the last guests must have left. And now, beneath that quiet roof, there remained only Mrs. Waddington, no doubt trying out blistering phrases in the seclusion of her boudoir—here, discarding an incandescent adjective in favour of a still zippier one that had just suggested itself: there, realizing that the noun 'worm' was too mild and searching in Roget's *Thesaurus* for something more expressive. Mr. Waddington paused on the door-step, half inclined to make for the solitude of the tool-shed.

Manlier counsels prevailed. In the tool-shed there would be nothing to drink, and, cost what it might, a drink was what his suffering soul demanded. He crossed the threshold, and leaped nimbly as a dark figure suddenly emerged from the telephone-booth.

"Oosh!" said Mr. Waddington.

"Sir?" said the figure.

Mr. Waddington felt relieved. It was not his wife. It was Ferris. And Ferris was the one person he particularly wanted at that moment to meet. For it was Ferris who could most expeditiously bring him something to drink.

"Sh!" whispered Sigsbee H. "Anyone about?"

"Sir?"

"Where is Mrs. Waddington?"

"In her boudoir, sir."

Sigsbee H. expected as much.

"Anyone in the library?"

"No, sir."

"Then bring me a drink in there, Ferris. And don't tell anybody you've seen me."

"Very good, sir."

Mr. Waddington shambled to the library and flung himself

down on the chesterfield. Delicious, restful moments passed, and then a musical tinkling made itself heard without. Ferris entered with a tray.

"You omitted to give me definite instructions, sir." said the butler, "so, acting on my own initiative, I have brought the whisky-decanter and some charged water."

He spoke coldly, for he disapproved of Mr. Waddington. But the latter was in no frame of mind to analyse the verbal nuances of butlers. He clutched at the decanter, his eyes moist with gratitude.

"Splendid fellow, Ferris!"

"Thank you, sir."

"You're the sort of fellow who ought to be out West, where men are men."

The butler twitched a frosty eyebrow.

"Will that be all, sir?"

"Yes. But don't go, Ferris. Tell me about everything."

"On what particular point did you desire information, sir?"

"Tell me about the wedding. I wasn't able to be present. I had most important business in New York, Ferris. So I wasn't able to be present. Because I had most important business in New York."

"Indeed, sir?"

"Most important business. Impossible to neglect it. Did the wedding go off all right?"

"Not altogether, sir."

"What do you mean?"

"There has been no wedding, sir."

Mr. Waddington sat up. The butler appeared to be babbling. And the one moment when a man does not want to mix with babbling butlers is immediately after he has returned home from a search through New York for a policeman named Mulcahy or Garrity.

"No wedding?"

"No, sir."

"Why not?"

"At the last moment a hitch occurred, sir."

"Don't tell me the new clergyman sprained his ankle, too?"

"No, sir. The presiding minister continues to enjoy good health in every respect. The hitch to which I allude was caused by a young woman who, claiming to be an old friend of the bride-groom, entered the room where the guests were assembled and created some little disturbance, sir."

Mr. Waddington's eyes bulged.

"Tell me about this," he said.

The butler fixed a fathomless gaze on the wall beyond him.

"I was not actually present at the scene myself, sir. But one of the lower servants, who chanced to be glancing in at the door, has apprised me of the details of the occurrence. It appears that, just as the wedding-party was about to start off for the church, a young woman suddenly made her way through the French windows opening on to the lawn, and, pausing in the entrance, observed 'George! George! Why did you desert me? You don't belong to that girl there. You belong to me,—the woman you have wronged!' Addressing Mr. Finch, I gather."

Mr. Waddington's eyes were now protruding to such a dangerous extent that a sharp jerk would have caused them to drop off.

"Sweet suffering soup-spoons! What happened then?"

"There was considerable uproar and confusion, so my informant tells me. The bridegroom was noticeably taken aback, and protested with some urgency that it was all a mistake. To which Mrs. Waddington replied that it was just what she had foreseen all along. Miss Waddington, I gather, was visibly affected. And the guests experienced no little embarrassment."

"I don't blame them."

"No, sir."

"And then?"

"The young woman was pressed for details, but appeared to be in an overwrought and highly emotional condition. She screamed, so my informant tells me, and wrung her hands. She staggered about the room and, collapsing on the table where the wedding-presents had been placed, seemed to swoon. Almost immediately afterwards, however, she appeared to recover herself and, remarking 'Air! Air! I want air!' departed hastily through the French windows. I understand, sir, that nothing was seen of her after that."

"And what happened then?"

"Mrs. Waddington refused to permit the wedding to take place. The guests returned to New York. Mr. Finch, after uttering certain protests which my informant could not hear distinctly but which appear to have been incoherent and unconvincing, also took his departure. Mrs. Waddington has for some little time past been closeted in the boudoir with Miss Waddington. A very unpleasant affair, sir, and one which could never have occurred at Brangmarley Hall."

One hates to have to record it, but it is a fact that the first emotion which came to Sigsbee H. Waddington after the waning of his initial amazement was relief. It was not the thought of this broken romance that occupied his mind, nor pity for the poor girl who had played the principal part in the tragedy. The aspect of the matter that touched him most nearly was the fact that he was not in for trouble after all. His absence had probably escaped notice, and that wifely lecture to which he had been looking forward so apprehensively would never be delivered.

And then, cutting through relief, came a sudden thought that chilled his satisfaction.

"What sort of a girl was it that came in through the window?"

"My informant describes her as small, sir, and of a neat figure. She had a *retroussé* nose and expressive black eyes, sir."

"Great Godfrey!" ejaculated Mr. Waddington.

He sprang from the sofa and, despite his aching feet, made good time along the hall. He ran into the dining-room and switched on the light. He darted across the room to the table where the wedding-presents lay. At first glance, they seemed to be all there, but a second look showed him that his suspicions had been well founded.

The case containing the necklace was gone.


## CHAPTER THIRTEEN

ONE of the most sustaining gifts a man can possess is the ability to look upon the bright side of disaster. It was a gift which, until now, Sigsbee H. Waddington had lacked almost entirely: but at this moment, owing perhaps to the fact that he had just introduced into his interior a healing drink of quite exceptional strength, he suddenly found himself discerning with a limpid clearness the fact that the elimination of that near-pearl necklace from the scheme of things was, from his point of view, the very best thing that could have happened.

It had not been his intention to allow his young assistant to secure the necklace and convert it to her own uses: but, now that this had happened, what, he asked himself, had he to worry about? The main thing was that the necklace had disappeared. Coming right down to it, that was the consummation at which he had aimed all along.

What it amounted to was that, when all the tumult and the shouting had died, he was three hundred dollars in hand and consequently in a position, if he ever met that policeman again and the policeman had not happened to hear the news which United Beef had told him, to . . .

At this point in his meditations Mr. Waddington suddenly broke off and uttered a sharp exclamation. For before his eyes in letters of fire there seemed to be written the one word

## GALLAGHER

Sigsbee H. Waddington reeled in his tracks. Gallagher! That was the name. Not Mulcahy. Not Garrity. Not Murphy. Gallagher!

Like many another good man before him, Sigsbee Waddington chafed at the fat-headed imbecility with which Memory can behave. Why should Memory have presented to his notice futile Mulcahys and Garritys and Murphys when what he had been asking for was Gallagher? Wasting his time!

But it was not too late. If he went straight back to New York now and resumed his quest, all might yet be well. And Fortune had, he perceived, presented him with the most admirable excuse for going straight back to New York. In a crisis like this, with a valuable pearl necklace stolen, it was imperative that a cool-headed, clear-thinking man of the world should take the next train up and place the facts in the possession of Police Head-quarters.

"Good enough!" said Mr. Waddington to his immortal soul: and hobbled stiffly but light-heartedly to the boudoir.

Voices reached his ears as he opened the door. They ceased as he entered, and Mrs. Waddington looked up peevishly.

"Where have you been, I should like to know?" she said.

Sigsbee H. was ready for this one.

"I took a long country walk. A very long country walk. I was so shocked, horrified and surprised by that dreadful scene that the house seemed to stifle me. So I took a long country walk. I have just got back. What a very disturbing thing to happen! Ferris says it could never have occurred at Brangmarley Hall."

Molly, somewhat red about the eyes and distinctly mutinous about the mouth, spoke for the first time.

"I'm sure there is some explanation."

"Tchah!" said Mrs. Waddington.

"I know there is."

"Then why did not your precious Finch condescend to give it ?"

"He was so taken aback."

"I don't wonder."

"I'm sure there was some mistake."

"There was," said Mr. Waddington. He patted his daughter's hand soothingly. "The whole thing was a put-up job."

"Kindly talk sense, Sigsbee."

"I am talking sense."

"What you call sense, perhaps, but not what anyone outside the walls of an institution for the feeble-minded would call sense."

"Is zat so ?" Mr. Waddington put his thumbs in the armholes of his waistcoat and felt rather conquering. "Well, let me tell you that girl simply pretended to be what she wasn't so as to fool you into thinking she wasn't what she was."

Mrs. Waddington sighed despairingly.

"Go away, Sigsbee," she said.

"That's all right about Go away, Sigsbee. I'm telling you that that girl was a crook. She couldn't get in any other way, so she pulled that discarded stuff. She was after the wedding presents."

"Then why did she not take them ?"

"She did. She took Molly's pearl necklace."

"What!"

"You heard. She took Molly's pearl necklace."

"Nonsense."

"Well, it's gone."

Molly had risen with shining eyes.

"I thought as much. So my dear darling George is innocent after all."

Very few people in this civilized world have ever seen a baffled tigress, but anybody who could have watched Mrs. Waddington's face at this moment would have gained a very fair knowledge of how baffled tigresses look.

"I don't believe it." she said sullenly.

"Well, the necklace has gone, hasn't it," said Sigsbee H. "And you don't suppose any of the guests took it, do you ? Though I wouldn't put it past that Lord Hunstanton guy. Of course that girl has got it. She fainted on the wedding-present table, didn't she ? She said she wanted air and rushed out, didn't she ? And nobody's seen her since, have they ? If it hadn't been for going for my long country walk, I'd have got on to this hours ago."

"I'm going straight to New York to see George and tell him," said Molly, breathing quickly.

"You will do nothing of the kind," said Mrs. Waddington, rising.

"And I'm going to New York to see the police," said Sigsbee.

"You are certainly not! I will go to New York, and I will inform the police. You and Molly will stay here."

"But listen . . ."

"I want no further discussion." Mrs. Waddington pressed the bell. "As for you," she said, turning to Molly, "do you suppose I am going to allow you to pay nocturnal visits to the apartments of libertines like George Finch?"

"He is not a libertine."

"Certainly not," said Sigsbee H. "A very fine young fellow. Comes from Idaho."

"You know perfectly well," Molly went on, "that what father has told us absolutely clears George. Why, the girl might just as well have come in and said that father had deserted her."

"Here!" said Mr. Waddington. "Hi!"

"She only wanted an excuse for getting into the house."

"It is possible," said Mrs. Waddington, "that in this particular instance George Finch is not so blameworthy as I had at first supposed. But that does not alter the fact that he is a man whom any mother with her daughter's happiness at heart must regard with the deepest suspicion. He is an artist. He has deliberately chosen to live in a quarter of New York which is notorious for its loose-thinking and Bohemian ways. And . . ."

The door opened.

"You rang, madam?"

"Yes, Ferris. Tell Bassett to bring the car round immediately. I am going into New York."

"Very good, madam." The butler coughed. "I wonder, madam, if it is not taking a liberty, if I might be permitted to ride on the box-seat beside the chauffeur?"

"Why?"

There are occasions in life when to give one's true reasons for some particular course of action would be tedious. The actual explanation of the butler's desire to visit the metropolis was that he wished to pay a call upon the editor of that bright and widely-read weekly paper, 'Town Gossip,' in order to turn an honest penny by informing him of the sensational scene which had occurred that day in the highest circles. Almost immediately after the facts of this scandal in high life had been called to his attention,

Ferris had started to telephone the 'Town Gossip' offices in order to establish communication, only to be informed that the editor was out of town. At his last attempt, however, a cautious assistant, convinced at length that the butler had something of real interest up his sleeve and was not disposed to reveal it to underlings, had recommended him to call upon L. Lancelot Biffen, the editor-in-chief, at his private address on the ninth floor of the Sheridan Apartment House, near Washington Square. Mr. Biffen, the assistant thought, would be back after dinner.

All this the butler could, of course, have revealed to his employer, but, like all men of intellect, he disliked long explanations.

"I have just received a communication informing me that a near relative of mine is ill in the city, madam."

"Oh, very well."

"Thank you, madam. I will inform Bassett at once."

"Besides," said Mrs. Waddington, as the door closed, going on where she had been interrupted, "for all we know, the girl's story may have been perfectly true, and her theft of the pearls the result of a sudden temptation on the spur of the moment."

"Mother!"

"Well, why not? I suppose she was in need of money. No doubt your Finch callously omitted to provide for her in any way."

"You've got it all wrong," said Sigsbee H.

"What do you know about it?" said Mrs. Waddington.

"Nothing," said Sigsbee H., prudently.

"Then kindly refrain from talking nonsense."

Mrs. Waddington left the room with ponderous dignity, and Sigsbee H., still prudent, closed the door.

"Say, listen, Molly," he said, "I've got to get up to New York right away. I've just got to."

"So have I. I certainly mean to see George to-night. I suppose he has gone back to his apartment."

"What'll we do?"

"Directly the car has gone, I'll run you up in my two-seater."

"'At-a-baby!" said Mr. Waddington fervently. "That's the way to talk."

He kissed his daughter fondly.

# CHAPTER FOURTEEN

## I

MRS. WADDINGTON found the authorities at Police Headquarters charming. It was some little time before they corrected their initial impression that she had come to give herself up to justice for committing a jewel-robbery: but, this done, they threw themselves heart and soul into her cause and became extraordinarily helpful. True, they were forced to admit that the description which she gave of the thief conveyed absolutely nothing to them: but if it had done, they assured her, she would have been amazed at the remorseless speed with which the machinery of the law would have been set working.

If, for instance, the girl had been tall and thin with shingled auburn hair, they would have spread the net at once for 'Chicago Kitty.' If, on the other hand, she had had a snub nose and two moles on her chin, then every precinct would have been warned by telephone to keep an eye out for 'Cincinatti Sue.' While, if only she had limped slightly and spoken with a lisp, the arrest of 'Indianapolis Edna' would have been a mere matter of hours. As it was, they were obliged to confess themselves completely baffled: and Mrs. Waddington came away with the feeling that, if she had not happened to possess large private means, she could have gone into the jewel-stealing business herself and cleaned up big without any fear of unpleasant consequences. It was wrong of her, of course, to call the chief detective a fat-faced goop, but by that time she had become a little annoyed.

She was still annoyed as she came out into the street, but the pleasant night air had a cooling effect. She was able now to perceive that the theft of the necklace was, after all, only a side issue, and that there lay before her sterner work than the mere bringing to book of female criminals. The consummation to which she must devote all her faculties was the downfall of George Finch.

It was at this point that she decided that she needed an ally, a sympathetic coadjutor who would trot along by her side and do what he was told and generally supply aid and encouragement in the rather tricky operations on which she was about to embark.

She went to a public telephone-office and invested five cents in a local call.

"Lord Hunstanton?"

"Hullo?"

"This is Mrs. Waddington."

"Oh, ah? Many happy returns."

"What are you doing just now?"

"I was thinking of popping out and having a bit to eat."

"Meet me at the Ritz-Carlton in ten minutes."

"Right-ho. Thanks awfully. I will. Yes. Thanks. Right Fine. Absolutely. Right-ho."

So now we find Mrs. Waddington seated in the vestibule of the Ritz-Carlton Hotel, watching the door like a cat at a mouse-hole and tapping the carpet impatiently with an ample shoe. Like everybody else who has ever waited five minutes for anybody in a restaurant, she had the illusion of having been there for several hours. But at last her patience was rewarded. An elegant figure shimmered through the doorway, and came towards her, beaming with happy anticipation. Lord Hunstanton was a man who combined a keen appetite with a rugged distaste for paying for his own meals, and the prospect of a dinner at the Ritz at somebody else's expense enchanted him. He did not actually lick his lips, but as he looked brightly up the stairs to where benevolent waiters were plying contented diners with food, there flitted across his face a radiant smile.

"Hope I'm not late," said Lord Hunstanton.

"Sit down," said Mrs. Waddington. "I want to talk to you." And proceeded to do so at some length.

Lord Hunstanton blinked pathetically.

"I'm awfully sorry," he said, as his companion paused for breath. "I know it's all frightfully interesting, but I don't seem somehow to follow. How would it be if we slid into the dining-room and thrashed the whole thing out quietly over a thoughtful steak or something?"

Mrs. Waddington eyed him with a distaste that bordered on contempt.

"You surely do not imagine that I propose to waste time eating?"

"Eh?" His lordship's jaw fell an inch. "Not eat?"

"Certainly not. I will repeat what I was saying, and please listen attentively this time."

"But I say! No dinner?"

"No."

"No soup ?"

"No."

"No fish ? No nourishment of any description ?"

"Certainly not. We have no time to lose. We must act promptly and swiftly."

"How about a sand— . . . ?"

"You were present at that appalling scene this afternoon," said Mrs. Waddington, "so there is no need to describe it to you. You will not have forgotten how that girl came into the room and denounced George Finch. You recall all she said."

"I do indeed. It was the real ginger."

"But unfortunately untrue."

"Oh ?"

"It was a ruse. She was a thief. She did it in order to steal a pearl necklace belonging to my step-daughter, which was among the wedding presents."

"No, really ? I say! Fancy that!"

"Unfortunately there seems to be no doubt of it. And so, instead of being appalled at George Finch's moral turpitude, my step-daughter looks upon him as a much-injured man and wishes the marriage to take place as arranged. Are you listening ?"

Lord Hunstanton started. There had come frolicking towards him from the dining-room a lively young smell composed principally of tournedos and gravy, and his attention had wandered.

"Sorry," he said. "Thinking of something else for the moment. You were saying that Miss Waddington was appalled at George Finch's moral turpitude."

"I was saying precisely the reverse. She is not appalled."

"No ? Very broad-minded, these modern girls," said Lord Hunstanton, turning away and trying not to inhale.

"But," proceeded Mrs. Waddington, "I am convinced that, although in this particular matter this Finch may be blameless, his morals, if we only knew it, are as degraded as those of all other artists. I feel as certain as I am that I am sitting here that George Finch is a loose fish."

"Fish!" moaned Lord Hunstanton.

"And I have made up my mind that there is only one thing to do if I am to expose the man in his true colours, and that is to go to the den which he maintains near Washington Square and question his man-servant as to his private life. We will start at once."

"But, I say, you don't need me ?"

"Certainly I need you. Do you imagine that I propose to call at this man's lair alone?"

Across the landing at the top of the stairs there passed a waiter bearing a tray with a smoking dish upon it. Lord Hunstanton followed him with haggard eyes: and, having watched him enter the restaurant, wished he had not done so, for there by one of the tables stood another waiter carving for a party of four what looked like the roast chicken of a lifetime,—one of those roast chickens you tell your grandchildren about. His lordship uttered a faint, whinnying sound and clenched his hands.

"Come!" said Mrs. Waddington. "Let us go."

The thought of defying this overpowering woman did not enter Lord Hunstanton's mind. Nobody ever defied Mrs. Waddington. And so, some little time later, a cab drew up outside the Sheridan Apartment House and two figures proceeded to climb the stairs—for it was one of the pleasing features of the Sheridan that the elevator was practically always out of order.

Arrived at the top floor, Lord Hunstanton rang the bell. The sound echoed faintly within.

"Seems to be out," said his lordship, having tried again.

"We will wait."

"What, here?"

"On the roof."

"How long?"

"Until this Finch's man-servant returns."

"But he may be hours."

"Then we will wait hours."

Lord Hunstanton's aching interior urged him to protest. 'Be brave!' it gurgled. And, whilst still not sufficiently courageous to defy, he nerved himself to make a suggestion.

"How would it be," he said, "if I just pushed round the corner somewhere and snatched a bite? I mean to say, you never know whether this man-servant fellow won't turn nasty. Sticking up for the young master, I mean to say. In which case, I should be twice the man with a bit of food inside me. With a dish of beans or something nicely poised within, I could do my bit."

Mrs. Waddington regarded him scornfully.

"Very well. But kindly return as soon as possible."

"Oh, I will, by Jove! Just wanted to pack away a hasty prune. I'll be back before you know I've gone."

"You will find me on the roof."

"On the roof. Right! Well, tinkey-tonk, then, for the moment." said his lordship, and pattered off down the stairs.

Mrs. Waddington mounted another flight, and came out under the broad canopy of heaven. She found herself with a choice of views, the glittering city that stretched away below and the dark windows of the Finch lair. She chose the windows and watched them narrowly.

She had been watching them for some considerable time, when suddenly the middles ones, the French windows, lit up. And, as she stepped forward, her rosiest dreams were realized. Across the yellow blind there passed a shadow which was plainly that of a young female person, no doubt of a grade of morality so low that in any other place but Washington Square it would have provoked the raised eyebrow and the sharp intake of the breath. Mrs. Waddington advanced to the window and tapped upon it imperiously.

There was a startled exclamation from within. The blind shot up, revealing a stoutish man in sober black. The next moment the window was opened, and the stoutish man popped his head out.

"Who's there?" he asked.

"I am," said Mrs. Waddington.

"Jiminy Christmas!" said the stoutish man.

II

Frederick Mullett had been in a nervous frame of mind all the afternoon, more nervous even than that of the ordinary bridegroom on his wedding day. For he had been deeply exercised for many hours past by the problems of what his bride had been up to that afternoon.

Any bridegroom would be upset if his newly-made wife left him immediately after the ceremony on the plea that she had important business to attend to and would see him later. Frederick Mullet was particularly upset. It was not so much the fact that he had planned a golden afternoon of revelry including a visit to Coney Island and had had to forgo it that disturbed him. That the delightful programme should have been cancelled was, of course, a disappointment: but what really caused him mental anguish was the speculation as to what from the view-point of a girl like Fanny constituted important business. Her reticence on this vital question had spoiled his whole day.

He was, in short, in exactly the frame of mind when a man who has married a pickpocket and has watched her go off on important business does not want to hear people tapping sharply on windows. If a mouse had crossed the floor at that moment, Frederick

Mullett would have suspected it of being a detective in disguise. He peered at Mrs. Waddington with cold horror.

"What do you want?"

"I wish to see and question the young woman who is in this apartment."

Mullett's mouth felt dry. A shiver ran down his spine.

"What young woman?"

"Come, come!"

"There isn't any young woman here."

"Tut, tut!"

"There isn't, I tell you."

Mrs. Waddington's direct mind was impatient of this attempt to deceive.

"I will make it worth your while to tell the truth," she said.

Mullett recoiled. The thought that he was being asked to sell his bride on the very day of their wedding revolted him. Not that he would have sold her at any time, of course, but being asked to do so on this day of all days made the thing seem, as Officer Garroway would have said, so peculiarly stark and poignant.

With a frenzied gesture of abhorrence he slammed the window. He switched off the light and with agonized bounds reached the kitchen, where Mrs. Frederick Mullett was standing at the range stirring a welsh rarebit.

"Hello, sweetie!" cooed his bride, looking up. "I'm just fixing the rabbit. The soup's ready."

"And we're in it." said Mullett hollowly.

"Why, whatever do you mean?"

"Fanny, where did you go this afternoon?"

"Just down into the country, dearie. I told you."

"Yes, but you didn't tell me what you did there."

"It's a secret for the present, darling. I want to keep it as a surprise. It's something to do with some money that's coming to us."

Mullett eyed her wanly.

"Fanny, were you doing a job this afternoon down there in the country?"

"Why, Freddy Mullett! What an idea!"

"Then what are the bulls here for?"

"The bulls!"

"There's a female dick out on the roof right now. And she's asking for you."

Fanny stared, round-eyed.

"Asking for me? You're crazy."

"She said 'I wish to see and question the young woman who is in this apartment.' Those were her very words."

"I'll take a peek at her."

"Don't let her see you," begged Mullett, alarmed.

"Is it likely!"

Fanny walked composedly to the sitting-room. She felt no concern. The most comforting possession in the world is, of course, a quiet conscience: but almost as good is the knowledge that you have left no tracks behind you. Fanny was positive that, on taking her departure from the Waddington home at Hempstead that afternoon, she had made a nice clean getaway and could not possibly have been followed to this place by even the most astute of female dicks. Mullett, she was convinced, must have misunderstood this woman, whoever she might be.

She drew the blind aside an inch and looked cautiously out. The intruder was standing so close to the window that it was possible even in the uncertain light to get an adequate view of her: and what she saw reassured Fanny. She returned to her anxious husband with words of cheer.

"That's no dick," she said. "I can tell 'em a mile off."

"Then who is she?"

"You'd better ask her. Listen, you go and kid her along and I'll sneak out. Then we can meet somewhere when you're through. It's a shame having to waste this nice supper, but we'll go to a restaurant. Listen, I'll be waiting for you at the Astor."

"But if she's not a dick, why not stay where we are?"

"You don't want people knowing that I'm here, do you? Suppose your boss heard of it, what would he say?"

"That's true. All right, then. Wait for me at the Astor. Though it's kind of a swell place, isn't it?"

"Well, don't you want a swell place to dine at on your wedding night?"

"You're right."

"I'm always right," said Fanny, giving her husband's cheek a loving pinch. "That's the first thing you've got to get into your head, now you're a married man."

Mullett returned to the sitting-room and switched on the light again. He felt fortified. He opened the window with something of an air.

"You were saying, ma'am?"

Mrs. Waddington was annoyed.

"What do you mean by going away and slamming the window in my face?"

"Had to see to something in the kitchen, ma'am. Is there anything I can do for you?"

"There is. I wish to know who the young woman is who is in the apartment."

"No young woman in this apartment, m'am."

Mrs. Waddington began to feel that she was approaching this matter from the wrong angle. She dipped in her bag.

"Here is a ten-dollar bill."

"Thank you, ma'am."

"I should like to ask you a few questions."

"Very good, ma'am."

"And I shall be obliged if you will answer them truthfully. How long have you been in Mr. Finch's employment?"

"About a couple of months, ma'am."

"And what is your opinion of Mr. Finch's morals?"

"They're swell."

"Nonsense. Don't attempt to deceive me. Is it not a fact that during your term of employment you have frequently admitted female visitors to this apartment?"

"Only models, ma'am."

"Models!"

"Mr. Finch is an artist."

"I am aware of it," said Mrs. Waddington with a shiver. "So you persist in your statement that Mr. Finch's mode of life is not irregular?"

"Yes, ma'am."

"Then," said Mrs. Waddington, twitching the ten-dollar bill neatly from his grasp, "it may interest you to know that I do not believe you."

"Here, hey!" cried Mullett, deeply moved. "You gave me that!"

"And I have taken it back," said Mrs. Waddington, replacing the bill in her bag. "You do not deserve it."

Mullett slammed the window, outraged in his finest feelings. For some moments he stood, fermenting. Then, seething with justifiable indignation, he switched off the light once more and went out.

He had reached the foot of the stairs, when he heard his name spoken, and, turning, was aware of a long policeman regarding him with a mild friendliness.

"Surely it is Mr. Mullett?" said the policeman.

"Hullo?" said Mullett, somewhat embarrassed. Habit is not easily overcome, and there had been a time when the mere sight of a policeman had made him tremble like a leaf.

"You remember me? My name is Garroway. We met some weeks ago."

"Why, sure," said Mullett, relieved. "You're the poet."

"It is very nice of you to say so," said Officer Garroway, simpering a little. "I am about to call at Mr. Beamish's apartment now with my latest effort. And how has the world been using you, Mr. Mullett?"

"All right. Everything hunky-dory with you?"

"Completely. Well, I must not detain you. No doubt you are on you way to some important appointment."

"That's right. Say!" said Mullett, suddenly inspired. "Are you on duty?"

"Not for the moment."

"But you wouldn't object to making a cop?"

"By no means. I am always willing—and, indeed, anxious—to make a cop."

"Well, there was a suspicious character on our roof just now. A woman. I didn't like the look of her."

"Indeed? This is extremely interesting."

"She was snooping around, looking in at our windows, and I don't think she's up to any good. You might go and ask her what she wants."

"I will attend to the matter immediately."

"If I were you, I'd pich her on suspicion. So long."

"Good night, Mr. Mullett."

Mullett, with the elation which comes from a good deed done, moved buoyantly off to his tryst. Officer Garroway, swinging his night-stick, climbed thoughtfully up the stairs.

III

Mrs. Waddington, meanwhile, had not been content with a policy of watchful waiting. She was convinced that the shadow which she had seen on the blind had been that of a young woman: and instinct told her that in an apartment near Washington Square where there was a young woman present events were not likely to remain static for any considerable length of time. No doubt the man she had questioned would have warned the young woman of her visit, and by now she had probably gone away. But she would return. And George Finch would return. It was simply a question of exercising patience.

But she must leave the roof. The roof was the first place the guilty pair would examine. If they found it empty, their fears

148

would be lulled. The strategic move indicated was to go downstairs and patrol the street. There she could stay until things began to happen again.

She was about to move away, and had already taken a step towards the door that led to the stairs when a slight creaking noise attracted her attention and she was surprised to observe the window swinging open.

It opened some six inches: then, caught by a gust of wind, closed again. A moment later, there was another creak and it moved outward once more. Apparently, in the agony of losing his ten dollars, the man had omitted to fasten the catch.

Mrs. Waddington stopped. She drew a step nearer. She grasped the handle and, pulling the window wide open, peered into the dark room. It seemed to be empty, but Mrs. Waddington was a cautious woman.

"My man!" she called.

Silence.

"I wish to speak to you."

More silence. Mrs. Waddington applied the supreme test.

"I want to return that ten-dollar bill to you."

Still silence. Mrs. Waddington was convinced. She crossed the threshold and started to feel round the walls for the switch. And, as she did so, something came to her through the throbbing darkness.

It was the smell of soup.

Mrs. Waddington stiffened like a pointing dog. Although when sitting in the vestibule of the Ritz-Carlton with Lord Hunstanton she had apparently been impervious to the fragrant scents which had so deeply affected his lordship, she was human. It was long past the hour at which she usually dined, and in the matter of sustenance she was a woman of regular habits. Already, while standing on the roof, she had been aware of certain pangs, and now she realized beyond all possibility of doubt that she was hungry. She quivered from head to foot. The smell of that soup seemed to call to the deeps of her being like the voice of an old old love.

Moving forward like one in a trance, she groped along the wall, and found herself in an open doorway that appeared to lead into a passage. Here, away from the window, the darkness was blacker than ever: but, if she could not see, she could smell, and she needed no other guide than her nose. She walked along the passage, sniffing, and, coming to another open door, found the scent so powerful that she almost reeled. It had become a composite odour now, with a strong welsh rarebit motif playing through it. Mrs. Waddington felt for the switch, pressed it down, and saw that she was in a kitchen. And there, simmering on the range, was a saucepan.

There are moments when even the most single-minded of women will allow herself to be distracted from the main object of her thoughts. Mrs Waddington had reached the stage where soup seemed to her the most important—if not the only—thing in life. She removed the lid from the saucepan, and a meaty steaminess touched her like a kiss.

She drew a deep breath. She poured some of the soup into a plate. She found a spoon. She found bread. She found salt. She found pepper.

And it was while she was lovingly sprinkling the pepper that a voice spoke behind her.

"You're pinched!" said the voice.

### IV

There were not many things which could have diverted Mrs. Waddington's attention at that moment from the plate before her. An earthquake might have done it. So might the explosion of a bomb. This voice accomplished it instantaneously. She spun round with a sharp scream, her heart feeling as if it were performing one of those eccentric South Seas dances whose popularity she had always deplored.

A policeman was standing in the doorway.

"Arrested, I should have said," added the policeman with a touch of apology. He seemed distressed that in the first excitement of this encounter he had failed to achieve the Word Beautiful.

Mrs. Waddington was not a woman often at a loss for speech, but she could find none now. She stood panting.

"I must ask you, if you will be so good," said the policeman courteously, "to come along with me. And it will avoid a great deal of unpleasantness if you come quietly."

The torpor consequent upon the disintegrating shock of this meeting began to leave Mrs. Waddington.

"I can explain!" she cried.

"You will have every opportunity of doing so at the station-house," said the policeman. "In your own interests I should advise you until then to say as little as possible. For I must warn you that in pursuance of my duty I shall take a memorandum of any statement which you may make. See, I have my notebook and pencil here in readiness."

"I was doing no harm."

"That is for the judge to decide. I need scarcely point out that your presence in this apartment is, to say the least, equivocal. You came in through a window—an action which constitutes breaking and entering,—and, furthermore, I find you in the act of purloining the property of the owner of the apartment,—to wit, soup. I am afraid I must ask you to accompany me."

Mrs. Waddington started to clasp her hands in a desperate appeal: and, doing so, was aware that some obstacle prevented this gesture.

It was suddenly borne in upon her that she was still holding the pepper-pot. And suddenly a thought came like a full-blown rose, flushing her brow.

"Ha!" she exclaimed.

"I beg your pardon?" said the policeman.

Everything in this world, every little experience which we undergo or even merely read about, is intended, philosophers tell us, to teach us something, to help to equip us for the battle of life. It was not, according to this theory, mere accident, therefore, which a few days before had caused Mrs. Waddington to read and subconsciously memorize the report that had appeared in the evening paper to which she subscribed of a burglary at the residence of a certain leading citizen of West Orange, New Jersey. The story had been sent to help her.

Of the less important details of this affair she retained no recollection: but the one salient point in connection with it came back to her now with all the force of an inspiration from above. Cornered by an indignant house-holder, she recalled, the West Orange burglar had made his escape by the simple means of throwing about two ounces of pepper in the householder's face.

What this humble, probably uneducated, man had been able to achieve was surely not beyond the powers of a woman like herself, —the honorary president of twenty-three charitable societies and a well-known lecturer on the upbringing of infants. Turning coyly sideways, she began to unscrew the top of the pot.

"You will understand," said the policeman deprecatingly, "that this is extremely unpleasant for me . . ."

He was perfectly right. Unpleasant, he realized a moment later, was the exact adjective which the most punctilious stylist would have chosen. For suddenly the universe seemed to dissolve in one great cloud-burst of pepper. Pepper tickled his mouth: pepper filled his nose: pepper strayed into his eyes and caressed his Adam's apple. For an instant he writhed blindly: then, clutching at the table for support, he began to sneeze.

With the sound of those titanic sneezes ringing in her ears, Mrs. Waddington bumped her way through the darkness till she came to the open window: then, galloping across the roof, hurled herself down the fire-escape.

V

The only thing in the nature of a policy or plan of action which Mrs. Waddington had had when making for the fire-escape had been a general desire to be as far away as possible from the representative of the Law when he stopped sneezing and opened his eyes and began to look around him for his assailant. But, as her feet touched the first rungs, more definite schemes began to shape themselves. Fire-escapes, she knew, led, if followed long enough, to the ground: and she decided to climb to safety down this one. It was only when she had descended as far as the ninth floor that, glancing below her, she discovered that this particular fire-escape terminated not, as she had supposed, in some back-alley, but in the gaily-lighted out-door premises of a restaurant, half the tables of which were already filled.

This sight gave her pause. In fact, to be accurate, it froze her stiff. Nor was her agitation without reason. Those of the readers of this chronicle who have ever thrown pepper in a policeman's face, and skimmed away down a fire-escape, are aware that fire-escapes, considered as a refuge, have the defect of being uncomfortably exposed to view. At any moment, felt Mrs. Waddington, the policeman might come to the edge of the roof and look down; and to deceive him into supposing that she was merely a dust-bin or a milk-bottle was, she knew, beyond her histrionic powers.

The instinct of self-preservation not only sharpens the wits, but at the same time dulls the moral sensibility. It was so with Mrs. Waddington now. Her quickened intelligence perceived in a flash that if she climbed in through the window outside which she was now standing she would be safe from scrutiny: and her blunted moral sense refused to consider the fact that such an action—amounting, as it did, to what her policeman playmate had called breaking and entering—would be most reprehensible. Besides, she had broken and entered one apartment already that night, and the appetite grows by what it feeds on. Some ten seconds later, therefore, Mrs. Waddington was once more groping through the darkness of somebody else's dwelling-place.

A well-defined scent of grease, damp towels and old cabbages told her that the room through which she was creeping was a kitchen: but the blackness was so uniform that she could see nothing of her surroundings. The only thing she was able to say definitely of this kitchen at the moment was that it contained a broom. This she knew because she had just stepped on the end of it, and the handle had shot up and struck her very painfully on the forehead.

"Ouch!" cried Mrs. Waddington.

She had not intended to express any verbal comment on the incident, for those who creep at night through other people's kitchens must be silent and wary: but the sudden agony was so keen that she could not refrain from comment. And to her horror she found that her cry had been heard. There came through the darkness a curious noise like the drawing of a cork, and then somebody spoke.

"Who are you?" said an unpleasant, guttural voice.

Mrs. Waddington stopped, paralysed. She would not, in the circumstances, have heard with any real pleasure the most musical of speech: but a soft, sympathetic utterance would undoubtedly have afflicted her with a shade less of anguish and alarm. This voice was the voice of one without human pity: a grating, malevolent voice; a voice that set Mrs. Waddington thinking quiveringly in headlines:

" 'SOCIETY LEADER FOUND SLAIN IN KITCHEN.' "

"Who are you?"

" 'BODY DISMEMBERED BENEATH SINK.' "

"Who are you?"

" 'SEVERED HEAD LEADS TRACKERS TO DEATHSPOT.' "

"Who are you?"

Mrs. Waddington gulped.

"I am Mrs. Sigsbee H. Waddington," she faltered. And it would have amazed Sigsbee H., had he heard her, to discover that it was possible for her to speak with such a winning meekness.

"Who are you?"

"Mrs. Sigsbee H. Waddington, of East Seventy-Ninth Street and Hempstead, Long Island. I must apologize for the apparent strangeness of my conduct in . . ."

"Who are you?"

Annoyance began to compete with Mrs. Waddington's terror. Deaf persons had always irritated her, for like so many women of an impatient and masterful turn of mind, she was of opinion that they could hear perfectly well if they took the trouble. She raised her voice and answered with a certain stiffness.

"I have already informed you that I am Mrs. Sigsbee H. Waddington . . ."

"Have a nut," said the voice, changing the subject.

Mrs. Waddington's teeth came together with a sharp click. All the other emotions which had been afflicting her passed abruptly away, to be succeeded by a cold fury. Few things are more mortifying to a proud woman than the discovery that she had been wasting her time being respectful to a parrot: and only her inability to locate the bird in the surrounding blackness prevented a rather unpleasant brawl. Had she been able to come to grips with it, Mrs. Waddington at that moment would undoubtedly have done the parrot no good whatever.

"Brrh!" she exclaimed, expressing her indignation as effectively as was possible by mere speech: and, ignoring the other's request—in the circumstances, ill-timed and tasteless—that she should stop and scratch its head, she pushed forward in search of the door.

Reaction had left her almost calm. The trepidation of a few moments back had vanished; and she advanced now in a brisk and business-like way. She found the door and opened it. There was more darkness beyond, but an uncurtained window gave sufficient light for her to see that she was in a sitting-room. Across one corner of this room lay a high-backed chesterfield. In another corner stood a pedestal desk. And about the soft carpet there were distributed easy chairs in any one of which Mrs. Waddington, had the conditions been different, would have been delighted to sit and rest.

But, though she had been on her feet some considerable time now and was not a woman who enjoyed standing, prudence warned her that the temptation to relax must be resisted. It was a moment for action, not repose. She turned to the door which presumably led into the front hall and thence to the stairs and safety: and had just opened it when there came the click of a turning key.

Mrs. Waddington acted swiftly. The strange calm which had been upon her dissolved into a panic fear. She darted back into the sitting-room: and, taking the chesterfield in an inspired bound, sank down behind it and tried not to snort.

"Been waiting long?" asked some person unseen, switching on the light and addressing an invisible companion.

The voice was strange to Mrs. Waddington: but about the one that replied to it there was something so fruitily familiar that she stiffened where she lay, scarcely able to credit her senses. For it was the voice of Ferris, her butler. And Ferris, if the truth was in him, should by now have been at the sick-bed of a relative.

"Some little time, sir, but it has caused me no inconvenience."

"What did you want to see me about?"

"I am addressing Mr. Lancelot Biffen, the editor-in-chief of 'Town Gossip'?"

"Yes. Talk quick. I've got to go out again in a minute."

"I understand, Mr. Biffen, that 'Town Gossip' is glad to receive and pay a substantial remuneration for items of interest concerning those prominent in New York society. I have such an item."

"Who's it about?"

"My employer,—Mrs. Sigsbee H. Waddington, sir."

"What's she been doing?"

"It is a long story . . ."

"Then I haven't time to listen to it."

"It concerns the sensational interruption to the marriage of Mrs. Waddington's step-daughter . . ."

"Didn't the wedding come off, then?"

"No, sir. And the circumstances which prevented it . . ."

Mr. Biffen uttered an exclamation. He had apparently looked at his watch and been dismayed by the flight of time.

"I must run," he said. "I've a date at the Algonquin in a quarter of an hour. Come and have a talk to me at the office to-morrow."

"I fear that will be impossible, sir, owing to . . ."

"Then, see here. Have you ever done any writing?"

"Yes, sir. At Little-Seeping-in-the-Wold I frequently contributed short articles to the parish magazine. The vicar spoke highly of them."

"Then sit down and write the thing out. Use your own words and I'll polish it up later. I'll be back in an hour, if you want to wait."

"Very good, sir. And the remuneration?"

"We'll talk about that later."

"Very good, sir."

Mr. Biffen left the room. There followed a confused noise,—apparently from his bedroom, in which he seemed to be searching for something. Then the front door slammed, and quiet descended upon the apartment.

Mrs. Waddington continued to crouch behind her chesterfield. There had been a moment, immediately after the departure of Mr. Biffen, when she had half risen with the intention of confronting her traitorous butler and informing him that he had ceased to be in her employment. But second thoughts had held her back. Gratifying as it would undoubtedly be to pop her head up over the back of the sofa and watch the man cower beneath her eye, the situation, she realized, was too complicated to permit such a procedure. She remained where she was, and whiled away the time by trying out methods to relieve the cramp from which her lower limbs had already begun to suffer.

From the direction of the desk came the soft cratching of pen on paper. Ferris was plainly making quite a job of it, putting all his energies into his task. He seemed to be one of those writers, like Flaubert, who spared no pains in the quest for perfect clarity and are prepared to correct and re-correct indefinitely till their artist-souls are satisfied. It seemed to Mrs. Waddington as though her vigil was to go on for ever.

But in a bustling city like New York it is rarely that the artist is permittted to concentrate for long without interruption. A telephone-bell broke raspingly upon the stillness: and the first sensation of pleasure which Mrs. Waddington had experienced for a very long time came to her as she realized that the instrument was ringing in the passage outside and not in the room. With something of the wild joy which reprieved prisoners feel at the announcement of release, she heard the butler rise. And presently there came from a distance his measured voice informing some unseen inquirer that Mr. Biffen was not at home.

Mrs. Waddington rose from her form. She had about twenty seconds in which to act, and she wasted none of them. By the time Ferris had returned and was once more engrossed in his literary composition, she was in the kitchen.

She stood by the window, looking out at the fire-escape. Surely by this time, she felt, it would be safe to climb once more up to the roof. She decided to count three hundred very slowly and risk it.

# CHAPTER FIFTEEN

MOLLY and Sigsbee Horatio, the latter muttering 'Gallagher! Gallagher! Gallagher!' to himself in order that the magic name should not again escape him, had started out in the two-seater about a quarter of an hour after the departure of Mrs. Waddinton's Hispano-Suiza. Half-way to New York, however, a blow-out had arrested their progress: and the inability of Sigsbee H. to make a quick job of fixing the spare wheel had further delayed them. It was not, therefore, till almost at the exact moment when Mrs. Waddington was committing the rash act which had so discomposed Officer Garroway, that Molly, having dropped her father at Police Headquarters, arrived at the entrance of the Sheridan.

She hurried up the stairs and rang George's front-door bell. For awhile it seemed as if her ringing was to meet with no response: then, after some minutes, footsteps made themselves heard coming along the passage. The door opened, and Molly found herself gazing into the inflamed eyes of a policeman.

She looked at him with surprise. She had never seen him before, and she rather felt that she would have preferred not to see him now: for he was far from being a pleasing sight. His nose, ears and eyes were a vivid red: and his straggling hair dripped wetly on to the floor. With the object of diminishing the agony caused by the pepper, Officer Garroway had for some time been holding his head under the tap in the kitchen: and he now looked exactly like the body which had been found after several days in the river. The one small point that differentiated him from a corpse was the fact that he was sneezing.

"What are you doing here?" exclaimed Molly.

"Achoo!" replied Officer Garroway.

"What?" said Molly.

The policeman, with a nobility which should have earned him promotion, checked another sneeze.

"There has been an outrage," he said.

"Mr. Finch has not been hurt? cried Molly, alarmed.

"Mr. Finch hasn't. I have."

"Who are you?"

"My name is Gar-hosh-hoosh-hish."

"What?"

"Gar-ish-wash-WUSH . . . Garroway," said the policeman, becoming calmer.

"Where is Mr. Finch?"

"I could not say, miss."

"Have you a cold?"

"No, miss, not a ker-osh-wosh-osh. A woman threw pepper in my face."

"You ought not to know such women," said Molly severely.

The injustice of this stung Officer Garroway.

"I did no know her socially. I was arresting her."

"Oh, I see."

"I found her burgling this apartment."

"Good gracious!"

"And when I informed her that I was compelled to take her into custody, she threw pepper in my face and escaped."

"You poor man!"

"Thank you, miss," said Officer Garroway gratefully. A man can do with a bit of sympathy on these occasions, nor is such sympathy rendered less agreeable by the fact that the one who offers it is young and charming and gazes at you with large, melting blue eyes. It was at this point that Officer Garroway began for the first time to be aware of a distinct improvement in his condition.

"Can I get you anything?" said Molly.

Officer Garroway shook his head wistfully.

"It's against the law, miss, now. In fact, I am to be one of a *posse* this very night that is to raid a restaurant which supplies the stuff."

"I meant something from a drug-store. Some ointment or something."

"It is extremely kind of you, miss, but I could not dream of putting you to so much trouble. I will look in at a drug-store on my way to the station-house. I fear I must leave you now, as I have to go and drish-hosh-hish."

"What?"

"Dress, miss."

"But you are dressed."

"For the purposes of the raid to which I alluded it is necessary for our *posse* to put on full evening drah-woosh. In order to deceive the staff of the rish-wish-wosh, and lull them into a false security. It would never do, you see, for us to go there in our uniforms. That would put them on their guard."

"How exciting! What restaurant are you raiding?"

Officer Garroway hesitated.

"Well, miss, it is in the nature of an official secret, of course, but on the understanding that you will let it go no further, the rosh-ow-wush is the Purple Chicken, just round the corner. I will wish you good night, miss, as I really must be off."

"But wait a moment. I came here to meet Mr. Finch. Have you seen anything of him?"

"No, miss. Nobody has visited the apartment while I have been there."

"Oh, then I'll wait. Good night. I hope you will feel better soon."

"I feel better already, miss," said Officer Garroway gallantly, "thanks to your kind sympathy. Good nish-nosh, miss."

Molly went out on to the roof, and stood there gazing over the million twinkling lights of the city. At this height the voice of New York sank to a murmur, and the air was sweet and cool. Little breezes rustled in the potted shrubs over which Mullett was wont to watch with such sedulous care, and a half-moon was shining in rather a deprecating way, as if conscious of not being at its best in such surroundings. For, like Sigsbee H. Waddington (now speeding towards his third Gallagher), the moon, really to express itself, needs the great open spaces.

Molly, however, found nothing to criticize in that pale silver glow. She felt a proprietary interest in the moon. It was her own private and personal moon, and should have been shining in through the windows of the drawing-room of the train that bore her away on her wedding-journey. That that journey had been postponed was in no way the fault of the moon: and, gazing up at it, she tried to convey by her manner her appreciation of the fact.

It was at this point that a strangled exclamation broke the stillness: and, turning, she perceived George Finch.

George Finch stood in the moonlight, staring dumbly. Although what he saw before him had all the appearance of being Molly, and though a rash and irreflective observer would no doubt have said that it was Molly, it was so utterly impossible that she could really be there that he concluded that he was suffering from an hallucination. The nervous strain of the exacting day through which he had passed had reduced him, he perceived, to the condition of those dying travellers in the desert who see mirages. And so he remained where he was, not daring to approach closer: for he knew that if you touch people in dreams they vanish.

But Molly was of a more practical turn of mind. She had come twenty miles to see George. She had waited for George for what seemed several hours. And here George was. She did the sensible thing. Uttering a little squeak of rapture, she ran at him like a rabbit.

"Georgie! My pet!"

One lives and learns. George found that he had been all wrong, and that his preconceived ideas about dreams and what could and could not happen in them must be revised. For, so far from vanishing when touched, his wraith appeared to be growing more substantial every moment.

He shut his eyes and kissed her tentatively. He opened his eyes. She was still there.

"Is it really you?" said George.

"Yes, really me."

"But how . . . what . . . ?"

It was borne in upon George—for he was a young man of good average intelligence—that he was spoiling a golden moment with unseasonable chatter. This was no time for talk. He talked, accordingly, no more: and there was silence on the roof. The moon looked down, well pleased. There is not much of interest for a moon to look at in a large city, and this was the sort of thing it liked best,—the only sort of thing, if you came right down to it, that made it worth a moon's while to shine at all.

George clung to Molly, and Molly clung to George, like two shipwrecked survivors who have come together on a wave-swept beach. And the world moved on, forgotten.

But the world will never allow itself to be forgotten for long. Suddenly George broke away with an exclamation. He ran to the wall and looked over.

"What's the matter?"

George returned, reassured. His concern had been groundless.

"I thought I saw some one on the fire-escape, darling."

"On the fire-escape? Why, who could it be?"

"I thought it might be the man who has the apartment on the floor below. A ghastly, sneaking, snooping fellow named Lancelot Biffen. I've known him to climb up before. He's the editor of 'Town Gossip,' the last person we want to have watching us."

Molly uttered a cry of alarm.

"You're sure he wasn't there?"

"Quite sure."

"It would be awful if anyone saw me here."

George silently cursed the too vivid imagination which had led him to suppose that he had seen a dark form outlined against the summer sky. He had spoiled the golden moment, and it could not be recaptured.

"Don't be afraid, dear," he said. "Even if he had seen you, he would never have guessed who you were."

"You mean he would naturally expect to find you up here kissing some girl?"

George was in the state of mind when a man cannot be quite sure what his words mean, if anything: but so positive was he that he did not mean this that he got his tongue tied in a knot trying to say so in three different ways simultaneously.

"Well, after what happened this afternoon . . ." said Molly.

She drew away. She was not normally an unkind girl, but the impulse of the female of the species to torture the man it loves is well-known. Women may be a ministering angel when pain and anguish wring the brow: but, if at other times she sees a chance to prod the loved one and watch him squirm, she hates to miss it.

George's tongue appeared to him to be now in the sort of condition a ball of wool is in after a kitten has been playing with it. With a supreme effort he contrived to straighten out a few of the major kinks, just sufficient to render speech possible.

"I swear to you," began George, going so far in his emotion as to raise a passionate fist towards the moon.

Molly gurgled delightedly. She loved this young man most when he looked funny: and he had seldom looked funnier than now.

"I swear to you on my solemn oath that I had never seen that infernal girl before in my life."

"She seemed to know you so well."

"She was a perfect, complete, total, utter and absolute stranger."

"Are you sure? Perhaps you had simply forgotten all about her."

"I swear it," said George, and only just stopped himself from adding 'by yonder moon.' "If you want to know what I think . . ."

"Oh, I do."

"I believe she was mad. Stark, staring mad."

Molly decided that the anguish had lasted long enough. A girl has to judge these things to a nicety. Sufficient agony is good for a man, stimulating his mind and keeping him bright and alert: but too much is too much.

"Poor old Georgie!" she said soothingly. "You don't really suppose for a moment that I believed a word of what she said, do you?"

"What! You didn't?"

"Of course I didn't."

"Molly," said George, weighing his words, "you are without exception the dearest, sweetest, loveliest, most perfect and angelic thing that ever lived."

"I know. Aren't you lucky?"

"You saw at once that the girl was mad, didn't you? You realized immediately that she was suffering from some sort of obsession, poor soul, which made her . . ."

"No, I didn't. I couldn't think what it was all about at first, and then father came in and said that my pearl necklace had disappeared, and I understood."

"Your pearl necklace? Disappeared?"

"She stole it. She was a thief. Don't you see? It was really awfully clever. She couldn't have got it any other way. But when she burst in and said all those things about you, naturally she took everybody's attention off the wedding-presents. And then she pretended to faint on the table and just snapped the necklace up and rushed out, and nobody guessed what had happened."

George drew in a whistling breath. His fists clenched. He stared coldly at one of the potted shrubs as if it had done him a personal injury.

"If ever I meet that girl . . ."

Molly laughed.

"Mother still insists that you had known her before and that the story she told was true and that she only took the necklace as an afterthought. Isn't she funny!"

"Funny," said George heavily, "is not the word. She is one long scream from the rise of the curtain, and ought to be beaten over the head with a blackjack. If you want my candid and considered opinion of that zymotic scourge who has contrived to hook herself on to your family in the capacity of step-mother to you and general mischief-maker to the rest of the world, let me begin by saying . . . However, there is no time to go into that now."

"No, there isn't. I must be getting back."

"Oh no!"

"Yes. I must go home and pack."

"Pack?"

"Just a suit-case."

The universe reeled about George.

"Do you mean you're going away?" he quavered.

"Yes. To-morrow."

"Oh, heavens! For long?"

"For ever. With you."

"With . . .?"

"Of course. Don't you understand? I'm going home now to pack a suit-case. Then I'll drive back to New York and stay the night at an hotel, and to-morrow we'll be married early in the morning, and in the afternoon we'll go off together, all alone, miles and miles from everybody."

"Molly!"

"Look at that moon. About now it ought to have been shining into our drawing-room on the train."

"Yes."

"Well, there will be just as good a moon to-morrow night."

George moistened his lips. Something seemed to be tickling his nose, and inside his chest a curious growth had begun to swell, rendering breathing difficult.

"And half an hour ago," he said, "I thought I would never see you again."

"Come down and put me in the car," said Molly briskly. "I left it at the door."

They descended the stairs. Owing to the eccentricity of the elevator, George had frequently had to go up and down these stairs before: but it was only now that he noticed for the first time a peculiarity about them that made them different from the stairs of every other apartment-house he had visited. They were, he observed, hedged about with roses and honeysuckle, and many more birds were singing on them than you would expect in an apartment-house. Odd. And yet, as he immediately realized all perfectly in order.

Molly climbed into the two-seater: and George mentioned a point which had presented itself to him.

"I don't see why you need hurry off like this."

"I do. I've got to pack and get away before mother gets home."

"Is that blas . . . is your step-mother in New York?"

"Yes. She came in to see the police."

Until this moment George had been looking on New York as something rather out of the common run of cities—he particularly liked the way those violets were sprouting up through the flag-stones: but on receipt of this information he found that it had lost a little of its charm.

"Oh, she's in New York, is she?"

"Probably on her way home by now."

"You don't think there's time for us to go and have a little dinner somewhere? Just a cosy little dinner at some quiet little restaurant?"

"Good gracious, no! I'm running it very fine as it is." She looked at him closely. "But, Georgie darling, you're starving. I can see it. You're quite pale and worn-out. When did you last have anything to eat?"

"Eat? Eat? I don't remember."

"What did you do after that business this afternoon?"

"I—well, I walked around for awhile. And then I hung about in the bushes for awhile, hoping you would come out. And then—I believe I went to the station and took a train or something."

"You poor darling! Go and eat something at once."

"Why can't I come back to Hempstead with you?"

"Because you can't."

"What hotel will you go to to-night?"

"I don't know. But I'll come and see you for a minute before I go there."

"What, here? You'll come here?"

"Yes."

"You'll come back here?"

"Yes."

"You promise?"

"Yes, if you will go and have some dinner. You look perfectly ghastly."

"Dinner? All right, I'll have some."

"Mind you do. If you haven't by the time I get back, I'll go straight home again and never marry you as long as I live. Good-bye, darling, I must be off."

The two-seater moved away and turned into Washington Square. George stood looking after it long after there was nothing to look at but empty street. Then he started off, like some knight of old on a quest commanded by his lady, to get the dinner on which she had so strongly insisted. She had been wrong, of course, in telling him to go and dine: for what he wanted to do and what any good doctor would have recommended him to do was to return to the roof and gaze at the moon. But her lightest wish was law.

Where could he go most quickly and get the repulsive task done with the minimum waste of time?

The Purple Chicken. It was just round the corner, and a resolute man if he stuck to their *prix fixe* table-d'hote at one-dollar-fifty, could shovel a meal into himself in about ten minutes —which was not long to ask the moon to wait.

Besides, at the Purple Chicken you could get 'it' if they knew you. And George, though an abstemious young man, felt that 'it' was just what at the moment he most required. On an occasion like this he ought, of course, to sip golden nectar from rare old crystal: but, failing that, synthetic whisky served in a coffee-pot was perhaps the next best thing.

## CHAPTER SIXTEEN

### I

THE Purple Chicken seemed to be having a big night. The room opening on to the street, when George reached it, was so crowded that there was no chance of getting a table. He passed through, hoping to find a resting-place in the open-air section which lay beyond: and was struck, as he walked, by the extraordinarily fine physique of many of the diners.

As a rule, the Purple Chicken catered for the intelligentsia of the neighbourhood, and these did not run to thews and sinews. On most nights in the week you would find the tables occupied by wispy poets and slender futurist painters: but now, though these were present in great numbers they were supplemented by quite a sprinkling of granite-faced men with knobby shoulders and protruding jaws. George came to the conclusion that a convention from one of the outlying States must be in town and that these men were members of it, bent upon seeing Bohemia.

He did not, however, waste a great deal of time in speculation on this matter, for, stirred by the actual presence of food, he had begun now to realize that Molly had been right, as women always are, and that, while his whole higher self cried out for the moon, his lower self was almost equally as insistent on taking in supplies. And at this particular restaurant it was happily possible to satisfy both selves simultaneously: for there, as he stepped into what the management called the garden—a flagged back-yard dotted with tables—was the moon, all present and correct, and there, also, were waiters waiting to supply the *prix fixe* table-d'hôte at one-dollar-fifty.

It seemed to George the neatest possible combination: and his only anxiety now was with regard to the securing of a seat. At first glance it appeared that every table was occupied.

This conjecture was confirmed by a second glance. But, though all the other tables had their full quota, there was one, standing beside the Sheridan's back wall and within a few feet of its fire-escape, that was in the possession of a single diner. This diner George approached, making his expression as winning as possible. He did not, as a rule, enjoy sharing a table with a stranger, but as an alternative to going away and trudging round in search of another restaurant it seemed a good plan now.

"Excuse me, sir," said George, "would you mind if I came to this table?"

The other looked up from the *poulet rôti aux pommes de terre* and *salade Bruxelloise* which had been engaging his attention. He was plainly one of the convention from the outlying State, if physique could be taken as a guide. He spread upwards from the table like a circus giant and the hands which gripped the knife and fork had that same spaciousness which George had noted in the diners in the other room. Only as to the eyes did this man differ from his fellows. They had had eyes of a peculiarly steely and unfriendly type, the sort of eyes which a motorist instinctively associates with traffic-policemen and a professional thief with professional detectives. This man's gaze was mild and friendly, and his eyes would have been attractive but for the redness of their rims and the generally inflamed look which they had.

"By no means, sir," he replied to George's polite query.

"Place very crowded to-night."

"Extremely."

"Then, if you won't mind, I'll sit here."

"Delighted," said the other.

George looked round for a waiter and found one at his elbow. However crowded the Purple Chicken might be, its staff never neglected the old habitué; and it had had the benefit of George's regular custom for many months.

"Good evening, sare," said the waiter, smiling the smile which had once broken hearts in Assisi.

"Good evening, Guiseppe," said George. "I'll take the dinner."

"Yes, sare. Sick or glear zoop?"

"Sick. Crowded to-night, Guiseppe."

"Yes, sare. Lots of guys here to-night. Big business."

"The waiter appears to know you," said George's companion.

"Oh, yes," said George, "I'm in here all the time."

"Ah," said the other, thoughtfully.

The soup arrived, and George set about it with a willing spoon. His companion became hideously involved with spaghetti.

"This your first visit to New York?" asked George, after an interval.

"No, indeed, sir. I live in New York."

"Oh, I thought you were up from the country."

"No, sir. I live right here in New York."

A curious idea that he had seen this fellow before somewhere came over George. Yes, at some time and in some place he could have sworn that he had gazed upon that long body, that prominent Adam's apple, and that gentle expanse of face. He searched his memory. Nothing stirred.

"I have an odd feeling that we have met before," he said.

"I was thinking just the same myself," replied the other.

"My name is Finch."

"Mine is Cabot. Delancy Cabot."

George shook his head.

"I don't remember the name."

"Yours is curiously familiar. I have heard it before, but cannot think when."

"Do you live in Greenwich Village?"

"Somewhat further up-town. And you?"

"I live in the apartment on top of this building here at the back of us."

A sudden light that seemed that of recognition came into the other's face. George observed it.

"Have you remembered where we met?"

"No, sir. No, indeed," said the other hastily. "It has entirely escaped me." He took a sip of ice-water. "I recall, however, that you are an artist."

"That's right. You are not one, by any chance?"

"I am a poet."

"A poet?" George tried to conceal his somewhat natural surprise. "Where does your stuff appear mostly?"

"I have published nothing as yet, Mr. Finch," replied the other sadly.

"Tough luck. I have never sold a picture."

"Too bad."

They gazed at one another with kindly eyes, two fellow-sufferers from the public's lack of taste. Guiseppe appeared, bearing deep-dish apple-pie in one hand, *poulet rôti* in the other.

"Guiseppe," said George.

"Sare?"

George bent his lips towards the waiter's attentive ear.

"Bzz . . . Bzz . . . Bzz . . ." said George.

"Yes, sare. Very good, sare. In one moment, sare."

George leaned back contentedly. Then it occurred to him that he had been a little remiss. He was not actually this red-eyed man's host, but they had fraternized and they both knew what it was to toil at their respective arts without encouragement or appreciation.

"Perhaps you will join me?" he said.

"Join you, sir?"

"In a high-ball. Guiseppe has gone to get me one."

"Indeed? Is it possible to obtain alcoholic refreshment in this restaurant?"

"You can always get if they know you."

"But surely it is against the law?"

"Ha, ha!" laughed George. He liked this pleasant, whimsical fellow. "Ha, ha! Deuced good!"

He looked at him with that genial bonhomie with which one looks at a stranger in whom one has discovered a sly sense of humour. And, looking, he suddenly congealed.

Stranger?

"Great Scott!" ejaculated George.

"Sir?"

"Nothing, nothing."

Memory, though loitering by the way, had reached its goal at last. The man was no stranger. George recollected now where he had seen him before—on the roof of the Sheridan, when the other, clad in policeman's uniform, had warned him of the deplorable past of Frederick Mullett. The man was a cop, and under his very eyes, red rims and all, he had just ordered a high-ball.

George gave a feverish laugh.

"I was only kidding, of course," he said.

"Kidding, Mr. Finch?"

"When I said that you could get it here. You can't, of course. What Guiseppe is bringing me is a ginger-ale."

"Indeed?"

"And my name isn't Finch," babbled George. "It —it is—er— Briskett. And I don't live in that apartment up there, I live in . . ."

He was aware of Guiseppe at his side. And Guiseppe was being unspeakably furtive and conspiratorial with a long glass and a coffee-pot. He looked like one of the executive staff of the Black Hand plotting against the public weal.

"Is that my ginger-ale?" twittered George. "My ginger-ale, is that what you've got there?"

"Yes, sare. Your ginger-ale. Your ginger-ale, Mr. Feench, ha, ha, ha! You are vairy fonny gentleman," said Guiseppe approvingly.

George could have kicked the man. If this was what the modern Italian was like, no wonder the country had had to have a dictatorship.

"Take it away," he said, quivering. "I don't want it in a coffee-pot."

"We always sairve the whisky in the coffee-pot, Mr. Feench. You know that."

Across the table George was appalled by a sinister sight. The man opposite was rising. Yards and yards of him were beginning to uncoil, and on his face there was a strange look of determination and menace.

"You're . . ."

George knew what the next word would have been. It would have been the verb 'pinched.' But it was never uttered. With a sudden frenzy, George Finch acted. He was not normally a man of violence, but there are occasions when violence and nothing but violence will meet the case. There flashed through his mind a vision of what would be, did he not act with promptitude and despatch. He would be arrested, hauled to jail, immured in a dungeon-cell. And Molly would come back and find no one there to welcome her and—what was even worse—no one to marry her on the morrow.

George did not hesitate. Seizing the table-cloth, he swept it off in a hideous whirl of apple-pie, ice water, bread, potatoes, salad and *poulet rôti*. He raised it on high, like a *retarius* in the arena, and brought it down in an enveloping mass on the policeman's head. Interested cries arose on all sides. The Purple Chicken was one of those jolly, informal restaurants in which a spirit of clean Bohemian fun is the prevailing note, but even in the Purple Chicken occurrences like this were unusual and calculated to excite remark. Four diners laughed happily, a fifth exclaimed "Hot pazazas!" and a sixth said 'Well, would you look at that!"

The New York police are not quitters. They may be down, but they are never out. A clutching hand emerged from the table-cloth and gripped George's shoulder. Another clutching hand was groping about not far from his collar. The fingers of the first hand fastened their hold.

George was not in the frame of mind to be tolerant of this sort of thing. He hit out and smote something solid.

"Casta dimura salve e pura! 'At-a-boy! Soak him again," said

Guiseppe, the waiter, convinced now that the man in the table-cloth was one who had not the best interests of the Purple Chicken at heart.

George did so. The table-cloth became still more agitated. The hand fell from his shoulder.

At that moment there was a confused noise of shouting from the inner room, and all the lights went out.

George would not have had it otherwise. Darkness just suited him. He leaped for the fire-escape and climbed up it with as great a celerity as Mrs. Waddington, some little time before, had used in climbing down. He reached the roof and paused for an instant, listening to the tumult below. Then, hearing through the din the sound of somebody climbing, he ran to the sleeping-porch and dived beneath the bed. To seek refuge in his apartment was, he realized, useless. That would be the first place the pursuer would draw.

He lay there, breathless. Footsteps came to the door. The door opened, and the light was switched on.

II

In supposing that the person or persons whom he had heard climbing up the fire-escape were in pursuit of himself, George Finch had made a pardonable error. Various circumstances had combined to render his departure from the Purple Chicken unobserved.

In the first place, just as Officer Garroway was on the point of releasing his head from the folds of the table-cloth, Guiseppe, with a loyalty to his employers which it would be difficult to over-praise, hit him in the eye with the coffee-pot. This had once more confused the policeman's outlook, and by the time he was able to think clearly again the lights went out.

Simultaneously, the moon, naturally on George's side and anxious to do all that it could to help, went behind a thick cloud and stayed there. No human eye, therefore, had witnessed the young man's climb for life.

The persons whom he had heard on the fire-escape were a couple who, like himself, had no object in mind other than a swift removal of themselves from the danger-zone. And so far were they from being hostile to George that each, had they seen him, would have urged him on and wished him luck. For one of them was Madame Eulalie and the other no less a man than J. Hamilton Beamish in person.

Hamilton Beamish, escorting his bride-to-be, had arrived at the Purple Chicken a few minutes after George, and, like George had found the place crowded to its last table. But unlike George, he had not meekly accepted this situation as unalterable. Exerting the full force of his majestic personality, he had caused an extra table to appear, to be set, and to be placed in the fairway at the spot where the indoor restaurant joined the outdoor annex.

It was a position which at first had seemed to have drawbacks. The waiters who passed at frequent intervals were compelled to bump into Mr. Beamish's chair, which is always unpleasant when one is trying to talk to the girl one loves. But the time was to arrive when its drawbacks were lost sight of in the contemplation of its strategic advantages. At the moment when the raid may be said to have formally opened, Hamilton Beamish was helping the girl of his heart to what the management had assured him was champagne. He was interrupted in this kindly action by a large hand placed heavily on his shoulder and a gruff voice which informed him that he was under arrest.

Whether Hamilton Beamish would have pursued George Finch's spirited policy of enveloping the man in the table-cloth and thereafter plugging him in the eye, will never be known: for the necessity for such a procedure was removed by the sudden extinction of the lights: and it was at this point that the advantage of being in that particular spot became apparent.

From the table to the fire-escape was but a few steps: and Hamilton Beamish, seizing his fiancée by the hand, dragged her thither and, placing her foot on the lowest step, gave her an upward boost which left no room for misapprehension. A moment later, Madame Eulalie was hurrying roofwards with Hamilton Beamish in close attendance.

They stood together at the end of their journey, looking down. The lights of the Purple Chicken were still out, and from the darkness there rose a confused noise indicative of certain persons unknown being rather rough with certain other persons unknown. It seemed to Madame Eulalie that she and her mate were well out of it, and she said so.

"I never realized before what a splendid man you were to have by one in an emergency, Jimmy dear," she said. "Anything slicker than the way you scooped us out of that place I never saw. You must have had lots and lots of practice."

Hamilton Beamish was passing a handkerchief over his dome-like forehead. The night was warm, and the going had been fast.

"I shall never forgive myself," he said, "for exposing you to such an experience."

"Oh, but I enjoyed it."

"Well, all has ended well, thank goodness . . ."

"But has it?" interrupted Madame Eulalie.

"What do you mean?"

She pointed downwards.

"There's somebody coming up!"

"You're right."

"What shall we do? Go out by the stairs?"

Hamilton Beamish shook his head.

"In all probability they will be guarding the entrance."

"Then what?"

It is at moments like these that the big brain really tells. An ordinary man might have been non-plussed. Certainly, he would have had to waste priceless moments in thought. Hamilton Beamish, with one flash of his giant mind, had the problem neatly solved in four and a quarter seconds.

He took his bride-to-be by the arm and turned her round.

"Look."

"Where?"

"There!"

"Which?"

"That."

"What?" Bewilderment was limned upon the girl's fair face. "I don't understand. What do you want me to specially loook at?"

"At what do you want me specially to look," corrected Hamilton Beamish mechanically. He drew her across the roof. "You see that summer-house thing? It is George Finch's open-air sleeping porch. Go in, shut the door, switch on the light . . ."

"But . . ."

"But . . ."

" . . . and remove a portion of your clothes."

"What!"

"And if anybody comes tell him that George Finch rented you the apartment and that you are dressing to go out to dinner. I, meanwhile, will go down to my apartment and will come up in a few minutes to see if you are ready to be taken out to dine." Pardonable pride so overcame Hamilton Beamish that he discarded the English Pure and relapsed into the argot of the proletariat. "Is that a cracker-jack?" he demanded with gleaming eyes. "Is that a wam? Am I the bozo with the big bean or am I not?"

The girl eyed him worshippingly. One of the consolations which we men of intellect have is that, when things come to a crisis, what captures the female heart is brains. Women may permit themselves in times of peace to stray after Sheiks and look languishingly at lizards whose only claim to admiration is that they can do the first three steps of the Charleston: but let matters go wrong; let some sudden peril threaten; and who then is the king pippin, who the main squeeze ? The man with the eight and a quarter hat.

"Jimmy," she cried, "its the goods!"

"Exactly."

"It's a life-saver."

"Precisely. Be quick then. There is no time to waste."

And so it came about that George Finch, nestling beneath the bed, received a shock which, inured though he should have been to shocks by now, seemed to him to turn every hair on his head instantaneously grey.

III

The first thing that impressed itself on George Finch's consciousness, after his eyes had grown accustomed to the light, was an ankle. It was clad in a stocking of diaphanous silk, and was joined almost immediately by another ankle, similarly clad. For an appreciable time these ankles, though slender, bulked so large in George's world that they may be said to have filled his whole horizon. Then they disappeared.

A moment before this happened, George, shrinking modestly against the wall, would have said that nothing could have pleased him better than to have these ankles disappear. Nevertheless, when they did so, it was all he could do to keep himself from uttering a stricken cry. For the reason they disappeared was that at this moment a dress of some filmy material fell over them, hiding them from view.

It was a dress that had the appearance of having been cut by fairy scissors out of moonbeams and star-dust: and in a shop-window George would have admired it. But seeing it in a shop-window and seeing it bunched like a prismatic foam on the floor of this bedroom were two separate and distinct things: and so warmly did George Finch blush that he felt as if his face must be singeing the carpet. He shut his eyes and clenched his teeth. Was this, he asked himself, the end or but a beginning ?

"Yes ?" said a voice suddenly. And George's head, jerking

173

convulsively, seemed for an instant to have parted company with a loosely-attached neck.

The voice had spoken, he divined as soon as the power of ought returned to him, in reponse to a sharp and authoritative kn ck on the door, delivered by some hard instrument which sounded like a policeman's night-stick: and there followed immediately upon this knock sharp and authoritative words.

"Open up there!"

The possessor of the ankles was plainly a girl of spirit.

"I won't," she said. "I'm dressing."

"Who are you?"

"Who are *you*?"

"Never mind who I am."

"Well, never mind who *I* am, then!"

There was a pause. It seemed to George, judging the matter dispassionately, that the ankles had had slightly the better of the exchanges to date.

"What are you doing in there?" aked the male duettist, approaching the thing from another angle.

"I'm dressing, I keep telling you."

There was another pause. And then into this tense debate there entered a third party.

"What's all this?" said the new-comer sharply.

George recognized the voice of his old friend Hamilton Beamish.

"Garroway," said Hamilton Beamish, with an annoyed severity, "what the devil are you doing, hanging about outside this lady's door? Upon my soul," proceeded Mr. Beamish warmly, "I'm beginning to wonder what the duties of the New York constabulary are. Their life seems to consist of an endless leisure, which they employ in roaming about and annoying women. Are you aware that the lady inside there is my fiancée and that she is dressing in order to dine with me at a restaurant?"

Officer Garroway, as always, cringed before the superior intelligence.

"I am extremely sorry, Mr. Beamish."

"So you ought to be. What are you doing here, anyway?"

"There has been some little trouble down below on the premises of the Purple Chicken, and I was violently assaulted by Mr. Finch. I followed him up here on the fire-escape . . ."

"Mr. Finch? You are drivelling, Garroway. Mr. Finch is on his wedding-trip. He very kindly lent this lady his apartment during his absence."

"But, Mr. Beamish, I was talking to him only just now. We sat at the same table."

"Absurd!"

The dress had disappeared from George's range of vision now, and he heard the door open.

"What does this man want, Jimmy?"

"A doctor, apparently," said Hamilton Beamish. "He says he met George Finch just now."

"But George is miles away."

"Precisely. Are you ready, darling? Then we will go off and have some dinner. What you need, Garroway, is a bromo-seltzer. Come down to my apartment and I will mix you one. Having taken it, I would recommend you to lie down quietly on the sofa and rest awhile. I think you must have been over-exercising your brain, writing that poem of yours. Who blacked your eye?"

"I wish I knew," said Officer Garroway wistfully. "I received the injury during the fracas at the Purple Chicken. There was a table-cloth over my head at the moment, and I was unable to ascertain the identity of my assailant. If, and when, I find him I shall soak him so hard it'll jar his grandchildren."

"A table-cloth?"

"Yes, Mr. Beamish. And while I was endeavouring to extricate myself from its folds, somebody hit me in the eye with a coffee-pot."

"How do you know it was a coffee-pot?"

"I found it lying beside me when I emerged."

"Ah! Well," said Hamilton Beamish, summing up, "I hope that this will be a lesson to you not to go into places like the Purple Chicken. You are lucky to have escaped so lightly. You might have had to eat their cheese. Well, come along, Garroway, and we will see what we can do for you."

IV

George stayed where he was. If he had known of a better 'ole, he would have gone to it: but he did not. He would have been the last person to pretend that it was comfortable lying underneath this bed with fluff tickling his nose and a draught playing about his left ear: but there seemed in the circumstances nothing else to do. To a man unable to fly there were only two modes of exit from this roof,—he could climb down the fire-escape, probably into the very arms of the constabulary, or he could try to sneak down the stairs, and most likely run straight into the vengeful Garroway. True, Hamilton Beamish had recommended the policeman after drinking his bromo-seltzer to lie down on the sofa, but who knew if he would follow the advice? Possibly he was even now patrolling the staircase: and George, recalling the man's physique and remembering the bitterness with which he had spoken of his late assailant, decided that the risk was too great to be taken. Numerous as were the defects of his little niche beneath the bed, considered as a spot to spend a happy evening, it was a good place to be for a man in his delicate position. So he dug himself in and tried to while away the time by thinking.

He thought of many things. He thought of his youth in East Gilead, of his manhood in New York. He thought of Molly and how much he loved her; of Mrs. Waddington and what a blot she was on the great scheme of things; of Hamilton Beamish and his off-hand way of dealing with policemen. He thought of Officer Garroway and his night-stick; of Guiseppe and his coffee-pot; of the Reverend Gideon Voules and his white socks. He even thought of Sigsbee H. Waddington.

Now, when a man is so hard put to it for mental occupation that he has to fall back on Sigsbee H. Waddington as a topic of thought, he is nearing the end of his resources: and it was possibly with a kindly appreciation of this fact that Fate now supplied something else to occupy George's mind. Musing idly on Sigsbee H. and wondering how he got that way, George became suddenly aware of approaching footsteps.

He curled himself up into a ball, and his ears stood straight up like a greyhound's. Yes, footsteps. And, what was more, they seemed to be making straight for the sleeping-porch.

A wave of self-pity flooded over George Finch. Why should he be so ill-used? He asked so little of Life,—merely to be allowed to lie quietly under a bed and inhale fluff: and what happened? Nothing but interruptions. Nothing but boots, boots, boots, boots, marching up and down again, as Kipling has so well put it. Ever since he had found his present hiding-place, the world had seemed to become one grey inferno of footsteps. It was wrong and unjust.

The only thing that could possibly be said in extenuation of the present footsteps was that they sounded too light to be those of any New York policeman. They had approached now to the very door. Indeed, they seemed to him to have stopped actually inside the room.

He was right in this conjecture. The switch clicked. Light jumped at him like a living thing. And when he opened his eyes he found himself looking at a pair of ankles clad in stockings of diaphanous silk.

The door closed. And Mrs. Waddington, who had just reached the top of the fire-escape, charged across the roof and, putting her ear to the keyhole, stood listening intently. Things, felt Mrs. Waddington, were beginning to move.

## v

For a moment, all that George Finch felt as he glared out at this latest visitation was a weak resentment at the oafishness of Fate in using the same method for his tormenting that it had used so short a while before. Fate, he considered, was behaving childishly, and ought to change its act. This ankle business might have been funny enough once: but, overdone, it became tedious.

Then to indignation there succeeded relief. The remarks of Hamilton Beamish in his conversation with the policeman had made it clear that the possessor of the ankles had been his old friend May Stubbs of East Gilead, Idaho: and, seeing ankles once again, George naturally assumed that they were attached, as before, to Miss Stubbs, and that the reason for her return was that she had come back to fetch something—some powder-puff, for example, or a lipstick—which in the excitement of the recent altercation she had forgotten to take along with her.

This, of course, altered the whole position of affairs. What it amounted to was that, instead of a new enemy he had found an ally. A broad-minded girl like May would understand at once the motives which led him to hide under the bed and would sympathize with them. He could employ her, it occurred to him, as a scout, to see if the staircase was now clear. In short, this latest interruption of his reverie, so far from being a disaster, was the very best thing that could have happened.

Sneezing heartily, for he had got a piece of fluff up his nose, George rolled out from under the bed: and, scrambling to his feet with a jolly laugh, found himself gazing into the bulging eyes of a complete stranger.

That, at lest, was how the girl impressed him in the first instant of their meeting. But gradually, as he stared at her, there crept into his mind the belief that somewhere and at some time he had seen her before. But where? And when?

The girl continued to gape at him. She was small and pretty, with vivid black eyes and a mouth which, if it had not been hanging open at the moment like that of a fish, would have been remarkably attractive. Silence reigned in the sleeping-porch: and Mrs. Waddington, straining her ears outside, was beginning to think that George could not be in this lair and that a further vigil was before her, when suddenly voices began to speak. What they were saying, she was unable to hear, for the door was stoutly built: but beyond a doubt one of them was George's. Mrs. Waddington crept away, well content. Her suspicions had been confirmed, and now it remained only to decide what it was best to do about it. She moved into the shadow of the water-tank, and there remained for a space in deep thought.

Inside the sleeping-porch, the girl, her eyes fixed on George, had begun to shrink back. At about the third shrink she bumped into the wall, and the shock seemed to restore her power of speech.

"What are you doing in my bedroom?" she cried.

The question had the effect of substituting for the embarrassment which had been gripping George a sudden bubbling fury. This, he felt, was too much. Circumstances had conspired that night to turn this sleeping-porch into a sort of meeting-place of the nations, but he was darned if he was going to have visitors looking on the room as their own.

"What do you mean, your bedroom?" he demanded hotly. "Who are you?"

"I'm Mrs. Mullett."

"Who?"

"Mrs. Frederick Mullett."

Mrs. Waddington had formed her plan of action. What she needed, she perceived, was a witness to come with her to this den of evil and add his testimony in support of hers. If only Lord Hunstanton had been present, as he should have been, she would have needed to look no further. But Lord Hunstanton was somewhere out in the great city, filling his ignoble tummy with food. Whom, then, could she enrol as a deputy! The question answered itself. Ferris was the man. He was ready to hand and could be fetched without delay.

Mrs. Waddington made for the stairs.

"Mrs. Mullett?" said George. "What do you mean? Mullett's not married."

"Yes, he is. We were married this morning."

"Where is he?"

"I left him down below, finishing a cigar. He said we'd be all alone up here, nesting like two little birds in a tree top."

George laughed a brassy, sardonic laugh.

"If Mullett thought anyone could ever be alone for five minutes up here, he's an optimist. And what right has Mullett to go nesting like a little bird in my apartment?"

"Is this your apartment?"

"Yes, it is."

"Oh! Oh!"

"Stop it! Don't make that noise. There are policemen about."

"Policemen!"

"Yes."

Tears suddenly filled the eyes that looked into his. Two small hands clasped themselves in a passionate gesture of appeal.

"Don't turn me over to the bulls, mister! I only did it for ma's sake. If you was out of work and starvin' and you had to sit and watch your poor old ma bendin' over the wash-tub . . ."

"I haven't got a poor old ma," said George curtly. "And what on earth do you think you're talking about?"

He stopped suddenly, speech wiped from his lips by a stunning discovery. The girl had unclasped her hands, and now she flung them out before her: and the gesture was all that George's memory needed to spur it to the highest efficiency. For unconsciously Fanny Mullett had assumed the exact attitude which had lent such dramatic force to her entrance into the dining-room of Mrs. Waddington's house at Hempstead earlier in the day. The moment he saw those outstretched arms, George remembered where he had met this girl before: and, forgetting everything else, forgetting that he was trapped on a roof with a justly exasperated policeman guarding the only convenient exit, he uttered a short, sharp bark of exultation.

"You!" he cried. "Give me that necklace."

"What necklace?"

"The one you stole at Hempstead this afternoon."

The girl drew herself up haughtily.

"Do you dare to say I stole a necklace?"

"Yes, I do."

"Oh? And do you know what I'll do if you bring a charge like that against me? I'll . . ."

She broke off. A discreet tap had sounded on the door.

"Honey!"

Fanny looked at George. George looked at Fanny.

"My husband!" whispered Fanny.

George was in no mood to be intimidated by a mere Mullett. He strode to the door.

"Honey!"

George flung the door open.

"Honey!"

"Well, Mullett?"

The valet fell back a pace, his eyes widening. He passed the tip of his tongue over his kips.

"A wasp in the beehive!" cried Mullett.

"Don't be an idiot," said George.

Mullett was gazing at him in the manner of one stricken to the core.

"Isn't your own bridal-trip enough for you, Mr. Finch," he said reproachfully, "that you've got to come butting in on mine?"

"Don't be a fool. My wedding was temporily postponed."

"I see. And misery loves company, so you start in breaking up my home."

"Nothing of the kind."

"If I had known that you were on the premises, Mr. Finch," said Mullett with dignity, "I would not have taken the liberty of making use of your domicile. Come, Fanny, we will go to a hotel."

"Will you?" said George unpleasantly. "Let me tell you there's a little matter to be settled, before you start going to any hotel. Perhaps you are not aware that your wife is in possession of a valuable necklace belonging to the lady who, if it hadn't been for her, would now be Mrs. George Finch?"

Mullett clapped a hand to his forehead.

"A necklace!"

"It's a lie," cried his bride.

Mullett shook his head sadly. He was putting two and two together.

"When did this occur, Mr. Finch?"

"This afternoon, down at Hempstead."

"Don't you listen to him, Freddy. He's dippy."

"What precisely happened, Mr. Finch?"

"This woman suddenly burst into the room where everybody was and pretended that I had made love to her and deserted her. Then she fell on the table where the wedding-presents were and pretended to faint. And then she dashed out, and some time afterwards it was discovered that the necklace had gone. And don't," he added, turning to the accused, "say that you only did it for your poor old ma's sake, because I've had a lot to put up with to-day, and that will be just too much."

Mr. Mullett clicked his tongue with a sort of sorrowful pride.

Girls will be girls, Frederick Mullett seemed to say, but how few girls could be as clever as his little wife.

"Give Mr. Finch his necklace, pettie," he said mildly

"I haven't got any necklace."

"Give it to him, dearie, just like Freddie says, or there'll only be unpleasantness."

"Unpleasantness," said George, breathing hard, "is right!"

"It was a beautiful bit of work, honey, and there isn't another girl in New York that could have thought it out let alone gone and got away with it. Even Mr. Finch will admit it was a beautiful bit of work."

"If you want Mr. Finch's opinion . . ." began George heatedly.

"But we've done with all that sort of thing now, haven't we, pettie? Give him his necklace, honey."

Mrs. Mullett's black eyes snapped. She twisted her pretty fingers irresolutely.

"Take your old necklace," she said.

George caught it as it fell.

"Thanks," he said, and put it in his pocket.

"And now, Mr. Finch," said Mullett suavely, "I think we will say good night. My little girl here has had a tiring day and ought to be turning in."

George hurried across the roof to his apartment. Whatever the risk of leaving the safety of the sleeping-porch, it must be ignored. It was imperative that he telephone to Molly and inform her of what had happened.

He was pulling the French window open when he heard his name called: and perceived Mullett hurrying towards him from the door that led to the stairs.

"Just one moment, Mr. Finch."

"What is it? I have a most important telephone-call to make."

"I thought you would be glad to have this, sir."

With something of the air of a conjurer who, to amuse the children, produces two rabbits and the grand old flag from inside a borrowed top-hat, Mullett unclasped his fingers.

"Your necklace, sir."

George's hand flew to his pocket and came away empty.

"Good heavens! How . . ?"

"My little girl," explained Mullett with a proud and tender look in his eyes. "She snitched it off you, sir, as we were going out. I was able, however, to persuade her to give it up again. I reminded her that we had put all that sort of thing behind us now.

I asked her how she could expect to be happy on our duck-farm if she had a thing like that on her mind, and she saw it almost at once. She's a very reasonable girl, sir, when tactfully approached by the voice of love."

George drew a deep breath. He replaced the necklace in his inside breast-pocket, buttoned his coat and drew away a step or two.

"Are you going to let that woman loose on a duck-farm, Mullett?"

"Yes, sir. We are taking a little place in the neighbourhood of Speonk."

"She'll have the tail-feathers off every bird on the premises before the end of the first week."

Mullett bowed his appreciation of the compliment.

"And they wouldn't know they'd lost them, sir," he agreed. "There's never been anyone in the profession fit to be reckoned in the same class with my little girl. But all that sort of thing is over now, sir. She is definitely retiring from business,—except for an occasional visit to the department stores during bargain-sales. A girl must have her bit of finery. Good night, sir."

"Good night," said George.

He took out the necklace, examined it carefully, replaced it in his pocket, buttoned his coat once more, and went into the apartment to telephone to Molly.


## CHAPTER SEVENTEEN

### I

MRS. WADDINGTON had once read a story in which a series of emotions including fear, horror, amazement, consternation and a sickly dismay were described as 'chasing one another' across the face of a dastardly person at the moment of realization that his villainy had been discovered past concealment: and it was with the expectation of watching a similar parade on the moon-like countenance of Ferrrs, the butler, that she pressed the bell outside the door of the apartment of Mr. Lancelot Biffen on the ninth floor.

She was disappointed. Ferris, as he appeared in the doorway

in answer to her ring, lacked a little of his customary portentous dignity, but that was only because we authors, after a gruelling bout at the desk, are always apt to look a shade frazzled. The butler's hair was disordered where he had plucked at it in the agony of composition, and there was more ink on the tip of his nose than would have been there on a more formal occasion: but otherwise he was in pretty good shape, and he did not even start on perceiving the identity of his visitor.

"Mr. Biffen is not at home, madam," said Ferris equably.

"I do not wish to see Mr. Biffen." Mrs. Waddington swelled with justifiable wrath. "Ferris," she said, "I know all!"

"Indeed, madam?"

"You have no sick relative," proceeded Mrs. Waddington: though her tone suggested the opinion that anyone related to him had good reason to be sick. "You are here because you are writing a scurrilous report of what happened this afternoon at my house for a gutter rag called 'Town Gossip.'"

"With which is incorporated 'Broadway Whispers' and 'Times Square Tattle,'" murmured the butler, absently.

"You ought to be ashamed of yourself!"

Ferris raised his eyebrows.

"I venture to take issue with you, madam. The profession of journalism is an honourable one. Many very estimable men have written for the Press. Horace Greeley," said Ferris, specifying. "Delane . . ."

"Bah!"

"Madam?"

"But we will go into that later."

"Very good, madam."

"Meanwhile, I wish you to accompany me to the roof . . ."

"I fear I must respectfully decline, madam. I have not climbed since I was a small lad."

"You can walk up a flight of stairs, can't you?"

"Oh, stairs? Decidedly, madam. I will be at your disposal in a few moments."

"I wish you to accompany me now."

The butler shook his head.

"If I might excuse myself, madam. I am engaged on the concluding passages of the article to which you alluded just now, and I am anxious to complete it before Mr. Biffen's return."

Mrs. Waddington caused the eye before which Sigsbee H. had so often curled up and crackled like a burnt feather to blaze imperiously upon the butler. He met it with the easy aplomb of one who in his time has looked at dukes and made them feel that their trousers were bagging at the knees.

"Would you care to step inside and wait, madam?"

Mrs. Waddington was reluctantly obliged to realize that she was quelled. She had shot her bolt. A cyclone might shake this man, but not the human eye.

"I will not step inside."

"Very good, madam. For what reason do you desire me to accompany you to the roof?"

"I want you to—to look at something."

"If it is the view, madam, I should mention that I have already visited the top of the Woolworth Building."

"It is not the view. I wish you to look at a man who is living in open sin."

"Very good, madam." There was no surprise in Ferris's manner, only a courteous suggestion that he was always glad to look at men living in open sin. "I will be at your disposal in a few minutes."

He closed the door gently, and Mrs. Waddington, full of the coward rage which dares to burn but does not dare to blaze, abandoned her intention of kicking in a panel and stood on the landing, heaving gently. And presently there was borne up to her from the lower levels a cheerful sound of whistling.

Lord Hunstanton came into view.

"Hullo-ullo-ullo!" said Lord Hunstanton exuberantly. "Here I am, here I am, here I am!"—meaning, of course, that there he was.

A striking change had taken place in the man's appearance since Mrs. Waddington had last seen him. He now wore the care-free and debonair expression of one who has dined and dined well. The sparkle in his eye spoke of clear soup, the smile on his lips was eloquent of roast duck and green peas. To Mrs. Waddington, who had not broken bread since lunch-time, he seemed the most repellent object on which she had ever gazed.

"I trust you have had a good dinner," she said icily.

His lordship's sunny smile broadened and a dreamy look came into his eyes.

"Absolutely!" he replied. "I started with a spruce spoonful of Julienne and passed on by way of a breezy half-lobster on the shell to about as upstanding a young Long Island duckling as I have ever bitten."

"Be quiet!" said Mrs. Waddington, shaken to the core. The man's conversation seemed to her utterly revolting.

"Finishing up with . . ."

"Will you be quiet! I have no desire to hear the details of your repast."

"Oh, sorry! I thought you had."

"You have been away long enough to have eaten half-a-dozen dinners. However, as it happens, you are not too late. I have something to show you."

"That's good. Moral turpitude pretty strong on the wing, eh?"

"A few moments ago," said Mrs. Waddington, leading the way to the roof, "I observed a young woman enter what appears to be some kind of outdoor sleeping-porch attached to George Finch's apartment, and immediately afterwards I heard her voice in conversation with George Finch within."

"Turpy," said his lordship, shaking his head reprovingly. "Very turpy."

"I came down to fetch Ferris, my butler, as a witness, but fortunately you have returned in time. Though why you were not back half an hour ago I cannot understand."

"But I was telling you. I dallied with a mouthful of Julienne . . ."

"Be quiet!"

Lord Hunstanton followed her, puzzled. He could not understand what seemed to him a morbid distaste on his companion's part to touch on the topic of food. They came out on the roof, and Mrs. Waddington, raising a silent and beckoning finger, moved on tip-toe towards the sleeping-porch.

"Now what?" inquired his lordship, they paused before the door.

Mrs. Waddington rapped upon the panel.

"George Finch!"

Complete silence followed the words.

"George Finch!"

"George Finch!" echoed his lordship, conscious of his responsibilities as a chorus.

"Finch!" said Mrs. Waddington.

"George!" cried Lord Hunstanton.

Mrs. Waddington flung open the door. All was darkness within. She switched on the light. The room was empty.

"Well!" said Mrs. Waddington.

"Perhaps they're under the bed."

"Go and look."

"But suppose he bites at me."

Nothing is truer than that the secret of all successful operations consists in the overlooking of no eventuality, but it was plain that

Mrs. Waddington considered that in this instance her ally was carrying caution too far. She turned on him with a snort of annoyance: and, having turned, remained staring frozenly at something that had suddenly manifested itself in his lordship's rear.

This something was a long, stringy policeman: and though Mrs. Waddington had met this policeman only once in her life, the circumstances of that meeting had been such that the memory of him had lingered. She recognized him immediately: and, strong woman though she was, wilted like a snail that has just received a handful of salt between the eyes.

"What's up?" inquired Lord Hunstanton. He, too, turned. "Oh, what ho! the constabulary!"

Officer Garroway was gazing at Mrs. Waddington with an eye from which one of New York's Bohemian evenings had wiped every trace of its customary mildness. So intense, indeed, was the malevolence of its gleam that, if there had been two such eyes boring into hers, it is probable that Mrs. Waddington would have swooned. Fortunately, the other was covered with a piece of raw steak and a bandage, and so was out of action.

"Ah!" said Officer Garroway.

There is little in the word 'Ah' when you write it down and take a look at it to suggest that under certain conditions it can be one of the most sinister words in the language. But hear it spoken by a policeman in whose face you have recently thrown pepper, and you will be surprised. To Mrs. Waddington, as she shrank back into the sleeping-porch, it seemed a sort of combination of an Indian war-whoop, the Last Trump, and the howl of a pursuing wolf-pack. Her knees weakened beneath her, and she collapsed on the bed.

"Copped you, have I?" proceeded the policeman.

The question was plainly a rhetorical one, for he did not pause for a reply. He adjusted the bandage that held the steak, and continued his remarks.

"You're pinched!"

It seemed to Lord Hunstanton that all this was very odd and irregular.

"I say, look here, you know, what I mean to say is . . ."

"So are you," said Officer Garroway. "You seem to be in it, too. You're both pinched. And start any funny business," concluded the constable, swinging his night-stick in a ham-like fist, "and I'll bend this over your nut. Get me?"

There followed one of those pauses which so often punctuate

the conversation of comparative strangers. Officer Garroway seemed to have said his say. Mrs. Waddington had no observations to make. And, though Lord Hunstanton would have liked to put a question or two, the spectacle of that oscillating night-stick had the effect of driving the words out of his head. It was the sort of night-stick that gave one a throbbing feeling about the temples merely to look at it. He swallowed feebly, but made no remark.

And then from somewhere below there sounded the voice of one who cried 'Beamish! Hey, Beamish!' It was the voice of Sigsbee H. Waddington.

## II

Nothing is more annoying to the reader of a chronicle like this than to have somebody suddenly popping up in some given spot and to find that the historian does not propose to offer any explanation as to how he got there. A conscientious recorder should explain the exits and the entrances of even so insignificant a specimen of the race as Sigsbee H. Waddington: and the present scribe must now take time off in order to do so.

Sigsbee H., it may be remembered, had started out to search through New York for a policeman named Gallagher: and New York had given him of its abundance. It had provided for Mr. Waddington's inspection a perfect wealth of Gallaghers: but, owing to the fact that what he really wished to meet was not a Gallagher but a Garroway, nothing in the nature of solid success had rewarded his efforts. He had seen tall Gallaghers and small Gallaghers, thin Gallaghers and stout Gallaghers, a cross-eyed Gallagher, a pimpled Gallagher, a Gallagher with red hair, a Gallagher with a broken nose, two Gallaghers who looked like bad dreams, and a final supreme Gallagher who looked like nothing on earth. But he had not found the man to whom he had sold the stock of the Finer and Better Motion Picture Company of Hollywood, Cal.

Many men in such a position would have given up the struggle. Sigsbee H. Waddington did. The last Gallagher had been on duty in the neighbourhood of Bleecker Street: and Mr. Waddington, turning into Washington Square, tottered to a bench and sagged down on it.

For some moments, the ecstatic relief of resting his feet occupied his mind to the exclusion of everything else. Then there occurred to him a thought which, had it arrived earlier in the day, would have saved him a considerable output of energy. He suddenly recollected that he had met the missing policeman at the apartment of Hamilton Beamish: and, pursuing this train of thought to its logical conclusion, decided that Hamilton Beamish was the one person who would be able to give him information as to the man's whereabouts.

No tonic, however popular and widely-advertised, could have had so instantly revivifying an effect. The difference between Mr. Waddington before taking and after taking this inspiration was almost magical. An instant before, he had been lying back on the bench in a used-up attitude which would have convinced any observer that the only thing to do with a man in such a stage of exhausted dejection was to notify the City authorities and have him swept up and deposited in the incinerator with the rest of the local garbage. But now, casting off despair like a cloak, he sprang from his seat and was across the Square and heading for the Sheridan before such an observer would have had time to say 'What ho!'

Not even the fact that the elevator was not running could check his exhilarated progress. He skimmed up the stairs to Hamilton Beamish's door like a squirrel.

"Beamish!" he cried. "Hey, Beamish!"

Up on the roof, Officer Garroway started as a war-horse at the sound of the bugle. He knew that voice. And, if it should seem remarkable that he should have remembered it after so many days, having been in conversation with it but once, the explanation is that Mr. Waddington's voice had certain tonal qualities that rendered it individual and distinctive. You might mistake it for a squeaking file, but you could not mistake it for the voice of anybody but Sigsbee H. Waddington.

"Gosh!" said Officer Garroway, shaking like an aspen.

The voice had had its effect also on Mrs. Waddington. She started up as if the bed on which she sat had become suddenly incandescent.

"Siddown!" said Officer Garroway.

Mrs. Waddington sat down.

"My dear old constable," began Lord Hunstanton.

"Shut up!" said Officer Garroway.

Lord Hunstanton shut up.

"Gosh!" said Officer Garroway once more.

He eyed his prisoners in an agony of indecision. He was in the unfortunate position of wanting to be in two places at once. To rush down the stairs and accost the man who had sold him that stock would mean that he would have to leave these two birds, with the result that they would undoubtedly escape. And that they should escape was the last thing in the world that Officer Garroway desired. These two represented the most important capture he had made since he had joined the Force. The female bird was a detected burglar and assaulter of the police, and he rather fancied that, when he took him to headquarters and looked him up in the Rogue's Gallery, the male bird would prove to be Willie the Dude, wanted in Syracuse for slipping the snide. To land them in the coop meant promotion.

On the other hand, to go down and get his fingers nicely placed about the throat of the man downstairs meant that he would get his three hundred dollars back.

What to do? What to do?

"Oh, gosh! Oh, Gee!" sighed Officer Garroway.

A measured footstep made itself heard. There came into his range of vision an ambassadorial-looking man with a swelling waistcoat and a spot of ink on his nose. And, seeing him, the policeman uttered a cry of elation.

### III

"Hey!" said Officer Garroway.

"Sir?" said the new-comer.

"You're a deputy."

"No, sir. I am a butler."

"Say. Be-eeeee-mish!" bleated the voice below.

It roused the policeman to a frenzy of direct action. In a calmer moment he might have been quelled by the protruding green-grey eyes that were looking at him with such quiet austerity: but now they had no terrors for him.

"You're a deputy," he repeated. "You know what that means don't you, dumb-bell? I'm an officer of the Law and I appoint you my deputy."

"I have no desire to be a deputy," said the other with the cold sub-tinkle in his voice which had once made the younger son of a marquess resign from his clubs and go to Uganda.

It was wasted on Officer Garroway. The man was berserk.

"That's all right what you desire and don't desire. I've made you a deputy, and you'll be one or go up the river for resisting an officer of the Law, besides getting a dot over the bean with this stick that'll make you wish you hadn't. Now then?"

"The position being such as you have outlined," said the

butler with dignity, "I have no alternative but to comply with your wishes."

"What's your name?"

"Rupert Antony Ferris."

"Where do you live?"

"I am in the employment of Mrs. Sigsbee H. Wadddington, at present residing at Hempstead, Long Island."

"Well, I've got two birds in here that are wanted at headquarters, see? I'm locking them in." Officer Garroway slammed the door and turned the key. "Now, all you have to do is to stand on guard till I come back. Not much to ask is it?"

"The task appears to be well within the scope of my powers, and I shall endeavour to fulfil it faithfully."

"Then go to it," said Officer Garroway.

Ferris stood with his back to the sleeping-porch, looking at the moon with a touch of wistfulness. Moonlight nights always made him a little home-sick, for Brangmarley Hall had been at its best on such occasions. How often had he, then a careless, light-hearted footman, watched the moonbeams reflected on the waters of the moat and, with all the little sounds of the English country whispering in his ear, pondered idly on what would win the two o'clock race at Ally Pally next day. Happy days! Happy days!

The sound of some one murmuring his name brought his wandering thoughts back to the workaday world. He looked about him with interest, which deepened as he saw that he had apparently got the roof to himself.

"Ferris!"

The butler was a man who never permitted himself to be surprised, but he was conscious now of something not unlike that emotion. Disembodied voices which whispered his name were new in his experience. It could hardly be one of the two birds in the sleeping-porch that was speaking, for they were behind concrete walls and a solid door, and would have had to raise their voices far louder to make themselves heard.

"Ferris!"

Possibly an angel, thought the butler: and was turning his mind to other things when he perceived that in the wall by which he stood there was a small window high up in the concrete. So it was one of the birds, after all. Scarcely had he made the discovery of the window when the voice spoke again, and so distinctly this time that he was able to recognize it as that of his employer, Mrs. Sigsbee H. Waddington.

"Ferris!"

"Madam?" said Ferris.

"It is I, Ferris—Mrs. Waddington."

"Very good, madam."

"What did you say? Come closer. I can't hear you."

The butler, though not a man who did this sort of thing as a general rule, indulgently stretched a point and stood on tip-toe. He advanced his mouth towards the hole in the wall, and repeated his remark.

"I said, 'Very good, madam'," explained this modern Pyramus.

"Oh? Well be quick, Ferris."

"Quick, madam?"

"Be quick and let us out."

'You wish me to release you, madam?"

"Yes."

"H'm!"

"What did you say?"

The butler, who had found that the strain of standing on tip-toe a little hard on his fallen arches, reared himself up once more.

"I said 'H'm!' madam."

"What did you say?" asked the voice of Lord Hunstanton.

"He said 'H'm!'" replied the voice of Mrs. Waddington.

"Why?"

"How should I know? I believe the man has been drinking."

"Let me talk to the fellow," said Lord Hunstanton.

There was a pause. Then a male understudy took up Thisbe's portion of the performance.

"Hi!"

"Sir?" said Ferris.

"You out there, what's your name...."

"My name is—and has always been—Ferris, sir."

"Well, then, Ferris, listen to me and understand that I'm not the sort of man to stand any dashed nonsense or anything like that of any description whatsoever. Why, when this dear, good lady told you to let us out, did you reply 'H'm'? Answer me that—yes or no."

The butler raised himself on tip-toe again.

"The ejaculation was intended to convey doubt, your lordship."

"Doubt? What about?"

"As to whether I could see my way to letting you out, your lordship."

"Don't be a silly idiot. It's not so dark as all that."

"I was alluding to the difficulties confronting me as the result of the peculiar position in which I find myself situated, your lordship."

"What did he say?" asked the voice of Mrs. Waddington.

"Something about his peculiar position."

"Why is he in a peculiar position?"

"Ah! There you have me."

"Let *me* talk to the man."

There was a scuffling noise, followed by a heavy fall and a plaintive cry from a female in distress.

"I knew that chair would break if you stood on it," said Lord Hunstanton. "I wish I could have had a small bet on that chair breaking if you stood on it."

"Wheel the bed under the window," replied the indomitable woman beside him. She had lost an inch of skin from her right ankle, but her hat was still in the ring.

A grating noise proclaimed the shifting of the bed. There was a creak of springs beneath a heavy weight. The window, in its capacity of loud speaker, announced Mrs. Waddington calling.

"Ferris!"

"Madam?"

"What do you mean? Why is your position peculiar?"

"Because I am a deputy, madam."

"What does that matter?"

"I represent the Law, madam."

"The what?" asked Lord Hunstanton.

"The Law," said Mrs. Waddington. "He says he represents the Law."

"Let *me* speak to the blighter!"

There was another interval, which the butler employed in massaging hs aching insteps.

"Hi!"

"Your lordship?"

"What's all this rot about your representing the Law?"

"I was placed in a position of trust by the officer who has recently left us. He instructed me to guard your lordship and Mrs. Waddington and to see that you did not effect your escape."

"But, Ferris, try not to be more of an ass than you can help. Pull yourself together and use your intelligence. You surely don't suppose that Mrs. Waddington and I have done anything wrong?"

"It is not my place to speculate on the point which you have raised, your lordship."

"Listen, Ferris. Let's get down to the stern, practical side of this business. If the old feudal spirit hadn't died out completely, you'd do a little thing like letting us out of this place for the pure love of service, if you know what I mean. But, seeing that we live in a commercial age, what's the figure ?"

"Are you suggesting that I should accept a bribe, your lordship ? Am I to understand that you propose that, in return for money, I should betray my trust ?"

"Yes. How much ?"

"How much has your lordship got ?"

"What did he say ?" asked Mrs. Waddington.

"He asked how much we'd got."

"How much what ?"

"Money."

"He wishes to extort money from us ?"

"That's what it sounded like."

"Let *me* speak to the man."

Mrs. Waddington came to the window.

"Ferris."

"Madam ?"

"You ought to be ashamed of yourself."

"Yes, madam."

"Your behaviour surprises and revolts me."

"Very good, madam."

"You cease from this moment to be in my employment."

"Just as you desire, madam."

Mrs. Waddington retired for a brief consulation with her companion.

"Ferris," she said, returning to the window.

"Madam ?"

"Here is all the money we have,—two hundred and fifteen dollars."

"It will be ample, madam."

"Then kindly make haste and unlock this door."

"Very good, madam."

Mrs. Waddington waited, chafing. The moment passed.

"Madam."

"Well, what is it now ?"

"I regret to have to inform you, madam," said Ferris respectfully, "that, when the policeman went away, he took the key with him."

# CHAPTER EIGHTEEN

IT had taken George some considerable time to establish connection with the Waddington home at Hempstead: but he had done it at last, only to be informed that Molly did not appear to be on the premises. She had driven up in her two-seater, a Swedish voice gave him to understand, but after remaining in the house a short while had driven off again.

"Fine!" said George, as his informant was beginning to relapse into her native tongue.

A yeasty feeling of pleasure and good-will towards his species filled him as he hung up the receiver. If Molly had started back to New York, he might expect to see her at any moment now. His heart swelled: and the fact that he was in the unfortunate position of being a fugitive from justice and the additional fact that the bloodhound of the Law most interested in his movements was probably somewhere very close at hand, entirely escaped him. Abandoning the caution which should have been the first thought of one situated as he was, he burst into jovial song.

"Hey, Pinch!"

George, who had been climbing towards a high note, came back to earth again, chilled and apprehensive. His first impulse was to dash for his bedroom and hide under the bed—a thing which he knew himself to be good at. Then his intelligence asserted itself and panic waned. Only one man of his acquaintance could have addressed him as 'Hey, Pinch!'

"Is that Mr. Waddington?" he murmured, opening the door of the sitting-room and peering in.

"Sure, it's Mr. Waddington." The reek of a lively young cigar assailed George's nostrils. "Don't you have any lights in this joint?"

"Are there any policemen about?" asked George in a conspiratorial undertone.

"There's one policeman down in young Beamish's apartment," replied Mr. Waddington with a fruity chuckle. "He's just sold me all his holdings in the Finer and Better Motion Picture Company of Hollywood, Cal., for three hundred smackers: and I've come here to celebrate. Set up the drinks," said Mr. Waddington, who was plainly in as festive a mood as a man can be without actually breaking up the furniture.

George switched on the light. If the enemy was in as distant a spot as Hamilton Beamish's apartment, prudence might be relaxed.

"'At's right," said Mr. Waddington, welcoming the illumination. He was leaning against a book-shelf with his hat on the back of his head and a cigar between his lips. His eyes were sparkling with an almost human intelligence. "I've got a smart business head, Pinch," he said, shooting the cigar from due east to due west with a single movement of his upper lip. "I'm the guy with the big brain."

Although all the data which he had been able to accumulate in the course of their acquaintanceship went directly to prove the opposite, George was not inclined to combat the statement. He had weightier matters to occupy him than an academic discussion of the mentality of this poor fish.

"I found that girl," he said

"What girl?"

"The girl who stole the necklace. And I've got the necklace."

He had selected a subject that gripped. Mr. Waddington ceased to contemplate the smartness of his business head and became interested. His eyes widened, and he blew out a puff of poison-gas.

"You don't say!"

"Here it is,"

"Gimme!" said Mr. Waddington.

George dangled the necklace undecidedly.

"I think I ought to hand it over to Molly."

"You'll hand it over to me," said Mr. Waddington with decision. "I'm the head of the family, and from now on I act as such. Too long, Pinch, have I allowed myself to be trampled beneath the iron heel and generally kicked in the face with spiked shoes, if you get my meaning. I now assert myself. Starting from to-day and onward through the years till my friends and relatives gather about my bier and whisper "Doesn't he look peaceful, what I say goes. Give me that necklace. I intend to have it reset or something. Either that, or I shall sell it and give Molly the proceeds. In any case, and be that as it may, gimme that necklace!"

George gave it him. There was a strange new atmosphere of authority about Sigsbee H. to-night that made one give him things when he asked for them. He had the air of a man whom somebody has been feeding meat.

"Pinch," said Mr. Waddington.

"Finch," said George.

"George," said a voice at the window, speaking with a startling abruptness which caused Mr. Waddington to jerk his cigar into his eye.

A wave of emotion poured over George.

"Molly! Is that you?"

"Yes, darling. Here I am."

"How quick you've been."

"I hurried."

"Though it seems hours since you went away."

"Does it really, precious?"

Mr. Waddington was still shaken.

"If I had been told that any daughter of mine would come and bark at me from behind like that," he said querulously, "I would not have believed it."

"Oh, father! There you are. I didn't see you."

"There," said Mr. Waddington, "is right. You nearly scared the top of my head off."

"I'm sorry."

"Too late to be sorry now," said Mr. Waddington moodily. "You've gone and spoiled the best ten-cent cigar in Hempstead."

He eyed the remains sadly: and, throwing them away, selected another from his upper waistcoat pocket and bit the end off.

"Molly, my angel," said George vibrantly, "fancy you really being with me once more!"

"Yes, Georgie, darling. And what I wanted to say was, I believe there's somebody in your sleeping-porch."

"What!"

"I'm sure I heard voices."

Come right down to it, and there is no instinct so deeply rooted in the nature of Man as the respect for property—his own property, that is to say. And just as the mildest dog will tackle bloodhounds in defence of its own back-yard, so will the veriest of human worms turn if attacked in his capacity of householder. The news that there was somebody in his sleeping-porch caused George to seethe with pique and indignation. It seemed to him that the entire population of New York had come to look on his sleeping-porch as a public resort. No sooner had he ejected one batch of visitors than another took their place.

With a wordless exclamation he rushed out upon the roof, closely followed by Molly and her father. Molly was afraid he would get hurt. Sigsbee H. was afraid he would not. It had been a big night for Sigsbee H. Waddington, and he did not want it to end tamely.

"Have your gun ready," advised Sigsbee H., keeping well in the rear, "and don't fire till you see the whites of their eyes."

George reached the door of the sleeping-porch, and smote it a lusty blow.

"Hi!" he cried. He twisted the handle. "Good heavens, it's locked."

From the upper window, softened by distance, came a pleading voice.

"I say! I say! I say!" To Lord Hunstanton the beating on the door had sounded like the first guns of a relieving army. He felt like the girl who heard the pipers skirling as they marched on beleagured Lucknow. "I say, whoever you are, dear old soul, let us out, would you mind."

George ground his teeth.

"What do you mean—whoever you are? I'm George Finch, and that sleeping-porch belongs to me."

"Good old George! Hunstanton speaking. Let us out, George, old top, like the sportsman you are!"

"What are you doing in there?"

"A policeman locked us in. And a blighter of a butler, after promising to undo the door, told some thin story about not being able to find the key and legged it with all our available assets. So play the man, dear old George, and blessings will reward you. Also and moreover, by acting promptly you will save the life of my dear good friend and hostess here, who has been hiccoughing for some little time and is, I rather fancy, on the point of hysterics."

"What are you talking about?"

"Mrs. Waddington."

"Is Mrs. Waddington in there with you?"

"Is she not, laddie!"

George drew in his breath sharply.

"Mother," he said reproachfully, through the keyhole. "I had not expected this."

Sigsbee H. Waddington uttered a fearful cry.

"My wife! In there! With a man with a toothbrush moustache! Let *me* talk to them!"

"Who was that?" asked Lord Hunstanton.

"Mr. Waddington," replied George. "Who was that?" he said, as a scream rent the air.

"Mrs. Waddington. I say, George, old man," queried his lordship anxiously, "what's the precedure when a woman starts turning blue and making little bubbling noises?"

Sigsbee H., finding that a man of his stature could not hope to speak to any advantage through the window unless he stood on something, had darted across the roof and was now returning with one of the potted shrubs in his arms. The wildness of his eyes and the fact that even in this supreme moment he had gone on puffing at his cigar gave him a striking resemblance to a fire-breathing dragon. He bumped the tub down and, like a man who rises on stepping-stones of his dead self to higher things, elevated himself upon it.

This brought him nicely within range of the window and enabled him to push Lord Hunstanton in the face—which was all to the good. His lordship staggered back, leaving the way clear for the injured man to gaze upon his erring wife.

"Ha!" said Sigsbee H. Waddington.

"I can explain everything, Sigsbee!"

Mr. Waddington snorted.

"Nerve," he said, "in its proper place and when there's not too much of it, I admire. But when a woman has the crust to disparage the morals of one of the finest young fellows who ever came out of the golden West and then I happen to pop into New York on important business and find her closeted with a man with a toothbrush moustache and she has the audacity to say she can explain everything . . ."

Here Mr. Waddington paused to take in breath.

"Sigsbee!"

"It's living in this soul-destroying East that does it," proceeded Mr. Waddington, having re-filled his thoracic cavities. "If I've said it once, I've said it a hundred times, that . . ."

"But, Sigsbee, I couldn't help it. It's quite true what Lord Hunstanton was saying. A policeman locked us in."

"What were you doing up here, anyway?"

There was a brief silence within.

"I came to see what that Finch was doing. And I heard him in here, talking to an abandoned creature."

Mr. Waddington directed a questioning gaze at George.

"Have you been talking to any abandoned creatures to-night?"

"Of course he hasn't," cried Molly indignantly.

"I have spoken with no one of the opposite sex," said George with dignity, "except the girl who stole the necklace. And that was a purely business discussion which would not have brought a blush to the cheek of the sternest critic. I said 'Hand over that necklace!' and she handed it over, and then her husband came and took her away."

"You hear?" said Mr. Waddington.

"No, I don't," said Mrs. Waddington.

"Well, take it from me that this splendid young man from the West is as pure as driven snow. So now let's hear from you once more. Why did the policeman lock you in?"

"We had a misunderstanding."

"How?"

"Well, I—er—happened to throw a little pepper in his face."

"Sweet artichokes of Jerusalem! Why?"

"He found me in Mr. Finch's apartment and wanted to arrest me."

Mr. Waddington's voice grew cold and grim.

"Indeed?" he said. "Well, this finishes it! If you can't live in the East without spending your time throwing pepper at policemen, you'll come straight out with me to the West before you start attacking them with hatchets. That is my final and unalterable decision. Come West, woman, where hearts are pure, and there try to start a new life."

"I will, Sigsbee, I will."

"You bet your permanent henna hair-wash you will!"

"I'll buy the transportation to-morrow."

"No, sir!" Mr. Waddington with a grand gesture nearly overbalanced the tub on which he stood. "I will buy the transportation to-morrow. You will be interested to learn that, owing to commercial transactions resulting from the possession of a smart business head, I am now once more an exceedingly wealthy man and able to buy all the transportation this family requires and to run this family as it should be run. I'm the big noise now. Yes, me—Sigsbee Horatio. . . ." The tub tilted sideways, and the speaker staggered into the arms of Officer Garroway who had come up to the roof to see how his prisoners were getting on and was surprised to find himself plunged into the middle of what appeared to be a debating society.

" . . . Waddington," concluded Sigsbee H.

The policeman eyed him coldly. The fever of dislike which he had felt towards this man had passed, but he could never look on him as a friend. Moreover, Mr. Waddington, descending from the tub, had stamped heavily on his right foot, almost the only portion of his anatomy which had up till then come unscathed through the adventures of the night.

"What's all this about?" inquired Officer Garroway.

His eyes fell upon George: and he uttered that low, sinister growl which is heard only from the throats of leopards seeking their prey, tigers about to give battle, and New York policemen who come unexpectedly upon men who have thrown table-cloths over them and hit them in the eye.

"So there you are!" said Officer Garroway.

He poised his night-stick in his hand, and moved softly forward. Molly flung herself in his path with a cry.

"Stop!"

"Miss," said the policeman, courteously as was his wont in the presence of the sex. "Oblige me by getting to hell out of here."

"Garroway!"

The policeman wheeled sharply. Only one man in the world would have been able to check his dreadful designs at that moment, and that man had now joined the group. Clad in a sweater and a pair of running-shorts, Hamilton Beamish made a strangely dignified and picturesque figure as he stood there with the moonlight glinting on his horn-rimmed spectacles. He wore soft shoes with rubber soles, and he was carrying a pair of dumb-bells. Hamilton Beamish was a man who lived by schedule: and not all that he had passed through that day could blur his mind to the fact that this was the hour at which he did his before-retiring dumb-bell exercises.

"What is the trouble, Garroway?"

"Well, Mr. Beamish . . ."

Confused voices interrupted him.

"He was trying to murder George."

"He's got my wife locked up in this room."

"The brute!"

"Darned fresh guy!"

"George didn't do a thing to him."

"My wife only threw a little pepper in his face."

Hamilton Beamish raised a compelling dumb-bell.

"Please, please! Garroway, state your case."

He listened attentively.

"Unlock that door," he said, when all was told.

The policeman unlocked the door. Mrs. Waddington, followed by Lord Hunstanton, emerged. Lord Hunstanton eyed Mr. Waddington warily, and sidled with an air of carelessness towards the stairway. Accelerating his progress as he neared the door, he vanished abruptly. Lord Hunstanton was a well-bred man who hated a fuss: and every instinct told him that this was one. He was better elsewhere, he decided.

"Stop that man!" ejaculated Officer Garroway. He turned back, baffled, with a darkening brow. "Now he's gone!" he said sombrely. "And he was wanted up in Syracuse."

Sigsbee H. Waddington shook his head. He was not fond of that town, but he had a fair mind.

"Even in Syracuse," he said, "they wouldn't want a man like that."

"It was Willie the Dude, and I was going to take him to the station-house."

"You are very much mistaken, Garroway," said Hamilton Beamish. "That was Lord Hunstanton, a personal acquaintance of mine."

"You knew him, Mr. Beamish?"

"Quite."

"Do you know her?" asked the policeman, pointing to Mrs. Waddington.

"Intimately."

"And him?" said Officer Garroway, indicating George.

"He is one of my best friends."

The policeman heaved a dreary sigh. He relapsed into silence, baffled.

"The whole affair," said Hamilton Beamish, "appears to have been due to a foolish misunderstanding. This lady, Garroway, is the step-mother of this young lady here, to whom Mr. Finch should have been married to-day. There was some little trouble, I understand from Mr. Waddington, and she was left with the impression that Mr. Finch's morals were not all they should have been. Later, facts which came to light convinced her of her error, and she hastened to New York to seek Mr. Finch out and tell him that all was well and that the marriage would proceed with her full approval. That is correct, Mrs. Waddington?"

Mrs. Waddington gulped. For a moment her eye seemed about to assume its well-known expression of a belligerent fish. But her spirit was broken. She was not the woman she had been. She had lost the old form.

"Yes. . . . Yes. . . . That is to say . . . I mean, yes," she replied.

"You called at Mr. Finch's apartment with no other motive than to tell him this?"

"None. . . . Or, rather . . . No, none."

"In fact, to put the thing in a nutshell, you wished to find your future son-in-law and fold him in a mother-in-law's embrace. Am I right?"

This time the pause before Mrs. Waddington found herself able to reply was so marked and the look she directed at George so full of meaning that the latter, always sensitive, could not but wonder whether in refraining from punching her on the nose he was not neglecting his duty as a man and a citizen. She gazed at him long and lingeringly. Then she spoke.

"Quite right," she said huskily.

"Excellent," said Hamilton Beamish. "So you see, Garroway, that Mrs. Waddington's reason for being in the apartment where you found her were wholly admirable. That clears up that point."

"It doesn't clear up why she threw pepper in my face."

Hamilton Beamish nodded.

"There, Garroway," he said, "you have put your finger on the one aspect of Mrs. Waddington's behaviour which was not completely unexceptionable. As regards the pepper, you have, it seems to me, legitimate cause for pique and, indeed, solid grounds for an action for assault and battery. But Mrs. Waddington is a reasonable woman, and will, no doubt, be willing to settle this little matter in a way acceptable to all parties."

"I will pay him whatever he wants," cried the reasonable woman. "Anything, anything!"

"Hey!"

It was the voice of Sigsbee H. He stood there, forceful and dominant. His cigar had gone out, and he was chewing the dry remains aggressively.

"Say, listen!" said Sigsbee H. Waddington. "If there's any bribing of the police to be done, it's my place to do it, as the head of the family. Look me up at my little place at Hempstead to-morrow, Gallagher, and we'll have a talk. You will find me a generous man. Open-handed. Western."

"Capital," said Hamilton Beamish. "So everything is happily settled."

There was not much of Officer Garroway's face that was not concealed by the bandage and the steak, but on the small residuum there appeared a look of doubt and dissatisfaction.

"And what about this bird here?" he asked, indicating George.

"This individual before me," corrected Hamilton Beamish. "What about him, Garroway?"

"He soaked me in the eye."

"No doubt in a spirit of wholesome fun. Where did this happen?"

"Down there in the Purple Chicken."

"Ah! Well, if you knew that restaurant better, you would understand that that sort of thing is the merest commonplace of everyday life at the Purple Chicken. You must overlook it Garroway."

"Can't I push his head down his throat?"

"Certainly not. I cannot have you annoying Mr. Finch. He is to be married to-morrow, and he is a friend of mine."

"But . . ."

"Garroway," said Hamilton Beamish, in a quiet, compelling voice, "Mr. Finch is a friend of mine."

"Very well, Mr. Beamish," said the policeman resignedly.

Mrs. Waddington was plucking at her husband's sleeve.

"Sigsbee."

"Hello?"

"Sigsbee, dear, I'm starving. I have had nothing to eat since lunch. There is some wonderful soup in there."

"Let's go," said Sigsbee H. "You coming?" he said to George.

"I thought of taking Molly off somewhere."

"Oh no, do come with us, George," said Mrs. Waddington winningly. She drew closer to him. "George is it really true that you hit that policeman in the eye?"

"Yes."

"Tell me about it."

"Well, he was trying to arrest me, so I threw a table-cloth over his head and then plugged him a couple of rather juicy ones which made him leave go."

Mrs. Waddington's eyes glistened. She put her arm through his.

"George," she said, "I have misjudged you. I could wish Molly no better husband."


Hamilton Beamish stood in the moonlight, swinging his dumbbells. Having done this for awhile, he embarked on a few simple setting-up exercises. He stood with his feet some six inches apart, his toes turned slightly out: then, placing his hands on his hips, thumbs back, bent slightly forward from the shoulders—not from the hips. He retracted the lower abdomen, and holding it retracted, leaned well over to the left side, contracting the muscles of the left side forcibly. He kept his legs straight all the time, his knees stiff. He reversed to right side, and repeated twenty times—ten right, ten left. This exercise was done slowly and steadily, without jerking.

"Ah!" said Hamilton Beamish, relaxing. "Splendid for the transversalis muscle, that, converting it into a living belt which girds the loins. Have you ever given considered thought to the loins, Garroway?"

The policeman shook his head.

"Not that I know of," he said indifferently. "I've seen 'em in the Bronx Zoo."

Hamilton Beamish eyed him with concern.

"Garroway," he said, "you seem distrait."

"If that's how a feller is when he's been hit and punched and stepped on and had pepper thrown at him and table-cloths put over his head I've got a swell licence to seem distrait," replied the policeman bitterly. "And on top of all that, when I thought I had made a cop . . ."

"Brought about an arrest."

" . . . brought about an arrest which would have got me promotion, I find they're all friends of yours and have to be allowed to make a clean getaway. That's what jars me, Mr. Beamish."

Hamilton Beamish patted him on the shoulder.

"Every poet, Garroway, has to learn in suffering before he can teach in song. Look at Keats! Look at Chatterton! One of these days you will be thankful that all this has happened. It will be the making of you. Besides, think of the money you are going to get from Mr. Waddington to-morrow."

"I'd give it all for one long, cool drink now."

"Mr. Garroway."

The policeman looked up. Molly was standing in the window.

"Mr. Garroway," said Molly, "a most mysterious thing has happened. Mr. Finch has found two large bottles of champagne in his cupboard. He can't think how they got there, but he says would you care to come in and examine them and see whether they are good or not."

The cloud which had hung about the policeman's face passed from it as if beneath some magic spell. His tongue came slowly out of his mouth and moved lovingly over his arid lips. His one visible eye gleamed with the light which never was on land or sea.

"Are you with me, Mr. Beamish?" he asked.

"I precede you, Mr. Garroway," said Hamilton Beamish.

# BY THE SAME AUTHOR

## Life At Blandings

'For Wodehouse there has been no fall of Man ... the gardens of Blandings Castle are the original gardens from which we are all exiled' – Evelyn Waugh

The tranquil idyll of life at Blandings is once again shattered by scrapes and skulduggery, mishaps and mix-ups in:

## Galahad at Blandings

A major mix-up at the Castle, in which Gally introduces yet another impostor to Lord Emsworth's residence, and the Empress of Blandings somehow gets drunk in her sty.

## Heavy Weather

Forced to seek alternative employment when his editorials for *Tiny Tots* magazine become too adult, Monty Bodkin has been engaged as Lord Emsworth's personal secretary.

*also published*

FULL MOON
LEAVE IT TO PSMITH
A PELICAN AT BLANDINGS
PIGS HAVE WINGS
SERVICE WITH A SMILE
SOMETHING FRESH
SUMMER LIGHTNING
SUNSET AT BLANDINGS
UNCLE FRED IN THE SPRINGTIME

*and the omnibus*

LIFE AT BLANDINGS

### The Adventures of Sally

Pretty, impecunious Sally never dreamed a fortune could be a disadvantage until she became an heiress. Life in New York became complicated enough, but a trip to England seemed only to make matters worse.

### Bachelors Anonymous

Their methods were borrowed from Alcoholics Anonymous: whenever a member felt the urge to take a woman out to dinner, he relied on the others to reason with him until the madness passed. But even the most hardened bachelor can occasionally fall by the wayside . . .

### Cocktail Time

Uncle Fred, off the leash and into the Drones Club, cannot resist firing a well-aimed Brazil nut at the hat of Beefy Bastable. From this incident springs the injured barrister's mistaken exposé of the misdeeds of the younger generation, in a novel which causes only trouble for its hapless author.

*also published*

**At first there seems no reason why the courtship of a wealthy bachelor like George Finch should not run sweetly to its natural conclusion.**

But George has fallen in love with the adorable Molly Waddington, daughter of one of the most formidable matrons in America. And Mrs Waddington vastly prefers the idea of an eligible aristocrat to the reality of George, whom she strongly suspects is half-witted. In fact, without the intervention of the small bachelor's dearest friend, the inventive and resourceful J. Hamilton Beamish, and the help of the bride's father, Sigsbee H. Waddington, millionaire and thwarted cowboy, it is doubtful whether George's story could ever have had a happy ending.

Cover illustration by Ionicus

 **A PENGUIN BOOK**
Fiction

ISBN 0-14-008506-8

90401

9 780140 085068